Blood's Fury

Deadly Beauties, Book 1

C.M. Owens

Blood's Fury

Deadly Beauties Series

Chapter One

"Maybe tomorrow we can find someone to take care of the rest of your furniture," my mother breathlessly releases, as we finish heaving my far too heavy couch into the living room.

"Or we could finish now since I have to start work tomorrow," I chirp with a grin.

I know she's not tired, but she's very opposed to doing things the *human* way. Too bad. That's what I plan to be for as long as I can.

"I could go persuade some of your hunky new neighbors to help us out," she says while flashing me a scandalous grin.

The candles in the house flicker before rising to a flame as the fire starts to spread over her eyes, making me scowl in response.

"No magic in my house," I caution while standing up and heading back out.

"It would be a hell of a lot easier to get your stuff in using magic," she huffs as the candles stop their blazing intent without leaving a smoky trail.

"Not concerned about getting it done easily," I chuckle out. "That's sort of the point of my new start."

She follows me to the oversized truck I rented, and we start lugging out the next set of furnishings.

"It's part of you, Alyssa. The sooner you start accepting it, the better. You're so pow-"

"Don't say it," I interrupt, holding a hand up. "If you say it, I'll finish unpacking by myself."

She crosses her arms in protest, but I roll my eyes as I head back into the house while carrying my two lamps. As soon as I walk in, a growl of agitation slips through my tight lips. All of my furniture, clothes, and everything else has been put into place. Even my pictures are hanging on the damn walls.

"Seriously?" I gripe, knowing damn well she's out there laughing.

She walks in, a smug look on her face, and I roll my eyes.

"What? You can't expect me to spend all day sweating and toiling over all this unnecessary labor when I'm not going to see my daughter for months."

Guilt. She always uses guilt. Amazing.

"Fine. I'll order a pizza, and you can grab some wine out of the grocery bags I have over-" I look up to see they've also been taken care of. "Never mind. You can find the wine wherever you put it."

She lets a bit of a chuckle escape and the television turns on as she passes by.

"Really? You're so lazy you can't even use the remote?"

"Not lazy, dear, just special… like you."

Oh you're special all right.

I somehow refrain from letting that snarky comment out.

"Get your hair out from behind your ears. You know I absolutely hate that."

And she wonders why I'm moving out.

Like a small child, I do as my mother says and pull my hair out from behind my ears. It's her biggest pet peeve. After the little stunt she just pulled, I should keep both sides of my hair tucked behind my ears all day.

My attention is drawn to the television when four pictures of young girls my age flash across the screen.

"If you see these women, please contact the police. They were last seen together on Midwalk Avenue."

The television mutes when I press the button, and then I flip the channel quickly, hoping Mom didn't hear.

"I guess that means you didn't check to see what other immortals were roaming around here?" Mom asks as she walks back in with her phone at her face, reading. "Fifteen girls have gone missing this month alone. I don't like this."

"There are a variety of immortals all over the world, Mom. It's not like I can avoid living among *all* of them. Besides, they're apparently blood drinkers, which means they'll be moving along soon enough, and this will be one of the safest places around."

"It's not safe right now, and you're not immortal yet, meaning you can die as easily as a human."

And let the fight begin.

"I'm marked, Mom. If someone gets too close, I'll show them what I'm meant to become."

She scoffs, "That won't matter. If they give you the chance to show them, they'll just deny it if it comes to war. No one wants another dark ages, so our council will dismiss it as an accident."

I sigh as I head over to the pantry to pull out some popcorn. I'm exhausted from the move and the woman I stupidly asked to help me get situated in my new place.

"They're probably vampires or changers, considering the pretty girls they took. I'll just steer clear of pretty boys for a while."

She groans while rolling her eyes.

"Don't say vampires. It's so... juvenile. And pretty boys aren't the only night stalkers or changers. Pretty girls are night stalkers and changers too. Besides, this could be lycans, werewolves, werecats, dark users... the list goes on and on, Alyssa. I knew this was a bad idea. Just come home with me."

Turning around, I shake my head, meeting her determined gaze with my defiant glower. "No. I'm twenty, and I've already been knocked out of going to college because of your paranoia. You swore one of my professors was a changer you knew hundreds of years ago."

"He was," she growls.

Again, I'm forced to huff. She's impossible.

"The point is, this world is deadly for anyone, yet humans exist daily, living to be of old age and dying of natural causes. The chances of me actually

6

running into harm are astronomical. Stop worrying so much."

She breathes out heavily, and then she vanishes briefly to reappear on the couch. That's one bit of magic I wouldn't mind having. It would save me from trying to afford a car.

"It just worries me. Promise me you'll use your powers if one of them comes after you."

Finally.

"I have no problem using paranormal against paranormal," I say with a shrug. "I just don't want magic to be my life, not yet. I happen to like living like a regular girl. It's… comforting. Now, where's my wine?"

She smirks before vanishing again, and I hear a cork being pulled free from the bottle.

Chapter Two

The diner isn't what I was expecting. You'd think a small town would have small business, but I've hardly had a chance to breathe, due to the ridiculous volume of customers.

"Thanks," I murmur to the guy who hands me a ten for a tip.

"My pleasure. You new around here?" he asks, his eyes staring into mine with an obvious agenda.

I check his eyes for sparks of blue to infuse, showing me his true identity, but they stay brown as he stares at me. His hair is too light to be a night stalker, and his thudding heartbeat is too quick to be a changer. I could be wrong, but judging by his pitiful posture and terrible wardrobe, I'd say I'm in the clear.

Just a horny human.

"Very new." I smile sweetly, and then I start to walk away when he pulls at my hand, catching me off guard.

"We're having a large dock party tonight. You're welcome to come. I could introduce you to some of the locals, help you make some friends."

He seems harmless enough, but vampires... er... I mean, night stalkers... are strongest under the moonlight. If they're here, they'll be hunting at night. My mother would flip the hell out if I was attacked, and knowing her, she'd level the town before our council could pass a verdict.

"Um, maybe," I lie, having no intentions of risking it.

"Here," he says, releasing my hand and scribbling down an address on a napkin. "If you decide to show, just come here. We might take one of the boats for a cruise later tonight. There will be a bonfire on shore."

I smile, showing a little gratitude, and then I wave sweetly at him after taking the proffered address.

"Thanks."

Walking away, I felt his eyes on me. He was cute, but not my type. Unfortunately, I've got a nasty habit for being drawn to the bad, bad, very bad boys. I sure as hell don't want to end up like my mother. She has worse taste in men than I do.

"Alyssa, can you stay until nine tonight?" Francine asks as I walk behind the counter. "Darlene just called in, and we don't have anyone to cover."

"Um, yeah. I could use the extra cash."

Crap. So much for enjoying my first night alone in my new house.

"Thank you. You're a life saver."

At least now I'll be one step closer to getting a car.

The streets are dark, and my feet are killing me. I was supposed to get to leave at nine, but I ended up having to stay until eleven. What a *great* first day.

The night is perfect at least, just a slight breeze. Putting the diner to my back, I start walking home. I hate walking.

A chill hits my neck, as if a breath is being blown against it, but I turn to see nothing. Then I feel it again, and I roll my eyes.

"You can show yourself, Frankie."

No one answers, and my skin crawls. I assumed it was Frankie, my mother's best friend. He loves scaring the shit out of me. But he usually always starts laughing by now.

"Frankie?" I prompt, my hand tingling at my side as my magic starts to stir, ready to be used.

Nothing happens, and no one answers. Sighing, I turn around and slam into a hard body, almost falling to the ground before strong arms wrap around me, pulling me back to a safe balance.

"You okay?" a smooth voice asks, and I grumble to myself as I try to look up at him.

My knees wobble, my heart thuds, and my palms begin sweating as I stare into the gorgeous green eyes of a dark haired beauty. The way I'm shivering over him means he has to be terrible for my health.

His strong, chiseled face is nothing but flawless, and his dark hair sways with the wind, making me jealous of the fact I can't touch it with such ease.

I blush when I realize my hands are resting on his incredible waist, and he smirks in a way that makes me damn near dissolve.

"I said, are you okay?" he repeats, making my cheeks heat more when I realize I've forgotten how to damn speak.

"Um… yeah… you just startled me. Where'd you come from?"

He shrugs, nodding his head toward the diner.

"I was heading toward the diner for some pie, but I see I was too late. They sometimes stay open a little later if there are customers lingering around."

His smile is disarming, far too perfect. He's too frigging hot to be part of this small town… or human.

"Oh, yeah. Sorry. I just finished locking up."

I start walking off, but he jogs up beside me, surprising me a little.

"You aren't from around here."

I pause, not sure if I should continue trying to speak to him. If he's a changer, I should probably keep from turning my back on him again. If he's a night stalker, I definitely don't want to turn my back on him.

"Um, is that a question or an observation?"

"Both, I suppose."

He smiles bigger, making my heart trip over itself. Stupid deadly beauty bullshit. What is he?

"You're right. I just moved here from Colorado."

He stays at my side, keeping my pace as his hands cross behind his back.

"So are you going to the dock party? I hear it's supposed to be pretty great, and it's just up the road."

I look up, expecting to see a glisten of something in his eyes, but there's nothing there. I can't show him my mark until he reveals himself. It could kill a human to see it.

"No. I don't think so. I'm exhausted."

I start walking faster, and he keeps stride with me, his steps even and not seeming rushed like mine.

"Is Frankie your boyfriend?" he asks.

"Huh?"

"You were calling for a Frankie back there," he murmurs softly, not sounding winded like me.

"Oh. No. Frankie is my mom's friend. I thought I saw him."

Or thought he was trying to scare the shit out of me.

"Ah. Your mom lives here with you then?"

I almost stumble, but I quickly regain my composure before he has to catch me again. I almost wish my mother did live with me right now. She's made me a fucking basket case, and I'm freaking out a little.

For all I know, this is just one hot human. It's not like every sexy creature is an immortal.

"Um, no. I assumed she sent him out here to check up on me. He likes to scare me, so I thought he was lingering in the parking lot."

He bites back a grin, seeming amused by something. He keeps his hands behind his back, casually enjoying the night while I clamber down the sidewalk.

"You seem… scared. Am I scaring you?"

Hell yes.

"A little… are you following me home?" I worry, trying to provoke him into revealing himself and ending this cat-and-mouse game if he's really a blood drinker.

"Not at all," he laughs. "I'm going to the dock party. It's just around the corner up there. I thought it would seem creepier if I was walking behind you."

I let out a nervous laugh, finally relaxing a little, and he smiles his panty-dropping grin that makes the junction between my legs heat up and pulsate.

"Oh. Sorry. I'm just a little freaked out after seeing the news about the missing girls," I mutter, gauging his reaction with subtle scrutiny.

He nods, his smile fading as seriousness takes place.

"You should be. It's unnerving. Just be careful, and try not to walk home so late. Why did they make you shut down alone?"

Because I'm the new girl and a sucker.

"Because the other girls wanted to go to the dock party."

"Ah. Well, personally, I feel no party gets going good until close to midnight."

"Midnight, eh?" I ask, feeling all the more relaxed now.

Not immortal, just a bad boy human. Crap. I think that's even worse.

Midnight is the showing hour, and all blood drinkers loathe it because they're forced to reveal the monster they are. It's when their fangs show against their will, and their eyes glow their true color, even though they're not ready to show themselves.

"Well, it was odd but nice meeting you. Sorry I wasn't better company," I murmur as I start off the sidewalk and down my gravel path to my house.

"You live here?" he asks, seeming surprised, possibly a little confused.

"Yeah, why?"

"It's just… what made you choose this house?"

It was the first affordable house I found that was far away from my overbearing, paranoid, ridiculously protective mother.

"It was cheap, I needed something close to town, and it's small. Why? Is something wrong with it?"

He shakes his head, obviously hiding something. "Not at all. A friend of mine lived here a while back. I didn't realize she was selling it."

"I bought it from a woman in her early thirties. Jessica… Richards? I think."

"Sounds about right," he murmurs to himself, staring at the house as though he's looking for something... someone.

He seems confused.

"Were you close to her?" I muse.

"Not really, it's just odd this place made it back on the market without my knowing."

Okay. I'm curious now, but I'd rather talk about something other than the prior owner of my house.

He concentrates on the house for a second longer, giving me a chance to examine him better under the moonlight. He's so much hotter than I initially thought now that I can truly gawk at him.

"I should get going," I strain out, knowing Mom would kick my ass for speaking to a dark-haired beauty in the middle of the night. "It was nice meeting you…"

"Kane," he says softly, giving me his delicious, dissolving smile once again.

"Nice to meet you, Kane."

"I'm sure you'll see me around. Especially since you work at the diner. It's my main source of nourishment."

Butterflies ruffle through my stomach, and I smile involuntarily.

I don't know if I should stay or go. Now that I finally believe he's human, I'm almost considering going to the dock party.

"I should head on before all the booze is gone. I'll see you around, Alyssa," he says while turning away, making me sick at my stomach.

"How did you know my name?" I release in a crackle.

He just laughs, turning back, mocking my fear.

"You're still wearing your tag," he says while motioning to my shirt, and then he winks at me before walking away.

I look down to my uniform, and I roll my eyes when I see the big slab advertising my name.

Idiot.

I've officially made myself look like an absolute wreck now that I've freaked out for no real reason.

I turn around and head inside, hoping to fall right to sleep. A shadow passes through the room, and I squeal out.

"Ha! Knew I'd scare you," Frankie murmurs as he appears in front of me.

"Stupid warlocks," I grumble. "I knew you were here."

He laughs harder, reveling in his successful plot to leave me shaking and breathing hard.

"I know, that's why I didn't bother showing myself back at the diner. By the way, who was that guy you were walking with?"

A delicious human that I made myself look like a psycho in front of.

"Spying much?" I scoff while walking by him.

Frankie looks much younger and acts much younger than he actually is. His soft eyes and timeless face remind me of what's to come.

"You told your mother you wouldn't be getting involved with any guys until the disappearances stop."

"I'm not getting involved with anyone, Frankie. Besides, he's human."

"You're sure?"

He runs his hand through his blond hair as he stares worriedly at me.

"He would have tried something. The streets were deserted. All he did was accompany me on my walk since it was on his way."

"So you showed him your mark?" he asks naively.

Though he's my mother's best friend, he doesn't know all of my dark, jaded secrets. Mom's poor taste in men left her with a daughter too strong for her own damn good.

"Um, it wasn't necessary."

He sighs and grips his head.

"Your mother isn't going to be happy about this."

"Happy about what?" I can't think of absolutely anything I've done wrong. Hell, I've spent all day at work.

"You coming home so late, talking to a handsome stranger, and then letting him walk away after finding out where you live."

I'm sick of this. I've literally been one day without my mother, and already I'm getting scolded by her spy. She's not going to make me feel like a child in my own house. That was the entire reason I moved all the way out here to Pine Shore.

"My mother can't control my life. Neither can you. Now go loiter in someone else's home. I'm taking a shower and going to bed."

He tightens his lips, knowing better than to argue with me.

"Fine, but I'll be around. This place is crawling with immortals. I can feel their energy. It's a good thing your mother can't do the same, otherwise *she'd* be the one stalking you right now."

"Overbearing, untrusting, arrogant immortals," I mumble under my breath while heading to my room.

"I heard that," he calls from the living area, but I ignore him as I hear the front door shut behind him.

My first night, and I'm getting treated like a child who is still living with her crazy mother. Just for that, screw them. I'm going to the dock party.

I walk up, tugging at the ends of the dress I didn't realize was this short, and my eyes fall on all the drunken fools acting out. Everyone is completely wasted right now, and I haven't had a sip. This could either be really fun, or incredibly annoying.

"You came," a voice says from behind, and I turn to meet the guy who invited me, though he's staggering drunk.

I don't even know how he recognizes me with his heavy duty beer-goggles on.

"I thought we had a moment."

"A moment?" I muse, stifling a laugh as he reaches for me and misses.

"Yeah," he says as he tries to figure out which of the many images is actually me.

"Seeing double?" I giggle out.

"Seeing quadruple," he jokes while shaking his head. "It's fucking wonderful since there're four of you and one of me."

When he finally finds me, his arm wraps around my waist to pull me to him.

"Hey, whoa. Easy, Romeo," I say through my snickers while escaping his hold.

"I can show you Romeo," he slurs while leaning toward me again, and I take a step back, bumping into someone.

I look up to see Kane towering over me, and my heartbeat quickens to the point of feeling like I'm going to explode.

"I thought you weren't coming," he says with a deviously sexy smile.

"I changed my mind," I mutter softly while turning to face him, and his eyes fall down to my chest before popping back up to meet mine.

"Yo, dude, she's with me," the drunken mess murmurs while tugging at my hand.

"Please stop," I huff while struggling to pull my hand free.

Then I feel Kane leaning over me and freeing me from the grasp.

"Actually, I think Alyssa is with me, considering I'm sober."

"So am I," he says while laughing ridiculously hard. "Alyssa is a pretty name."

I'm tempted to make his hand go crazy and splash his beer in his face, but I refrain from using magic.

Kane pulls me back behind him, tucking me safely in his grasp, and then he gently murmurs, "Actually, she's my girl. Better luck next time, Mark."

Mark huffs and slumps down to the ground. Fortunately, he's too drunk to even try to counter. I smirk as Kane pulls my hand in his and leads me toward the bonfire.

"*Your girl*, eh?" I tease.

He laughs a little, and then he looks over his shoulder.

"It worked, didn't it? You're here without anyone to help you rebuff their attempts, and you're wearing that," he says, motioning to my dress, his brow rising.

He offers me a glance that makes me blush, and he smirks before looking away.

"Are you trying to say you like my dress?" I flirt, and his smile grows.

He props up against the side of a truck and studies me intently, making me feel a little on display. The intensity of his green eyes is mesmerizing, and the way his dark hair plays with the wind is breathtaking.

"You're a little confusing, Alyssa," he says while tilting his head. "You seemed terrified of me earlier, and yet now you're here, flirting with me."

Way to be obvious, Alyssa.

"I thought *your girl* was supposed to flirt with you," I say jokingly to lighten the mood, praying I don't look like the mess I feel I do.

"Cute. So, why'd you change your mind about coming?" he says softly, shifting as he puts his hands in his pocket.

Five seconds ago he seemed so confident, and now he seems nervous.

"Long story. So, are these people your friends?"

He lets his eyes drift around, taking in the partiers as he mulls that over.

"Some of them. You want me to introduce you around?" he asks curiously while hopping up on the tailgate of a truck.

"Um, nah. I'm not staying long. I just wanted to see what all the fuss was about."

And I secretly wanted to see him again - possibly to piss my mother off. *Great.* I had to move out before I had the courage to start acting rebellious.

"Well, now you see a bunch of lake-loving drunks. Some fun, huh?" he says through a laugh, making me chuckle lightly while nodding in agreement.

I look down to see it's almost midnight.

"So much for your theory - the fun gets started at midnight. It looks like it gets sloppy after eleven."

He laughs ridiculously hard, and then he lifts me up, as though I weigh nothing, to pull me beside him on the tailgate of the truck. His unexpected touch makes my breath hitch, but I play it off without letting him know how he just affected me.

"You'll have to come to one of my parties sometime. This one shouldn't be setting the bar for this place. I wouldn't have come if I had known it'd be this pathetic."

"You live close to here?" I muse, given the way he said it.

"Yeah, two houses over. You should come by sometime, seriously. We have a party at least once a week. My roommates are relentless hell-raisers."

I smile lightly, and then I tug at my dress when I see it has risen almost too high. He looks down and smirks.

"Pink's a good color on you," he murmurs, his eyes motioning to my dress.

I start to thank him when a group of people walk up to us. They're laughing and talking

"Hey, Kane," one girl says. "We're ditching the dud party and having the after party at our place. You coming?"

He looks to me and smirks. "Told you."

I force a smile, but my stomach is almost queasy. There's no way this many hot-as-hell people are all in one group without them being some sort of immortals. Maybe they're harmless though.

Or maybe you just think he's hot and now you're making excuses.

Girls are missing. And here is a group of immortals, but I know Kane isn't. They're not blood drinkers,,, they can't be. It's now after midnight, and no one is revealing themselves. Midnight is the waking hour when their victims' deaths force the curse of revelation. They're planning to party, not hide.

"You coming?" a guy prompts, his eyes questioning Kane. "You can bring your… new girl."

His eyes rake over me once before looking to Kane to give him a smile of approval, and Kane lets out a laugh.

"I'll see. You guys head on."

They all start walking off, though one girl turns around to burn through me with her glare. She's the only girl without a guy's arm draped around her, and I start wondering if she's into Kane. I sure as hell don't need to make enemies with her until I know what she is.

"Girlfriend?" I muse as she turns around, my eyes still watching her carefully.

"Don't have one."

I turn back to see his eyes staring into mine, his far too sexy grin making my skin heat up, and I almost shiver in response.

"Cold?" he asks while leaning toward me.

"No, um… I just…. I need to get going."

I struggle to slide off the truck gracefully when my legs stick to the tailgate. Suddenly I'm being lifted and sliding down a wonderfully hard body as Kane lowers me to the ground.

Oh damn.

Everything on me is tingling to be touched by him right now, and I'm almost looking forward to the sort of mistakes I could make.

He brushes my hair from my shoulder while wrapping his arm around my waist, and then he starts ushering me through the crowd.

"I'll walk you home. It's late, and you shouldn't be walking back by yourself."

If he really is human, along with his model friends, then I'd be the one protecting him. If he's not human, and I'm being played, my mom is going to kick my ass.

"I'll be fine. You should probably go monitor your party-animal roommates."

He lets free a grin that sends the most heated chills through my bones, making my heart thud loudly.

"So, it's not me you're scared of, but being alone with me? I think you might have a bit of a crush, Alyssa," he teases, his green eyes burning into mine without fear.

I'm such a damn girl.

"Um… I don't… we… I-"

"Look, I'm walking you home. You can't go walking around by yourself this late right now. I'd like to see you again - somewhere other than the missing flyers."

I swallow hard, and he takes my hand in his as he starts pulling me away from the party. Now I want to go to his party.

"So… what about going to your party?" I ask, surprising myself.

"You want to go?" he muses, his smile etching up more.

"Is it going to be like this?" I laugh lightly, trying to sound more respectable than a stammering fool.

"Not at all. It'll be more laid back."

"Then… yeah. I want to go."

Cop lights begin flashing as sirens squeal out, and Kane shakes his head while pulling out his phone.

"You might want to can the after party. The cops are here," he says into the phone, and then he hangs up and turns to me. "How old are you?"

"Um, twenty. Why?"

"You're underage. Come on. I'll get you out of here."

He tugs me through a wooded area, forcing me to quicken my pace. He stays quiet and alert, checking from side to side with each step. I can't help but admire the view he's giving me, letting me walk behind him. I'm so pathetic.

Before I know it, we've hit the sidewalk of the streets.

"That was one hell of a short cut. I wish I had known about it on the way there."

He turns to me, stopping our retreat and shakes his head.

"Don't go through those woods without me. It's crazy dangerous, especially at night. Two of the girls that are missing went in one night, and they were never seen again."

I smile a little at his protective tone.

"And you think you can protect me?" I ask, delighting in the warm feeling his words have given me.

"I know I can," he says with that damn heart-stopping grin before pulling me again.

Our fingers stay interlocked as we head down the sidewalk, and then I frown when I see my house coming into view.

"Do you think the cops will be at your house?"

"Probably," he chuckles out. "We've had so many parties interrupted by them that it's just common for us to get the blame. It'll be fine though. We're all legal adults."

"Oh," I say somewhat disappointedly.

I was hoping for an excuse to invite him in without looking like a lusting, hormonal fool. Something about him makes my blood stir with primal need. I wanted to feel those perfectly smooth lips on my skin, devouring me.

"Your eyes," he murmurs softly. "Wow."

Oh shit.

I quickly look away, praying my eyes die down. Fucking mood stone eyes.

"It's like they were turning different colors," he says with a touch of suspicion.

I laugh dismissively, trying to downplay the slip up. "Turning on the smooth talk?"

Out of all the immortals, my eyes are the only ones to do this. No one in my family knows why, and I hate it. Every emotion I have comes through almost too clearly when it gets too strong. I was definitely feeling a strong emotion - desire.

"Not at all," he says with a smile as he walks me to my front door. "I suppose I'll see you tomorrow."

"Tomorrow?" I ask, feeling my eyes fully back to normal.

"At the diner."

"Oh… yeah."

"I'm going to vote they make this your new uniform," he says with a devious grin while motioning to my showy dress.

I let out a small laugh, but then I'm trapped in his eyes as he props up against my door and stares at me. It's like time has slowed, and I'm considering risking everything and pulling him inside.

"Are you going in?" he asks, his smile growing.

My cheeks flush, and I look down at my feet.

"Yeah. Sorry. Bye," I mumble as I wiggle my keys in the lock.

When my door opens, I step inside and turn to see him again just as he walks off my porch. I *really* thought he was going to at least try to kiss me.

"You know where I live if you need me for anything," he says with his back turned.

"Actually, I don't," I say, smiling, and he turns to face me before I continue. "You said you lived two houses down, but you didn't say in which direction."

He smiles this time, and then he shrugs before walking back toward me. He gets dangerously close, letting his breath find my lips for a split second, and then he pulls back with my phone in his hand.

I was so enthralled and entranced by his near kiss that I never felt him pulling my phone out of my hand. My breaths are heavy now, and then I hear a phone ringing - the sound coming from his pocket. He smirks as it quits and hands me back my phone.

"Now you've got my number. It's up to you whether or not you want to program it."

He starts walking away again, and I prop up while murmuring, "That goes both ways."

He turns around with his phone in his hand and waves it in front of him.

"Already done."

My heart flips over, and then the shadows swallow him as he disappears into the woods again.

Oh damn.

Obviously, I program his number in my phone before I even shut the damn door. I glance around one last time before stepping inside, but something catches my eye before I can lock up.

There's a tall, lean figure in the distance across the street, and I hear the breaths growing rasp as a second figure goes limp in his arms. Though they're in the shadows and between two houses, I can still somewhat make out what's going on, horrified by the reality I had hoped I wouldn't run into.

Night stalker.

Without any regard for my own safety, I throw off my heels and take off running, throwing my arms out to release my attack, and impacting him with my invisible force. The feeding figure flies backwards, thudding against a house, and an alarm sounds as a window shatters.

Lights from several of the houses around us flash on in response to the loud wails. The lights cast a bright glow on the scene of the crime, and I hear a hissing noise as the dark figure disappears into the shadows to avoid sight. I rush over to the collapsed body on the ground, and my heartbeat charges fiercely as I slip her blond hair to the side to see the marks of proof on her neck.

Definitely a night stalker. Changers have larger fangs, leaving bigger bite marks. Lycans and Were are beasts who only feed in changed form, and that was a man's silhouette.

A guy rushes out of a house with his boxers and robe on - his white, hairy belly bouncing as he charges toward us with a bat. He stumbles to a halt and turns pale when he sees the barely breathing girl's head cradled in my arms.

"Call an ambulance!" I scream. "She's dying!"

Others rush out, and within seconds, I hear the whooping sounds of help on the way. I only pray no one saw my release of power. The council will string me up if they did.

Chapter Three

"Are you crazy, Alyssa?" Mom scolds through the phone.

No, just really unlucky.

"He was killing her. What was I supposed to do?"

No good deed goes unpunished. Calypso Coldwell punishes me for every good deed I do.

"It's not your place to get involved. Night stalkers kill to live. You can't go painting yourself a target by interrupting their meal."

"He was feeding in the open. If anything, he painted himself a target. Besides, they don't have to kill in order to live, they just need blood. They don't have to pick young, pretty girls, but they choose to. I simply reminded him that they're not the only ones in the damn universe, and some of us don't approve of killing."

She groans, exasperation in her long, drawn-out breath. "Alyssa, you're still incredibly vulnerable right now. Going after a feeding night stalker is suicide. That's it. I'm coming to stay with you."

"You can't, Mom. They need you in Tibet for the ceremonies. You're the priestess. I'm fine. I can handle myself, and he never saw my face. Don't worry."

"Then I'm calling Frankie to follow you."

"If Frankie starts following me, I'm going to be on edge. His favorite pastime is scaring the shit out of me. Definitely not."

She sighs loudly, her mind searching for a way to keep me safe. I tuck the phone closer to me as I walk up to the diner.

"Look, I've got to head into work right now. I'll be fine. Don't worry. You do need to say something to the night... um... *their* council about openly eating dinner... if you know what I mean."

"Oh believe me, I will."

I nod, as if she can see me, and then I hang up the phone before she has time to reprimand me more. I'm the only person in the world who gets in trouble for saving a life.

Sheesh.

"Thanks for staying late again, Alyssa," Mary, another waitress murmurs as she strips off her apron.

"It's fine. It's dead in here anyway. I should be able to handle it by myself."

I have one customer who is simply here for the Wifi. He's about my age with black hair, tattoos peeking up from his shirt collar, and a piercing on his right eyebrow. I've studied him too much, since it's a little dull in here tonight.

I've barely seen his face though. He's kept his back to us since he arrived an hour ago.

Mary smiles, offering me a farewell-wave, and heads out to throw her arms around a beefed up guy who is leaning against his car. I smirk as they entangle in a rather showy kiss, and then I flip on my phone to pick up reading my book where I left off.

"Need anything?" I ask the guy who has no interest in spending a dime in the diner.

"No, still fine," he chirps.

I hear the door open, and I look up to see a tan guy with onyx, glistening hair, as he walks in. His eerie smile sends shivers down my spine, and I glance over to see the human in the corner shiver too.

Looking back, I see his glowing blue eyes spark and flicker before dying back down to a deep brown.

Shit. Vampire.

Swallowing hard, I murmur, "Can I help you?"

He smiles bigger, malice burning in his eyes as he sits down at the bar directly in front of me.

"What time do you close?"

"Um, an hour."

"Ah. Then I'll take some coffee while I wait."

I get sick as he stares at me, and I slowly back up, refusing to pull my eyes away. He knows who I am, and I know who he is. He's the night stalker from last night.

"You shouldn't be in here right now. You know what I am," I almost whisper.

"You shouldn't have meddled in my meal and then sent the council after me," he growls.

I narrow my eyes as I place the cup of coffee in front of him, and then I do my best to act composed and in control.

"You shouldn't have been in the open. You risk us all when you kill like that," I murmur in a nearly muted tone.

The sparks in his eyes ignite more fiercely as he smirks all the more - the devil's air in his breath.

"Well, I was famished, and there she was - drunk and alone."

"That's not how things work and you know it."

"Neither is interrupting one's kill. You're just lucky no one wants a damn war."

I laugh a little louder than I meant to, and he glares at me.

"No one would start a war over this shit," I daringly release through my mocking laughter. "You're a speck in a world far larger than you. Interrupting your brazen, open kill was nothing but warranted in the eyes of everyone's councils. I pray someone caught it on tape, and then they'll exterminate you."

He shakes his head, smiling more. "If they saw me, they saw you. You might want to recant that last little bit."

My feigned confidence doesn't waver, and I keep the conversation below the register a human can hear. "The force I used was invisible. You had a girl bent backwards with your fangs dug in. All they'll see is you mysteriously flying backwards and me screaming for help as I rush to her body. Believe me, I've ran through it a time or two."

He snarls, his eyes sparking blue again and his fangs slip free.

"How about I just pick up with you where I left off with her?"

He smirks as he stands, acting as though he's about to prove he hasn't just made an empty threat. But then the door sounds out as new customers arrive, halting him from trying anything.

Thank God.

He snarls louder as he turns, and a wave of butterflies crash through my stomach when I see Kane and his friends walking in.

He smiles as he walks toward the counter, and then his smile falls when he sees the damn vampire still ready to rip my throat out.

"Hey," he says softly, his eyes returning to me and studying my face.

I try to seem casual, not wanting to give this fanged son of a bitch any ideas about going after Kane in order to get revenge on me.

"Hi," I say very professionally, showing indifference instead of pure lust. "What can I get you?"

He frowns, feeling my chilly demeanor, and then he shrugs. "Um, five coffees and a slice of pie each," he murmurs with a bit of disappointment.

I glance back to the night stalker, and then I head over to the coffee. He won't attack with eyes on us. He's in enough trouble as it is.

"I'll bring it to your table," I say with my back turned, and I hear a slight huff as Kane walks away.

"Thanks."

When I turn back, the night stalker is staring at me, slowly sipping his coffee, but I ignore him as I head over to Kane's table - the oversized corner booth. The girl who glared at me the night before is sitting by his side, her body touching his.

Maybe it's good I'm being cold. It seems he has someone already much too into him, and he obviously doesn't mind the attention, since he's sitting by her.

Without speaking, I pass out the coffee and pie, avoiding eye contact with Kane, and then I force an obligatory smile before wandering back behind the counter. They're too close for the night stalker to say more, so he continues to stare at me, trying to scare me.

This could get bad when we're alone, so I decide to text Frankie. I know he's still in town.

Night stalker in diner. Could use your help.

This will cement my mother's fear, and I know she'll be out here as soon as she's finished with the ceremonies.

Crap.

Almost instantly, the door swings open, and in walks Frankie. Kane's head turns to investigate, and he watches the night stalker watching me as Frankie takes a seat at his side.

I smirk as Frankie cracks his fingers, warming up to intimidate the fanged asshole. "I'll take some coffee, Miss."

I stifle a laugh, and I serve him his coffee as requested, my eyes studying the night stalker who is oblivious to the immortal on his side. Realizing we're out of cream, I head to the back to grab a fresh stash.

As I turn around, I gasp for air when I see a body standing too close. I sigh in relief when I see it's Kane.

"You keep scaring the shit out of me," I grumble, shoving him lightly, and he smirks.

"I was starting to wonder if you recognized me." He almost pouts, making me tingle in *all* the wrong places.

I can't fight my foolish grin, and then I roll my eyes. "I recognize you, but I'm at work."

He smiles as he leans over, and his arm presses against the wall over my head.

"Is that guy bothering you? You seem a little rattled around him."

Knowing he'd probably say something to him, I decide it's best to lie. I don't need Kane throwing himself in the middle of a vampire/witch debacle.

"No. I'm just not used to working so long. Apparently the new girl gets used and abused the first few days."

He smiles bigger, and then he leans back.

"What are you doing after work?" he asks while propping up on some crates behind him.

"Why? You having another party?"

He lets out a small laugh and shakes his head. "No party, but I wouldn't mind you coming over… if you want to that is."

"You wouldn't *mind* me coming over? That doesn't sound like much of an invitation," I tease while stacking a few more boxes of stuff in the corner, pretending to stay busy so I don't fall prey to his emerald green eyes.

"I suppose it didn't. Let me rephrase it. Would you like to come over after work?"

Trying not to grin like a girly idiot, I shrug as I turn around. "I could, but it'll be late. I'm closing up at eleven, and then I'll need to go change and wash away the diner."

"I could come to your place if you prefer," he suggests, his lips turning up in a seductive grin.

We'd be alone at my place, and I don't know if that's a good idea… Definitely not a good idea.

"That sounds better, actually," I blurt out. *What?* "You want to meet me there around eleven thirty?"

I've lost my damn mind.

"I'll just swing by and walk you home. I don't like the vibe I'm getting from that guy. I don't mind waiting in your living room."

Oh damn. Tell him no. Tell him never mind.

"Sounds good."

Dumbass girl.

"Great," he says with a smile, and then he ushers me back out.

I glance over to the counter to see Frankie sipping his coffee beside the night stalker who seems a little paler now. Frankie gives me a wink, letting me know he just gave the lone stalker a hint that I have backup.

Kane glances over his shoulder, making butterflies stir when his eyes meet mine, and then he slides back into the booth beside the girl who is now fuming.

"Would you like some more coffee, sir?" I ask while staring at the less antagonistic night stalker.

"No thank you," he says, and then clears his throat. "I should be on my way."

He stands up and throws a ten on the table before walking out with his tail between his legs. I smile at Frankie who leans back with a triumphant grin.

"Well, that's that."

"What'd you say to him?" I whisper.

"Nothing. Sometimes words aren't necessary," he whispers back, and then he gives me a menacing wink. "Just give me a call if you have any more problems."

He stands up and then waves before walking out the door.

Kane turns around and comes to the counter as I wipe it clean and cash out the night stalker's coffee.

"So, it's almost eleven. Can I just stick around?" he asks as his friends come up to leave their money behind on the counter.

"Um, if you want to," I murmur a little shakily.

He smiles as he sits down, and they all start filtering out the door.

"You coming, Kane?" one of the guys asks.

"Nah. I'll be home later. Don't wait up."

I blush fiercely at the way that has to sound, and the guy chuckles in response, while the girl with a black, short bobbed haircut glares at me once again.

"We're supposed to do something tonight," she grumbles.

"Do it without me," he says nonchalantly.

She rolls her eyes and follows the others out, and then Kane props up on the counter as I cash out all the tickets and pocket the extra change as my tip.

"Are you sure she's not your girlfriend?" I ask with a tense tone, my eyes not meeting his.

They're supposed to do something? What does that mean?

"Positive," he exhales very dramatically. "She's just a roommate, but she's got a crush… like you do."

Blushing again, I roll my eyes and walk away from his teasing grin.

"I think you're a little full of yourself," I mumble.

"Hey, you're the one who blushes every time I say something," he menaces, and I turn to see his smoldering gaze burning through me.

"You're the one in my place of work asking to come home with me," I daringly counter, my own sizzling gaze meeting his.

"I never said I don't have a crush."

I blush again, and he leans back while propping his hands up behind his head. The lone guy in the corner with his laptop finally stands and heads out the door without so much as a *thank you.*

"He sat in here all night, taking up a booth, and never even ordered anything," I murmur softly to change the subject.

"Are you ready?" Kane asks, his attempt to seduce me refusing to be deterred as he ignores my statement.

I glance over my shoulder to look at the clock, and see it's five minutes past eleven.

"I suppose so. Just give me a second to wipe down your booth and ring out the register."

"I'll get the booth, you get the register," he says with a grin before picking up my rag and heading away.

I try not to smile like a fool as I rush through the closing process. As soon as I'm done, Kane walks over to hold the door open for me.

Locking it quickly, I turn around to see him staring at me with a gaze so sexy I'm worried my eyes are going to shift again.

"So," I murmur, looking away, "what do you want to do at my place?"

He stifles a laugh, making me blush harder, and then I shake my head.

"Not what I meant," I mumble as he walks side by side with me.

"I didn't say anything," he murmurs, feigning innocence.

"You didn't have to."

He laughs harder as we cross the road in the quiet, still night.

"I thought a movie and popcorn, if you have either. If not, we could just head down to the lake or something."

I'd love to go to the lake with him, but we'd have no privacy there. That's probably better. I don't need to be alone with him. The lake it is.

"I've got a movie and popcorn, so you're in luck."

Apparently my brain and my mouth are no longer linked together. *Good grief.*

"So I should probably ask for your last name," he murmurs while running a hand through his hair. "It's not on your tag."

I chuckle lightly and then say, "Coldwell."

He tilts his head to the side, and then he nods.

"And yours?" I muse. "I suppose I should have asked before inviting you home with me."

A devilish upturn of his lips makes me feel as though I'm coming down with a fever. "You should have. That's very irresponsible of you," he seductively plays. Then he sighs out before answering. "It's... don't laugh... Ice."

I do laugh because he's full of shit, and he lets out a laugh of his own.

"Seriously, what is it?" I giggle out.

He pulls out his wallet while smiling and hands me his license. My eyes fall on his surname that truly says *Ice*.

"Wow. Kane Ice. Unbelievable."

"I know," he says while putting his proof back in his back pocket. "I've caught hell a time or two. When people call me *Vanilla* I get a little agitated."

I giggle louder, and then I feel his hand grazing my back to turn me when I almost walk by my own house.

"Thanks," I murmur softly.

He bites back his grin for my completely stupid move, and he follows me up to the porch as I nervously fumble for my keys.

"If this is making you uncomfortable, we can go back to my place. There will be plenty of people around."

Good idea. Say yes.

"No, I'm fine," I lie, forcing a smile.

What's wrong with me?!

I push open the door, and then I quickly flip on the light to show him my very girly decorated home.

"The diner must pay more than I thought," he murmurs as he looks at my furnishings.

I smile lightly while shaking my head. "Everything you see was a housewarming gift from my mother. I paid for the house out of my savings, which was also started by my mother."

"Well, nevertheless, I'm impressed. I'll wait here for you," he says while flipping on the television and sitting down on my couch.

Suddenly, the flashy sectional looks so much sexier with him on it. His long, perfectly sculpted body makes my body start to sweat as I gape openly at his marvelous physique.

"Yeah," I finally force out, and then I quickly disappear into my bedroom.

I start tossing clothes around, trying to find something that doesn't scream *slut*, while also looking for something that won't make me look undesirable. I suck at mediums.

I hear the shower turn on, and scowl at myself for letting my magic out. The room flies into place, cleaning up my accidental mess, and then I scowl again.

Great. Seeping magic in front of a human. Just what I need.

My phone rings just as I walk into the bathroom, and I roll my eyes when I see who it is.

"Hey, Mom," I murmur casually.

"What are you doing with a boy in your house, Alyssa?" she scolds.

She's lost her mind, and Frankie deserves an ass kicking now. Keeping my voice in a whisper too low to even be heard by an immortal not standing directly beside me, I answer with agitation.

"Tell Frankie thanks for ratting me out."

"It could be dangerous. After last night-"

"He's human. Besides, I'm sure you've got Frankie watching the house for any possible intruders."

"You're sure he's human?" she worries.

"Very. I've been around him at midnight. He's also been alone with me and hasn't tried anything"

She huffs out, not enjoying her total lack of control.

"Well, if something happens, just call for Frankie. He's tuned in."

He might want to tune out.

"Sure will."

"And be careful. Right now, you're less than a year away from your immortality. Your emotions, hormones… everything will be a little out of whack. Don't lose your innocence to some random guy simply because you don't have the control to stop."

"Not having this conversation," I grumble.

"If it gets too intense, just eat some of the carnations I left behind and a drop of honey."

I'm not eating flowers to keep from being horny.

"Got it."

I hang up quickly, and then I rush myself through the shower to cleanse away the burger and fries smell.

Staring at my drowned-rat imagery in the mirror, I sigh. Against all my better judgment, I use my magic to dry and style my hair while also making my makeup appear.

"Breaking my own damn rules so I can hurry up and be with a guy," I mumble under my breath, disgusted with my eagerness.

Deciding not to dwell on my pathetic excitement, I pull on tight pair of jeans and a shirt that drapes off the side of one of my shoulders. Feeling satisfied, I walk out to see Kane is no longer on the couch. A twinge of worry spreads as the thought of the night stalker making his way into my house crosses my mind.

"Kane?" I say a little too crackly.

"In here," he murmurs from the kitchen. "I hate burnt popcorn so I'm watching very closely. I thought you were getting ready."

I smirk as I walk into the kitchen, and he turns to face me with a smile until his eyes fall on my fully redone self. His smile falls, his eyes widen, and his mind becomes clogged with transparently scandalous thoughts.

"Something wrong?" I almost tease.

He swallows hard and then bites back a smile. "Not at all. I just wasn't expecting you to… well, you clean up fast."

"I learned to be quick, thanks to my mother. She's constantly bouncing around from one task to the next."

"Well, I'm impressed again."

I grin as I smell the hint of something familiar, and then my eyes point to the microwave.

"I thought you said you hate burnt popcorn."

"Huh?" he asks with a stupefied stare, and then he turns to follow my gaze. "Shit," he spews while jerking open the door. He frowns as he opens the bag, and then he shakes his head. "Sorry."

"I happen to like it that way," I say with a laugh while pulling down a bowl.

His body brushes up against mine as he pours it in, and I feel my heartbeat quickening from the accidental graze. He swallows hard, and I look up to see him staring at me.

"You look… really good," he murmurs softly.

"Thanks," I murmur while blushing again.

His thumb reaches up to stroke my blushing cheek, and my breath catches in my throat.

"Pink really is a good color on you."

Considering I'm wearing a red top and blue jeans, it's obvious he's now referring to my blushing hue.

"Movie," I strain out, my whole body suddenly aching to feel his hands somewhere else.

He smirks lightly, and takes the popcorn from the counter to start heading into the living area.

"I picked a zombie flick. I thought horror would be better than a chick flick, and those two were quite literally your only options."

I laugh a little and then nod. "Sounds good."

He sits down on the large sectional with the remote in his hand, and I sit down a safe distance away from him.

"You won't be able to reach the popcorn from there. I don't bite… unless you want me to," he jokes, his eyes sizzling through me.

I swallow hard and force a smile as I move in closer. Our legs graze each other's and I stiffen up a little. The smallest touch from him seems to be igniting fires all over my body, and unless he plans to extinguish them, I'll burn alive with too much contact.

"You okay?" he asks as the movie starts.

"Yeah," I shakily release while cramming some of the burnt popcorn into my mouth.

Bring on the blood and gore and kill this lust.

The movie is almost over, and despite the blood and guts, I'm starting to burn worse than the popcorn I almost single handedly demolished. My leg has pushed against his more, and he's slouched down with his hand resting on his leg, close to mine.

So close to my change, my hormones really are at an all time uncontrollable level. This was so stupid. I hate to admit this, but I should have listened to my mother.

"I'll be right back," I murmur uncomfortably while standing up.

He pauses the movie before tilting his head.

"Too much?" he asks, motioning toward the horror scene.

Not enough. I need something to completely kill my desire to rip his clothes off right now.

"Um, nah. I just need something to drink. You want something?"

"Do you have any wine or anything?" he asks curiously.

"Yeah. White or red?"

"White, please."

I smile and nod while diving into the kitchen. I grab the carnations that are resting in the window and bite through the petals while digging around the cabinets for my honey. As soon as I find it, I turn it up and let the slow-falling, sticky mess fall into my mouth.

I swallow hard, and then cringe as the two combine. I grab a cup of water to force it all down, and then I take in a deep breath.

Slowly, the intense feelings start to relieve, and I sigh almost happily.

"Need some help?" Kane asks as he walks in, making me squeal a little from the surprise.

"Sorry," he chuckles out. "I suppose I shouldn't subject you to zombies and then sneak up on you."

I laugh uneasily, and then I turn to start pulling down the wine glasses.

"It's fine. I'm always a little jumpy."

I turn back around to see him propped up, looking far too damn good, and all the relief the carnations and honey gave me dissipates. The look he's giving me is just as carnal and raw as the one I'm giving him.

My control doesn't merely waver, it snaps, and I launch myself at him. I grip him behind the neck to pull him down, and his hands curl around my ass to jerk my hips against him.

His perfect, soft lips collide with mine in the most incredible way, and then his tongue slips in with a commanding force, exploring my mouth. Everything south on me heats up, and then he jerks me up and spins me around to put me on the counter.

I moan into his mouth, making him pull me tighter to him as my legs wrap around his waist, locking him to me. His arousal digs into the center of my pants, making me all the hotter as my fingers slide up to tangle in his hair.

Before I know what's going on, his hand slides under my shirt, finding one of my breasts through my bra, making me moan all the harder.

"Damn, you taste good," he murmurs against my lips, and then suddenly my shirt is over my head and on the floor as his hands slip over my bra strap to unclasp it.

I should stop him. This can't be sane.

Instead, I jerk him tighter to me, bringing his lips back to mine as my chest becomes bare. I hear the clap of my bra slapping the floor, and then I feel him lifting me from the counter and carrying me toward the bedroom.

I gasp when my back hits the bed, and then his lips start trailing down my neck, heating me to my core. I suck in a breath when his hot, wet breath finds my nipple to send tingling shots of excitement shooting through me.

I grip his head, bringing him closer as he starts unbuttoning my pants.

"Alyssa, I can slow down," he murmurs while letting his lips travel to my other breast to give it some attention.

"Please don't."

His ravaging motions pick up, and I tug his shirt over his head to reveal a body I only thought I was prepared to see.

"Oh damn," I breathe, and he smiles salaciously as he finishes unclasping my pants.

"I should be the one saying that. You're fucking ridiculous," he murmurs while his lips find the hollow of my neck.

His hands push down the open pants, and his fingers slide down to find the slick telltale proof of my arousal.

A deep moan exudes from the back of his throat, and I keep my eyes closed to prevent him from seeing the rolodex of crazy shades my eyes are flooding through right now.

"Damn, you're so wet," he murmurs, only making me want him inside me all the more.

I start undoing his belt, and he rips my pants free while I struggle. I can't look. I know my eyes are in hyper-drive right now, and he'd freak the hell out if he saw them.

Then I feel his bare body between mine - apparently he decided to help me out. His erection brushes up against my leg as his lips find the center of my breastbone, and my whole body arches as my panties become drenched from his touch.

His lips slide back up to meet mine, dragging out the suspense. All I can think about is getting him inside me, and I just learned his last name. I met him yesterday. This is crazy.

"Kane," I exhale with my heavy breath, making his moans louder as his erection presses against me through my underwear.

I've never wanted anyone so badly in all my life, and I barely even know him.

Someone pounds on my door, interrupting our crazy hot moment, and he leaps up from the bed to grab his pants.

"Are you expecting anyone?" he breathlessly releases.

"No. Don't answer it," I grumble, knowing damn well Frankie is here to douse our fire.

He drops back down to me, even though now his jeans have been pulled back up. He falls between my legs, and his mouth begins owning mine once again.

"Kane," a guys voice yells through the door.

"Shit," Kane gripes as he stands up again. "I'm so sorry."

"Who is it?" I murmur with a bit of a frazzled tone while covering up with my sheet.

"It's Deke, one of my roommates. I'll be right back."

I watch as he quickly buttons his pants, and then he pulls his shirt on while rushing out the door.

How did he know where I live?

"What the hell, man?" I hear Kane gripe.

"Sorry, it's Amy. She's kind of… gone. I think she got upset about you going off with this chick. We need to find her before-"

"Fine. Fuck," Kane interrupts. "Just give me a second."

Amy? The chick who's obviously in love with him?

I hear him rushing back through, and suddenly I feel incredibly stupid for having allowed myself to be with him. I should have known he had a damn girlfriend.

"Hey," he murmurs as he walks back into the room. "Something came up, and I have to go. I'm really, really sorry, but can I see you tomorrow?"

He walks over to the bed and takes a seat on the edge as I cling to the covers.

"Um, I don't know. Just call me, and I'll see what I've got going on."

He looks at me sideways, as if he's trying to see through me.

"Alyssa, I swear this is the last thing I want to do right now, but I have to. Will you please see me tomorrow… or later today rather?" he asks while looking at the absurd hour on the clock.

"I told you, call me. I don't know what I'll have going on," I murmur, my chill extinguishing the roaring flames.

He sighs out while gripping his head as Deke yells, "Come on, Kane. We've got to get going before she does something stupid."

Kane cringes, apparently not wanting me to hear that, and I look away, not letting on I've already heard more.

"Alyssa, I'll call you after while. I'm sorry," he murmurs while leaning over to kiss me.

I offer him my weakest, coldest kiss, and he pulls back looking torn about what to do. It's just sex he's passing up. He's doing me a huge favor by bailing out before I offer my first time to a creep.

He groans as he finally gets up, and then he walks out to leave me in my shameful bed that is laughing at me for my nearly foolish decision.

I hear the door shut, and then it wiggles as he checks to make sure it's locked. I feel sick at my stomach, and I rise up to rush to the bathroom and expel the proof of my shame.

"So stupid," I mumble while leaning over the toilet.

Wiping my mouth, I stand up and head back into my room to pull on a pajama shirt and a pair of pants that match. A huff falls free when I see his boxers he failed to put on his haste. I pick them up and carry them to the wash, along with my uniform and clothes that all smell like him.

Tossing them all in at once, I flip on the wash and head back to my living room to finish watching the zombie movie still that is paused.

"Bring on the blood, guts, and death."

Chapter Four

My phone buzzes for the fifth time during my shift, and I silence it when I see Kane's number. I groan inwardly and lean over the counter, burying my head in my hands while yawning.

Butterflies and nerves rattle around aimlessly when I look up to see him and two of his guy roommates heading toward the diner.

Squealing lightly, I rush to the back to hide from the mistake I desperately wanted to make. Cindy, another waitress, gasps while putting out her cigarette she's not supposed to be smoking inside.

"Please don't tell," she squeaks.

"I won't if you'll make Kane and the others believe I'm not at work."

She tilts her head. "Kane Ice? He's here to see you and you don't want to see him?" she gushes in disbelief.

"Please," I urge.

She nods hesitantly and then heads around to do my dirty work for me. I listen in to Kane's smooth voice talking to someone else.

"Can I speak to Alyssa Coldwell, please?"

"She's-"

"Actually," Cindy interrupts, "Alyssa left earlier today. We felt sort of bad for making her work over so much two nights in a row, so I told her I'd cover for her tonight."

"Oh. Did she say where she'd be going?" he asks disappointedly.

"I think she was going to meet one of her friends."

Damn it, Cindy. I'm new to town. I don't have any friends yet.

"Sounds like you fucked up," one of his friends chuckles.

Kane lets out a trapped breath of air before responding. "If you see Alyssa, will you tell her I stopped by?"

"Sure," Cindy chirps.

He sighs reluctantly, and I peek around the corner as he and his friends disappear out the door. Cindy squeals in excitement as she rejoins me, and then she throws her hands up like what-the-hell.

"Seriously?" she releases in a girly octave. "Kane Ice is into you and you're hiding from him? What is wrong with you?"

I'm a witch on the verge of turning immortal and I want to fuck his brains out. Probably shouldn't say that.

"He's… too… complicated," I murmur in a huff while returning to the floor to start refilling drinks.

"You've lost your mind. If Kane Ice is looking to talk to you, you run toward him, not away."

She continues following me around like a new puppy as I smile and refill drinks, and then I turn to see her with her hands on her hips.

"I knew blonds have all the fun," she gripes, and I glance in the mirror to see my hair has gotten lighter and lighter. In less than a month, I've gone from having a light brown color to a nearly solid, golden blond.

Crap. Soon I'll match my mother too damn much.

"Well, it's not as much fun as it looks. Listen, just drop it, please. I'm not trying to get involved with anyone right now."

Her shoulders drop as she silently pouts. "Fine," she grumbles. "So, tonight, will you-"

"No. I can't work over tonight. My shift ends in an hour, and I'm going to get off my feet for one night," I crankily murmur as I glance to see it's nearly six.

She chuckles a little and shakes her head. "I wasn't going to ask you to stay over. Some friends of mine are having a little party up the road, and I was wondering if you'd come. Apparently you draw in the right attention."

The praise in her eyes doesn't go unnoticed. She really thinks I've got something special. She'd feel stupid for thinking such a thing if she knew he ran off to be with *Amy* - while I was naked!

I offer a tight smile, and then I glance around the diner to see if I'm finished for now.

"Sure. I've got nothing better to do."

"Great," she squeals, clapping her hands once after jumping up.

"Kane won't be there, will he?" I worry.

"He's never come to one of their parties before. It's usually just a small gathering of the same old people, but tonight they've got some of the vacationers coming. There're supposed to be some serious hotties."

I smile and then head back behind the counter just as my phone buzzes again.

Kane.

Eventually he'll take a hint. For now, I've just got to dodge and ignore him.

Cindy's arm loops through mine as we head into the house too close to where Kane lives. I hadn't realized how very close we'd be, or I would have said no.

"You're sure he won't be here?" I rattle out nervously.

"Like I said, he's never come before. One of his roommates doesn't get along with Heath, my friend's husband."

"Okay," I murmur with some relief.

"So, what's the deal?" she muses. "With Kane I mean."

He's the bad boy I almost threw my virginity at, only to have him run out in the middle of the night to go be with another girl after she got upset.

"Long, weird, terrible story. Where's the booze?"

She laughs and then grabs me a cup full of a liquid stout enough to raise the dead.

"Whoa," I cough out

She laughs and then clanks her plastic cup against mine before sucking it back. I cringe as the tart, bitter taste lingers in my mouth after I've forced it down, but at least I should be able to get drunk.

"Hey," a tall, blond, smoking hot guy murmurs far too close to me.

"Hey yourself," I lightly flirt while turning my cup up again.

"Hey," Cindy squeaks, her red curls bouncing with excitement.

He smiles at her briefly, and then he turns his attention back to me.

"I'm Thad. And you?" he asks curiously.

"Alyssa. Are you a vacationer?"

"No, I just moved in a little across the way, close to Midbrook and Holtz."

"Awesome, Alyssa lives around there," Cindy interjects.

He tilts his head to the side, and then he leans up beside me while clanking the side of his cup to mine.

"Here's to new neighbors then," he says with a sexy grin, making me flush a little. Another bad boy. Just my luck.

"I suppose so."

Cindy frowns, possibly feeling ignored, and she wanders off to leave me alone with Mr. Blond Heaven.

"So, how long have you lived here?" he asks while getting a little closer.

"Less than a week," I chuckle out, and he lets a laugh free as well.

"Well then, I guess we're both the new kids on the block."

"I guess we are," I murmur while turning up the glass. "So how do you know the people that live here?"

"I don't," he laughs. "I'm a total party crasher. I guess I'm busted, but I thought it'd be a good way to meet some of the locals."

"Well, instead you met me. Another newbie."

He smirks, but doesn't laugh like I do. "I'd say this was a party worth crashing."

I blush lightly, and then Cindy walks back in.

"Hey, Alyssa, come here. I want to introduce you to Misty and Heath."

I turn to face the platinum blond vision, and then I hold my hand out to shake his.

"I guess I should go mingle. It was nice meeting you, Thad."

He smiles, pulling my hand to his lips instead of shaking it, and then he plants a soft, sweet kiss on the back. "It was very nice to meet you, Alyssa."

The way he looks at me makes me blush again, and I turn away, happy that someone else is interested in me besides Kane - the asshole who left me naked in bed while he went to find his missing girlfriend.

Time to drink until I can quit thinking about him.

The howls of the drunk exude the howls of the wild as I giggle over every stupid joke told. Staggering, I make my way outside where Heath is standing.

"This is a great party," I slur.

He laughs, though nothing is funny, and I laugh too while hanging off the back deck overlooking the lake.

"I'm glad you came."

"Me too," I chirp while chugging another guzzle.

He smiles as he leans toward me, and a sick feeling strikes my gut right before he jerks me forward into a kiss. I push him back with all my strength to shove him off while wiping his slobber from my face.

"What the hell?" I scold. "You're married."

He laughs and shakes his head. "Lighten up. It's a party."

He starts toward me again, and I dart underneath his drunken grasp and rush down the stairs to escape him, happy to reach the yard.

"Alyssa, I can play this game," he chuckles out, and I start scouring the party in search of Thad, praying he's still here.

I'm not surprised when I don't find him - since I haven't seen him in hours - and I start running to escape the drunken fool following too close behind.

My phone buzzes, and I juggle it up to my ear, hoping it's Frankie getting ready to scoop in and save me.

"Are you seeing this?" I ask, though my drunken stupor has made my words sound unintelligible and malformed. "Where the hell are you already, Frankie? I need your help."

"Alyssa? Are you drunk?" Kane's voice sounds out, and I get all the sicker as silence steals my breath, his voice concreting my feet to the ground. "Alyssa, where are you?"

The music blares louder as several drunken people stagger out of the house, and then I feel arms wrapping around me far too tightly.

"Let me go!" I yell while struggling under Heath's grasp.

"I've got you now," he chuckles out.

"Alyssa, damn it! Where are you?!" Kane demands.

"I swear I'll break you like a damn twig if you don't let me go right now!" I screech.

My phone drops to the ground as I start trying to free myself from this asshole's grip. If I use my power on him, I'm breaking the law of the light. If I don't use it, I'll probably end up dealing a consequence that I'm not willing to face.

I finally get enough leverage to stomp his foot, making him yelp and loosen his grip, and giving me the chance to start running again. I cry out as I stumble and crash to the ground, but knowing that scum is right behind me, I pull myself up and start running again.

I look over my shoulder to see Heath gaining on me, and suddenly I'm brought to an abrupt halt as I slam into a hard body. New arms wrap around me to keep me from collapsing to the ground.

"Alyssa," Heath chuckles out from not far behind, but when I look up, I see the fury burning in Kane's eyes as his grip on me tightens.

Shit! How'd he find me?

"Kane," Heath murmurs in surprise as his groggy eyes zoom in.

"Heath," Kane strains out through gritted teeth. "I think you should get back to your wife, don't you?"

His grip tightens on me more when my legs try to give out, and Heath's eyes glaze over with fear as Kane stares him down.

"Um, yeah," the stupid ass murmurs, and then he turns to walk away, leaving me alone with the guy I damn near gave something I couldn't get back.

He breathes out heavily, watching Heath until he staggers off into the shadows, and then he looks down to me.

"You okay?" he says too sincerely.

"Peachy," I mumble while trying to wobble free from his grip.

"Damn, you're so drunk right now," he sighs while catching me before I lose my footing again.

"So what?"

He doesn't have time to answer before the heel on my shoe breaks and I go falling forward. I tense up, but I'm suddenly going up before I hit the ground. Kane pulls me into his arms in a bridal-style carry.

"Kane, please put me down. I want to go home," I gripe while struggling.

"I'm sure you do, but you're too drunk to walk, and quite frankly, I'm not taking you home until I know you're not going to have alcohol poisoning."

"That's a little melodramatic," I scoff.

"No, ignoring me all day, staying away from your house, and then getting drunk at some random party where you don't have any friends there to have your back is melodramatic."

His tone is almost scolding, and I start to laugh at how absurd he sounds.

"Stalk me much?"

His jaw tenses, proving he's a little madder than I realized.

"Alyssa, you're obviously pissed, and all I want is a chance to explain about last night."

"It's fine. I'm sure *Amy* was thrilled to have you come after her, especially when she found out you left me naked in the bed to run out."

He huffs loudly, cursing under his breath, and then he murmurs, "You heard that? Why didn't you just say something?"

I squirm uselessly in his powerful grip. I'm too drunk to be very strong right now. Fuck it.

"Sounded like a personal problem, and it was obvious I was the other woman."

He groans, frustration rolling over him as he readies himself for the *big explanation.*

"Not even close to being the case. Yes, Amy is a little obsessed with me, but I've *never* been with her. She's just my damn roommate," he grumbles, as if he's exasperated. "She gets a little crazy, but we usually just calm her down."

"How? Do you put her back in her cage?" I mumble sardonically, not really meaning for him to hear, but he lets a laugh out.

"Something like that," he snickers.

Obviously I didn't say that as quietly as I meant to.

"How did you find me?"

He motions behind him with his head, though I have no idea what he's motioning to.

"The music. It's not like we haven't heard it thudding every time we go outside. We don't go to Heath's parties, but I would have shown up sooner, had I known you were there."

"Why? So you could tell me all about leaving me naked in the bed to go chase after another girl?"

His head drops back as he lets out another exasperated groan.

"You're really blowing this out of proportion. The last thing I wanted to do was leave you. Believe me, it was painful to do. But that's not why I would have shown up. Heath has a reputation for doing girls the way he tried to do you tonight."

"Oh," I mumble, looking away as a sick pang strikes.

That was way too damn close.

"So I suppose your mother's friend - Frankie - was supposed to be watching out for you?"

I thought so.

"I just assumed he was. I guess he would have been if I told him I was going out."

"I would have been if you had just talked to me."

I sigh, not really sure if I want to be talking to him right now. He definitely didn't do much for my confidence.

"Sorry, but I still don't feel right about all this. I shouldn't have even let you in my bed, and now you're whisking me away to who knows where."

"My house," he says as we start up the steps, making me look around.

My jaw drops when I see the three story cabin stretching wide. There's no way they can afford this beast. And he thought my place was impressive?

"Okay, this definitely doesn't feel right. I really don't want to be around Amy right now."

He frowns, and then he shakes his head.

"Don't worry about her. She knows not to mess with you, and she'll eventually get the hell over me."

Doubtful.

I sure as hell can't seem to stop thinking about him, and I just met him.

"Just take me home, please."

"If I take you home, I'm staying with you. I'm not leaving you alone tonight, not with the heavy amount of alcohol you've apparently taken in."

I can't let him stay with me because then I wouldn't be able to sneak out to get away.

"Fine," I huff. "I'll stay until I'm sober enough to leave."

He smirks, and then his delicious lips stroke my forehead as a guy opens the door to the cabin for us.

"Did you kick his ass?" he asks.

"No, but it was hard not to. Do me a favor, Zee, will you go grab Alyssa's phone? I think she dropped it around the midway point."

"Yeah, sure. Maybe I'll get the chance to run into Heath."

The menace in his eyes is unmistakable. They really hate Heath.

"Play nice. Don't cause a scene," Kane warns before walking through the enormous living area filled with gallant, large widows.

The others are stretched out on couches and chairs, some of them coupled up, and the others seeming causally engaged in whatever movie they're watching. Then I get sick when I see Amy staring at me with the scorned woman's fury.

"Should have kept her in that cage," I almost whisper, and Kane lets out a laugh again.

"You're probably right," he murmurs while kissing my forehead again.

"You alright?" one of the girls asks, seeming sincere in her concern.

"Fine, just drunk," I mumble.

She smirks and then she stands to walk to a door and opens it for us. Her soft auburn hair falls to her shoulders. Her eyes are dark, smoky blue, and they have a depth that shows experience beyond her years, giving her a delicate but mysterious edge.

"Heath is a total creep, and he knows it," she almost growls. "He's one person I'd like to break my no-violence rule for."

"I think that goes for all of us," Kane murmurs while carrying me through the doorway, and then I feel a plush bed beneath me as he puts me down.

"Let me know if you need anything," she says while shutting the door behind her.

"At least she's not psycho for you." I sigh while turning over on my side, avoiding looking at him.

"Definitely not. Sierra is Deke's girl, and she's pretty cool... like a sister to me." He walks over to a dresser and pulls out a tee-shirt, and then tosses it to me. "You can sleep in that, or I can see if Sierra has something you can borrow."

"I'll stay in my clothes because I'm leaving the second I'm sober."

His sweet face is taken over with agitation.

"Alyssa, you're not getting sober until you get some sleep. Change or I'll change you."

That shouldn't turn me on, so why does it?

"Fine. I'll change," I mumble while sitting up and pulling my shirt over my head.

He coughs and turns his back, and I let a laugh free.

"Like you didn't see more last night. Afraid you'll feel the urge to run off again?" I taunt.

He turns back around as I slip on his shirt, and then he walks over to me to pull my lips to his, devouring me by surprise. He jerks my hips to his and rips my pants free from my body.

Heat floods through my veins, burning me alive from the inside in the most divine way. *Damn he tastes so good.*

"Shit," he murmurs while backing away. "I didn't want to look because I knew it'd be hard as hell to stop myself, but I'm not some asshole like Heath who's ready to pounce on a girl while she's drunk."

"You didn't have a problem stopping yourself when I was completely sober."

My snarky comment forces a wince from him. He runs his hands through his hair, demonstrating how terribly frustrated he is.

"Please don't keep punishing me for that," he groans. "I've already explained it and told you I was sorry several times."

Sorry doesn't piece back together my dignity or my confidence. How's a girl supposed to feel?

"I'm not punishing you, I'm just stating the obvious."

I try to ignore the throbbing desire to straddle him right now, but it's almost overwhelming. One thing that helps me is the fact I really don't feel like being turned down a second time.

He sighs as he climbs into bed beside me, and then his arm drapes around my waist as he pulls me to him.

Now that he's touching me, it makes it all the harder to deny the throbbing ache inside me, pulsating at the spot no one has ever gone. When his arousal brushes against my back, I shiver.

"Kane, you're not exactly making this easy on me," I mumble, and his sharp intake of breath follows my words.

"Sorry. This isn't easy for me either."

He uncoils from my body, and then he rolls over to the other side of the bed to leave me all the more distraught and yearning for his touch.

I close my eyes tightly, praying for sobriety and sleep both. Maybe I can make it through the night without dreaming about him.

Chapter Five

The sun blinds me as it peers through the enormous window in front of my face. Shielding my eyes, I climb free from the bed to hear laughter and animated conversation on the other side of the door.

"Hey, I found the best new video," one of the guys laughs out. "You have to see it."

"Not right now. I'm trying to get Alyssa some breakfast ready before I take her home," Kane murmurs in objection, and I tense up.

I definitely don't want to see him right now… not after the idiot I looked like last night.

I start picking up my clothes and stepping into them as quickly as I can. My bra is nowhere to be found. Apparently I shed it during the night while I was sleeping, and right now I don't have time to find it.

I open the window to the balcony, and I grimace when I see how far down it is.

I hate using magic.

I force the ladder on the ground to rise to the window, and I tuck my high-heels under my arm as I climb down quickly. With a flick of my wrist, the ladder slides down and back into its place before I run like hell through the woods Kane forbid me to travel without him.

After the first briar tears at my foot, I pull on my heels, deciding to brave the woods in shoes never meant for hiking or running. I forgot I broke one of the heels off, so now I have to run like a gimp idiot through the patch of forest. This walk of shame is by far the worst one ever experienced, and I'm *still* a damn virgin.

I stumble onto the sidewalk, and then I remove my heels again as all the judgmental eyes of the quiet street fall on me.

Small town slut.

It'd be great if I actually got to have sex while being a slut.

I look over my shoulder, worried someone I actually *know* is going to see me, and then I feel myself colliding and arms wrapping around me to steady me as mail drops to the ground.

"Hey, whoa," a familiar voice chuckles out.

I turn to see Thad - fresh, clean, and looking just as sexy in the sun as he did under the moonlight.

"Hey," I bumble out.

"I guess you had a rough night," he says, amused, while staring at my bare, bleeding feet, my heels in my hand, and my previous night's clothing. Not to mention, I'm sure my hair is a hot mess.

"Um, yeah, you could say that. I ended up crashing with someone I know after getting a little too drunk to make it home."

My embarrassment has to be radiating from me with a blinding glare.

"I see," he says with his adorable grin, while his soft, blond hair strums through the fingers of the gentle breeze.

He kneels down and examines my bleeding feet, making me self conscious because I feel so icky right now. I'm glad humans can't read auras. I'd be mortified if he was an aura reader.

"Have you got anything to clean that up with?" he asks while standing back up.

"Um, I'm sure I do. Don't worry about it."

"Let me come help you. You definitely don't want an infection since you said you have to stand on your feet at work."

Sighing, I nod. I really don't know the first thing about cleaning up a wound. I've always had an overprotective mother to do that for me.

"You sure you don't mind?" I ask while walking by him, noticing his house is directly beside mine.

Great. As if I need another guy clogging up my head.

"Positive, where do you live?"

I let out a laugh as he picks his mail back up.

"Right beside you."

He smirks, a menacing twinkle flashes in his eye, and then he stands to his feet to follow me.

"I guess I should bring you a cup of sugar or something sometime."

I chuckle lightly at his corny joke.

He's so tall, like Kane, but he's tanner, and his shoulder are a little broader. His hips are still seductively narrow, like the dark-haired man who I've now slept with but still haven't *slept* with.

This town shouldn't be allowed to have so much sex appeal. It's too small. If the humans are this hot, I dread seeing the immortals.

"Wow, this is really nice," he murmurs as he follows me in.

"Thanks," I murmur softly as we head inside, then I feel a little sad as I think back to Kane walking in here just a couple of nights ago.

"So, let's see your foot," he ushers while motioning for me to sit down.

"It's both of them," I mumble while gripping my head in embarrassment.

"Should I ask why you felt it necessary to run home in broken shoes through the woods?"

I laugh bitterly while dropping my head back on the couch, and he gets up.

"Long story short, I didn't mean to spend the night with this person I know, so I snuck out while I could."

A knowing grin falls over his lips, and he bobs his head in a nod.

"Ah, one of *those* friends. Been there. So where's the alcohol, Band-Aids, and stuff like that?"

Not really one of those friends.

"Under the sink in the kitchen. Thank you for doing this, by the way," I murmur as he heads into the kitchen.

"What are neighbors for? The way I see it, small town people tend to band together and shut out outsiders. We'll have to start our own little gang."

I laugh lightly, amused by his positive outlook, and he smiles warmly as he walks back in while carrying an armload of supplies.

"Well, I owe you for this. My feet are not exactly very pretty right now."

He places a small bowl of water at my feet, and then he walks out again.

"I'll take care of it."

Suddenly my door swings open, and my head whips around to see Kane towering over me.

"Shit, Alyssa. You scared the hell out of me. How did you leave this morning?" He takes a steadying breath as he tries to calm down, surprising me with his worry.

I hadn't thought about my disappearance scaring him.

"You guys must have been in the kitchen or something," I lie.

"Why the hell did you just leave? And what's wrong with your feet?"

He slides around to be in front of me as he inspects my disgusting feet covered in dirt and matted blood. I didn't like Thad seeing them, but I sure as hell don't want Kane to see them.

I start curling them away from his view just as Thad walks back in with an awkward smile.

"I'm about to clean them up," he says, making Kane's head whip around, his eyes narrowing.

"And you are?" he prompts.

"I'm her neighbor. She sort of ran into me this morning - very literally - on her way in."

Kane relaxes slightly, returning his gaze to my dreadfully embarrassing feet.

"Ah, well, I'm here now. I'll take care of it," Kane says dismissively, picking up my foot.

"Stop, please. This is so embarrassing," I grumble while trying to pull my foot back.

"Did this happen last night or this morning?" he sighs.

I try cling to what shred of dignity I have left by refusing him an answer, but he stares at me expectantly, his eyes telling me he's more stubborn than I am.

"This morning," I mumble reluctantly.

Kane swears under his breath, scolding me with his eyes just before he resumes his examination.

"Alyssa? You okay with that?" Thad asks, putting me in an even more awkward position as he stares down Kane.

Kane snorts derisively, and I shrug while tightening my lips.

"Yeah, I guess so. I'll see you later, Thad. Thank you."

He doesn't seem too happy, but he puts the stuff on the floor beside Kane and walks around behind me.

"If you need me, you know I'm not far away. I'll see you after while."

Kane makes sure to shoot him a threatening glare, which confuses me, and Thad glowers back before walking out very reluctantly.

"I leave you alone for five seconds and the wolves are at the door," Kane grumbles as soon as the door shuts.

"He was just trying to help. I met him last night at the party before Heath went crazy."

His jaw tenses as he brings the bowl of water closer to him and starts the process of cleaning me up.

"Where was *Thad* when you were being chased around by a pervert?" he scoffs, his jealousy a little bit bemusing but somewhat exciting.

I bite back a smile as he washes away the dirt from my feet.

"I don't know. I think he had already left. I was there a while. Are you jealous?" I poke, and he stifles an embarrassed grin.

"I'm not crazy about you spending the night in my bed and then finding another guy in your house less than an hour later."

I laugh lightly as he starts towel-drying my feet.

"He was getting his mail when I came barreling down the sidewalk and slammed into him. He offered to help, and considering I have to go to work in a few hours, I decided I should let someone who knew what they were doing help out."

He looks up, his hands burning against the back of my leg as he stares into my eyes.

"Well, you're in luck. I happen to know a great deal about doctoring up scratches. You shouldn't let strangers into your house."

He looks back down, and I laugh again.

"Um, you realize *you're* still a stranger?" I muse.

He snickers lightly, and then he shakes his head.

"Yes, but I'm a stranger you can trust. You either don't realize how incredibly gorgeous you are, or you're far too trusting. Twice I've found you in a bad situation with a drunken ass at a party, and then I find some random guy in your house. A girl who looks like you shouldn't be so quick to trust."

I blush fiercely. Hearing his praises makes me start feeling hot in all the wrong places as his touch ignites that stupid, tempting fire I wish would stop blazing.

"I'm a little tougher than you might think."

He presses the alcohol swab against my cut, and I wince while reflexively jerking free from his grip when it burns.

"Yeah, you're superman alright," he sardonically releases after my whimpering reaction to the burning liquid.

"That's different," I huff, my lower lip pouting playfully.

His eyes suddenly shift from scolding concern to lusting desire, making me worry the windows in the house are all going to fog over.

"Please put that weapon away," he says with a wry grin.

"Weapon?" I murmur with a touch of breathlessness while falling prey to his gaze.

He abandons my foot, and jerks me to his body as he kneels between my legs. His lips attack mine as his tongue forces itself into my mouth, demanding my arousal.

He pulls back, his thumb strolling over my lower lip, and then he smirks.

"Yes, that weapon."

Swallowing hard, I pull him by the back of the neck back to my lips. His hand slides up my shirt, finding my breast and forcing a moan from my throat before his forceful touch starts becoming more urgent.

His passion and desire pours into my mouth. My hand slides down to feel his erection through his jeans, making me all the hotter as the firm piece of perfection tries to break free from the fabric.

"Alyssa, you're killing me," he groans against my lips while ripping me up from the couch. "I want you so damn bad."

"Then take me," I breathe, moaning louder when his lips reclaim mine.

My legs wrap around his waist as he starts carrying toward the bedroom. Then suddenly his phone starts buzzing.

No!

"Fuck," he grumbles while pulling back and lowering me to where my feet touch the ground.

I shift uncomfortably, confused by why I can't seem to say *no* to him. It's as though I lose all control and desire rules my body.

"What?" he snaps into the phone, and without thinking, my hand slides down the front of his pants to feel his delicious erection - hard, perfect, and ready to be inside me.

His breath hitches, and then he has to clear his throat. The phone is so quiet that I can't hear the person on the other side, which is unusual, given my exceptional inhuman hearing.

"You're going to have to take care of it without me... No, I'm not leaving...

I don't care."

He grips his head as my hand slides out of his pants, and then he looks at me as if he's tortured. I know that means he's about to have to leave, and I suddenly feel very dirty again.

"Fine. Fuck... Just meet me at the gallery in ten minutes."

He hangs up, and then he jerks me to his body before his lips crush mine, making me shiver before I push him away.

"Amy needs you again?" I mumble under my breath while turning away.

"Alyssa, it's not like that. Deke needs my help with something, but I swear I'll be back in no time. Please, please don't be mad at me."

My body officially hates him. This is twice I've been on the edge of finally getting rid of my damn innocence, and twice I've been blown off.

"I'm not mad. Go do what you have to. I need to... Hey, do you have my phone?" I murmur, ready to start picking up the pieces of my confidence that are still scattered around the floor of my room.

"Yeah." He sighs while pulling it out of his back pocket and hands it to me. "I meant to tell you it was ringing earlier."

"I have some calls to make." I groan inwardly when I see Frankie's number showing up at least ten times.

"Alyssa, please say I can see you in a little while."

I shrug, not really trusting myself not to fuck him if he returns. I should have more self respect than this.

"I don't know. I've got work, you've got... *stuff* to deal with. I guess we'll see," I murmur dismissively.

He huffs loudly, cursing to himself while gripping his head again.

"I swear I'll take you somewhere no one can find us," he almost pleads, and I let a laugh escape.

"It's probably for the best. This is all moving too fast anyhow. Just go help Deke. I've got to get a shower and put some stuff on my feet."

I start walking away, but he grabs my hand and whirls me around. Without giving me a second to protest, his lips find mine, his tongue invades, and his strong hands hold me to him, forcing my already throbbing center to start aching painfully.

"Say you'll see me later," he softly demands.

"I'll see you later," I murmur involuntarily - a little breathless - as my eyes burn into his.

I'm praying the mood stone craziness isn't going on right now, but I look away to be safe.

"I'll call you, and then I'll come pick you up before work. We'll go eat or something."

Or I'll go in to work early to avoid this.

"Sure."

He tightens his lips, and with exasperated reluctance, he releases me to rush through my door. Once I hear the click of the front door closing behind him, I let out my own huff.

I've never known of any girl having such a hard time losing her damn virginity.

I flip on the television to see something that makes me sick. Quickly turning up the volume, I lower myself to the couch when my legs try to fold.

"Samantha Taylor has been reported missing since late last night. She was supposed to close up at work, but her mother says she never came home. Police have found proof of a scuffle inside the diner where Samantha works, and they're currently running down every lead. If you have any information-"

I shut off the TV. I'm so sick and dizzy after hearing that. I just saw Samantha last night. I'm usually the one closing up. What if the night stalker who was after me decided to feast on Samantha in my absence?

Picking up my phone to dial Frankie, I head back into the living area, the weight of my guilt striking my heart. I saved one girl, but then I got another killed.

"It's about damn time you called me back," he gripes angrily, a little worked up.

"Sorry. Long story short, I lost my phone for a while. Where were you last night?"

"Why? Did something happen? Were you attacked?" The panic in his voice tells me I should downplay the occurrences from last night.

"Just some human issues. Nothing that couldn't be handled by a regular person."

Though Kane is far from regular.

Frankie sighs out his relief, and then suddenly he's walking through my front door as a shadow puff of smoke follows behind him, proving he just manipulated the air around him.

"Well," he says while putting down the phone, "I followed the night stalker you had a run-in with. I was worried he'd come after you, so I wanted to keep my eyes on him. I followed him three towns over, keeping my distance of course, and then I watched him get ripped apart."

My hand covers my gaping mouth as I gasp in disbelief.

"By who?"

"A group of them. I could tell by the way some of them were moving they were his own kind. There were lycans in the mix too - fully changed and snarling like vicious pets. Two lycans and three night stalkers working together. It's unusual for them to team up and kill one of their own."

"Did the night stalker I pissed off kill Samantha?" I whimper.

"Who?" he muses just as my phone rings.

I pick it up, recognizing the number from the diner, and hold up a finger to Frankie while answering.

"Hello?"

"Alyssa, this is Wade. I suppose you've seen the news," he murmurs with a heavy tension in his tone.

"Yeah, I just saw it. Are you okay?" I ask sincerely.

"Right now I'm just worried about Samantha. I pray she's okay. The reason I'm calling is because I'm closing the diner for the next few days while the police investigate. Whoever did this could come back. Whenever I reopen it, no one is to close alone."

"I understand," I murmur while glancing up at Frankie who has most likely overheard both sides of the conversation, given his look of dread.

I hang up, and Frankie grips his head.

"How is it you chose this town - one where night stalkers hang out with lycans, night stalkers kill openly, girls keep popping up missing almost daily... I mean, what's wrong with Miami or Palm Springs?"

I release an exasperated, dramatic laugh while dropping to the couch.

"Just my luck, I guess. Did you call Mom?" I sigh out.

"I tried, but she's apparently enthralled with the ceremonies. I'm sure she'll call me back when she's free."

"Great. I'm sure she'll yank me out of here the second she finds out a turf war is at play."

"This is bigger than a turf war. Last night, the other night stalkers stood by and watched the two lycan females drain the vampire's body of life and blood."

"Did you see them in human form?" I ask curiously.

"No. I couldn't ever get a look at the night stalkers either. It was too dark, and obviously, I kept my distance. I didn't want to be next on the menu."

Swallowing hard, I stand up and head for the wine. Despite the fact I got entirely too drunk last night, I really need a drink right now.

"I need a drink and a shower. You sticking around?" I ask curiously while heading to the kitchen.

"Yeah. I need to make some calls, find out how long your mother is going to be indisposed."

I nod, the feeling of dread cloaking me as I think of how royally pissed my mother is going to be, and then I pour my drink and carry the bottle of wine with me to the bathroom. One glass isn't going to cut it.

Chapter Six

"Any word from Mom yet?" I ask as I walk out fully dressed and towel-drying my hair.

"No," he sighs. "I can't get a hold of any of her guards either. They must be deep under."

I check to make sure my makeup isn't running, and then I head back into the kitchen in search of something to eat. A knock at the door interrupts my search, and Frankie stands up, ready to pounce.

"Chill, Frankie. It's probably my neighbor checking up on me."

He doesn't relax though, and as soon as I open the door, I tense up more than him.

"Kane," I murmur before sucking in a sharp breath, and he gives me a devilish smirk while stepping in.

"I decided to skip the phone calls. I wasn't going to risk you ignoring me again," he murmurs, his breath finding my neck as he pulls me to his body. "Damn you smell good."

His hands run through my wet hair as he crushes his lips to mine, and then my lips part to invite in his expert tongue.

"Ah hmm," Frankie says with a throat clearing chuckle.

Kane quickly cuts his gaze toward the warlock, and I let an embarrassed grin free.

"Another wolf?" He sighs, and I laugh a little when I see the sheer jealously blossoming in his perfectly green eyes.

"Sorry. Frankie, Kane. Kane, Frankie," I quickly introduce.

"Your mother's friend?" Kane muses. His body relaxes but his eyes continue to study Frankie curiously.

To the untrained eye, Frankie looks young - thirty at the most- but in all reality, Frankie has seen the realm of Author, the rise of the Roman Empire, the Trojan war... He's old as shit to put it bluntly.

"Well, I'd like to consider myself Alyssa's friend too," Frankie snickers.

Kane's grip on me doesn't loosen, but his hand does trail down my back to pull me into him.

"Um, Frankie, will you let me know something when she calls back?" I ask, hinting for him to get the hell out of the house.

"Yeah. I'm sure she'll want to talk to you soon."

I'm sure she will.

I'm definitely not leaving until I've at least had a chance to be with Kane. I know it's not possible to stay with a human, but I also want to be with him as long as I can. It's so ridiculous to have such feelings so early on, but I want him.

Frankie waves as he walks out, and Kane's arms return to pull me to him.

"So what was it this time?" I ask, trying not to sound bitter, but failing slightly.

"Deke needed some help with a... problem, so to speak. Zee and I went with him."

I back away, heading toward the kitchen once again, and he follows me.

"Is that all I get?" I sigh out, not sure if I even have the right to be prying.

"It's sort of a personal thing that you'd probably never understand. So, you hungry?" he asks as I pull out a prepackaged salad.

"Very, you?" I ask, checking my fridge for more.

"In more ways than one, but if you've got another salad, that will do," he says far too seductively. "Or we can go back to my place and I can make you something before you go to work."

I lean back while shaking my head, feeling my damp hair starting to seep through my shirt. *Crap.* I really wish I wasn't standing here with wet hair right now.

"Actually, they canceled work. A girl I work with was snatched from the diner last night just before she closed up. Wade is pretty upset, and he's not opening the place back up for a few days."

His eyes widen. "I haven't even heard about that. Shit. You've been closing."

"I know. It freaked me out a little, but I'm just worried about her right now."

"You're sure as hell not closing by yourself anymore. I don't care if I have to sit in there for your entire shift."

I bite back a smile, wondering how he can care so much when he barely knows me.

Without over thinking it, I drop the salad and jerk his lips to mine, feeling his immediate response trying to burst free from his pants as he moans into my mouth. Gripping my ass, he picks me up, forcing my legs to rise and straddle his waist as he starts carrying me to the bedroom once again.

I gasp as he drops me to the bed and then falls between my parted legs. He turns his phone off and then tosses it to the ground while smiling.

"No interruptions this time," he says with a devious grin.

My lower lip slides between my teeth as my anticipation builds, and he slowly runs his finger under the waistband of my pants.

A loud, obnoxious banging rattles us out of our moment, and his head drops to his chest.

"Are you fucking kidding me?" he growls.

"Why did you tell your friends where I live?" I huff as he stands to go answer the intruder.

"Because I'm stupid like that," he grumbles on his way to the door. "I swear I'm not leaving this time."

I flop down, waiting to hear why they have to have him right away, when suddenly Frankie's ashen face is in my room.

"What the hell?" I panic, and Kane quickly follows in behind him.

"Alyssa, come on. We've got to go. Your mom is missing."

My heart slaps my chest, my head spins, and I get dizzy and nauseated at once.

"I'll come with you," Kane quickly interjects while scooping up his shoes.

"Sorry, but you can't. This is family only right now," Frankie vaguely counters.

More like magic only. Shit. Mom, where are you?

"Yeah, let me grab my stuff. I'll meet you outside."

Kane looks so torn about what to do as I rush around to grab some stuff and throw it in a bag.

"Alyssa, please let me come help you out. I can be there for you when you have to talk to the cops."

There won't be any cops, just an immortal council.

"I'll call you as soon as I can, but right now I should just go with Frankie. I'm sorry," I murmur with tears teetering on my lids.

"Don't be sorry. Let me know if I can do anything. If you need me, I'll be there."

My heart melts, and if I wasn't in a complete panic over my mom, I'd probably say something really stupid right now.

"Thanks," I squeak out as the first tear finally falls.

He wipes it away, and then he kisses my forehead so sweetly before pulling me into a comforting embrace I don't want to leave.

"Alyssa!" Frankie prompts.

"I'm coming," I whimper out, and Kane follows me to the door as I rush to the car Frankie has apparently swindled from someone.

Kane props up against my porch railing as he watches me disappear into the car with Frankie. We pull away, and I feel his eyes still on me, wishing he could help me.

"What do they know?" I prompt, trying not to fall apart.

"All they'll tell me is that she's missing. When there's a blood relative alive, the council won't release the details to anyone else. When we get there, keep your eyes low. Some of these council members aren't far from dark users. They'll consider eye contact an insult, and it won't faze them to strike. I wouldn't even be letting you doing this if-"

"If you weren't secretly in love with my mother," I interrupt, making his breath catch. "I wouldn't let you not let me do this. She's my mother. She'd already be there if it was me. I wish you could vaporize me with you and get us there quicker."

"I could, but you'd die," he sighs. "Just hang on. This thing looks like a family car, but I've replaced the engine with something a little… faster."

The engine roars as he gasses it, snapping me back against the seat, and I close my eyes as we push forward.

"Thank you for coming out, Ms. Coldwell. I'm sorry we're not meeting under better circumstances," the frigid lady sitting near the end murmurs very insincerely.

I swallow the rude, foul thing I want to yell at her, and summon up my best cordial face, remembering to keep my eyes low and my tone humble.

"Thank you for seeing me. Could you please give me what information you have on my mother so that I may ask for permission to seek her?"

The arched table sits prestigiously in the place that resembles a gallant courtroom, with all of them being judge *and* jury. The prominent, stuffy asses behind the elongated table show no emotion as a man answers, "Her last whereabouts were in Tibet for the ceremonies, however, we believe it was a dark user she left with. We don't know if it was a nabbing or a simple disappearing act. Calypso has run off for decades at a time before, so it wouldn't be the first time. I suggest starting in Washington, near the Canadian border. Their roots of power are there, and if you're to find anything out of sorts, that's where she'll be."

I get sick, but I try to keep a straight face. My mom has been around for a long time. The longer you live, the harder you are to kill. They'd need the magic their dark roots have in order to do such a thing, but the council can't acknowledge that, not without telling me they know she was taken and they're not going to do anything about it.

"Calypso Coldwell is indeed very important to the light community. Without her, the ceremonies will have to stop until we can find someone strong enough to proceed. However, we cannot send you any means of help other than that of information for fear of sparking too much conflict. Light users are forbidden to travel around that area, so tread carefully."

Meaning these sorry, stick-up-their-asses cowards aren't going to risk their own necks to save the woman who has saved everyone here at some point and time.

I bite the inside of my jaw so hard the tang of blood strikes me.

"Of course," I murmur through strain, trying my best not to snap.

I bow, showing them respect they don't deserve, and then I walk out quickly to meet up with Frankie who's waiting by the door. "Have you called for plane tickets yet?" I mutter as we head down the hallway.

"We've got the next flight out."

"It looks like it's just the two of us. I've basically been forbidden to recruit anyone else."

He scowls. "I heard. Don't worry though. We'll get her out of there."

"We better, or else my estranged father will be getting a phone call."

His eyes grow wide, and then he turns to me. "You can't be serious. You know how dangerous he is, Alyssa. Your mother would-"

"I'm very serious. My mother would call him if it was me and she had to. He's dangerous, he's crazy, but he's also very protective of her. If he finds out, they'll all die, and I'll watch."

Chapter Seven

"I'm glad you called. I've been worried. Any word about your mother?" Kane asks.

I pull on my boots while slipping into my jacket, preparing to trudge through the rain, and then I sigh.

"Well, we're in Washington right now. I think she just got a little crazy and ran off with some friends. It's happened before," I lie, using the council's cop out. "They have a cabin up here, and right now we're trying to see if we can find it in this ridiculous wooded area."

"What section of woods?" he asks curiously.

I consider lying to him, but there's really no point. It's not like he can stop me from going in there, and I don't want to lie to him more than necessary.

"We're in Fenshaw, it's mostly all woods to be honest. When I track her down, I'll kick her ass for scaring Frankie and me."

At least I do well to mask my true fear.

"Alyssa, those woods are too dangerous. Hikers go missing all the time out there."

That's because they don't know what sadistic bastards lurk out here.

The worry in his tone is genuine, and if he knew the truth, he'd never feel the same about the world he lives in.

"Don't worry. Frankie knows a thing or two about the wilderness. I'll call you later. I doubt I'm going to have service once we get in there."

"Alyssa, just wait on me. I'll come out there and help you."

My heart sizzles in my chest. Knowing he'd do that makes the butterflies in my stomach ruffle.

"Don't be crazy. Washington is too far away for you to have to come. I'll take care of it. Thanks though."

He exhales loudly, and then he murmurs, "Well, if you need me, you know how to find me."

Something about the way he says it... He almost sounds angry that I won't let him help.

"Thanks. Really. I'll talk to you later, Kane."

"Yeah," he murmurs, and then the line goes quiet.

"You ready?" Frankie asks as I pull the battery out of my phone.

"Yeah, you?"

He does the same - pulling the battery out of his own phone - and then he puts the pieces on the table separately.

"Dark users are too good with tech."

"And black magic," I scoff while zipping up my jacket and heading out into the rain.

"And these woods," he sighs. "Stay close. I really don't even want you in here. Calypso will kill me for letting you come."

"She'll die if we don't find her."

He tightens his lips, and lets out a breath of defeat as we start heading into the creepy-as-hell forest. It's daylight, but between the rain and the shadows cast by the thick, leafy limbs of the forest giants, it's dark as night.

The wind whistles through a hollow log beside us, and Frankie evaporates only to reappear several yards in front of me.

"Really?" I scold in a whisper.

He shrugs and starts walking again until howling erupts from the far north, making Frankie evaporate once more only to reappear in a tree.

"I'm supposed to be the one who's scared," I grumble under my breath.

"Sorry," he murmurs as he reappears at my side.

"No more evaporating just because the wind rustles too loudly."

"Fine," he huffs, his body tensing as we slowly make our way through.

"If you want to evaporate so badly, then do it and grab Mom."

"You know it doesn't work that way. I can only travel short distances, and I have to see where I'm going and what I'm doing. If I could just pop in where she's at, I would have already done it. Not to mention, it'd make traveling a lot easier."

"I was being sarcastic," I mumble.

"Oh."

We continue walking in silence, making sure to investigate every shadowy form we see. Suddenly, a large, white bird, resembling a hawk, shoots free from a tree and rushes by us, making Frankie squeal and evaporate simultaneously.

Unbelievable.

I walk up just as he reappears, panting for air with his hands on his knees.

"That's it. Hand over your man-card. I'm having it revoked."

He straightens up, adjusting his shirt, and then scowls at me.

"I've been around a lot longer than you, meaning I've heard more horror stories about these woods than you."

"Meaning you've lost your balls along the way," I add, mocking him further.

He glares at me, but he doesn't come back with anything else as we continue on, warily checking over our shoulders with each step.

"How far until we reach their holy ground?" I ask, swallowing when I feel a chill in the air.

"At this pace? Three days."

I groan inwardly, and then I pull out a bottle of water from my pack. The only way to get there is on foot, and since I can't evaporate around the woods, this is going to be one hell of a three day trip.

Hours pass, leaving me exhausted and Frankie so tense that he's stiff as a board. I shiver as night really does descend, making me realize how much darker these woods can get. Frankie collapses to the ground, showing his own exhaustion - proving immortals aren't immune to being out of shape.

"We'll set up here for the night. I'll take first watch," Frankie says. He turns his jacket into a pillow for his back and props it between himself and a tree.

Reluctantly, I plop down. We can't see two steps in front of us right now, and we'll get lost if we keep trying to cipher our way through here.

"Wake me when you get tired." I yawn while resting my backpack under my head, praying the night doesn't hold any surprises.

A chill slithers up my back, and I wake up to the pitch black to see Frankie's eyes closed and his body limp as he snores.

Way to keep watch, Frankie.

I pull my jacket around me a little tighter as I stare at the streaks of moonlight escaping through the veil cast by the trees. My heart beats too quickly when I see several shadows appearing and evaporating in the distance.

Dark users.

"Frankie," I whisper while tugging at his jacket, but he doesn't move.

I slowly stand to my feet to kick him in the stomach, but still he doesn't move. It's then I realize his snoring is too deep. They've put him to sleep because they want me alone.

Fuck!

"Alyssssaaa," a phantom voice hisses too close, and I whip around just as the shadow turns to nothing.

They're playing with me.

"How do you know my name?" I demand, trying not to sound as terrified as I am.

"Alyssssaaa," the voice hisses again, and then suddenly I feel the air being knocked out of me as I'm thrown backwards, my body thudding hard against the ground as I collide.

"That's gonna leave a mark," I mumble under my breath while trying to stand up.

I feel another strike just as I stand, and I'm knocked backwards again. This time, I hit so hard my tongue gets chomped between my teeth, drawing blood.

I spit it out, steadying my breaths as I search for something to use my magic on. But it's hard to fight back when I can't see them coming.

I scream as my body gets lifted from the ground by a force I can't see, and then I get whisked up to nearly the tops of the trees just as several other shadows rush into the party from behind us.

Just when I accept my fate, I realize these shadows aren't evaporating, they're just fast as hell.

Screams erupt, and I'm dropped from the monstrous height, screaming all the way down. I brace for impact, but I feel swift, gentle arms catching me and then gently dropping me to the ground as the figures emerge more obviously.

Dark-hooded silhouettes rush from place to place as the dark users scream out their pain. The mystery people don't speak or slow down. Instead, they work together like a band of choreographed dancers fighting against my attackers.

Then I see it. Their faces are masked and their heads are covered, but I see the glowing blue eyes as they drain the dark users of their energy with the ease only one creature can hold.

Night stalkers!

Here I was, foolish enough to think I was being saved, only to find out I'm someone's next meal.

I slide over, and then kick Frankie's foot, trying to stir him awake, but it's no good. I watch in horror as the night stalkers continue to drain the dark users, deflecting their attacks as they feast, never fazed by their outnumbered circumstance.

Then I squeal as two lycans crash through the trees, roaring and shredding the dark users who were trying to rush the night stalkers from behind. One of the lycans spots me, and it snarls as it pounds the ground with its heavy paws.

The beast I've only ever heard about but never seen is far more terrifying than I imagined it to be. It's head is the size of seven human heads, and it stands six feet tall on all fours. I cower back, covering Frankie, offering myself as sacrifice.

The rabid beast snarls and rakes the ground with its dagger-like claws, readying itself for a charge as the battle behind it rages on. A pair of glowing blue eyes offer me a glance before a silhouette leaps over, kicking the beast in the stomach, sending it sailing.

I squeal, and shield my eyes momentarily. When I look up, I see the lycan is licking its paw, and then it charges back into the fight, no longer acknowledging me as it returns to shredding the dark users.

"Frankie!" I screech desperately, and he finally stirs just as the last of the dark users retreat.

"What?" he murmurs through sleepy yawns, and my eyes look up once more to see the glowing blues fade before the unlikely rescue team darts away, disappearing from sight instead of coming to drain me dry.

Both of the lycans disappear, leaving us behind in the darkness without a threat.

"What the hell just happened?" Frankie gushes as he rises up to see the bodies of the dark users lying around like limp, drained rag dolls.

"Believe it or not, night stalkers and lycans just saved our lives."

"Night stalkers and lycans took down a flock of dark users to help us?" he asks in disbelief.

I look around, understanding his shock. I watched it happen with my own eyes and I'm still struggling to find it true.

"Yeah. These dark users were apparently fairly new to their abilities, so they died easier."

"Those had to be some badass mother fuckers to do all this even if they were new to the change," he murmurs to continue our very whispered conversation.

I step over the bodies of the men and women shriveled up, their eyes glazed over with death's glare.

"That's creepy," Frankie shivers out.

"What's creepy is watching the dark ones of our kind trying to tear us apart and then watching our heroes be night stalkers and lycans."

Frankie shakes his head, still reeling from the absurdity of it all, and we continue to trek through the woods, not risking getting still again.

"How about casting an awake spell?" I whisper. "I'd prefer to have a little backup the next time they attack."

"Good idea," he mumbles before he starts chanting under his breath.

"There it is," he whispers as we stare through the thick brush at the black tree in front of us.

My clothes are filthy, my hair is a tangled mess, and we've been on foot for two days - no sleep since the attack - for this?

"How is this supposed to help us find Mom?"

"Like the Tree of Gaya - the root of the light - this is the tree of Tartarus, the root of the dark. If Calypso is close by, this will lead us there," he whispers, careful not to draw any unwanted ears our way.

Suddenly, a white hawk zooms down from the sky, barreling toward us as it screeches in protest.

"Get down, Alyssa! Changer!" Frankie yells.

I squeal and duck, but the hawk doesn't attack. Instead, it disappears behind the tree. I pull my hands up, ready to go on the offense, when I'm startled from behind.

"Don't use that tree. You'll awaken a thousand souls and yet you'll only have a riddle for what you need to know," a smooth voice says, and my eyes fall on his face in disbelief.

"Thad?" I gasp.

His lips thin, and then he nods while tossing a pair of pants beside the tree. I look over my shoulder to see an a guy pulling them on, his bare body making me blush, and then I whip my head back around.

"I'll tear you apart if you try to touch us," Frankie threatens.

"If I wanted to harm her, I would have already done so. I moved in next door to keep an eye on her once I found out she was living in a town full of night stalkers."

I tilt my head, still stunned into near silence.

"Why? You're a-"

"A vicious killer with a taste for blood?" he laughs out. "Not exactly. Just because I'm a changer, it doesn't make me a killer. I've only killed when necessary, never for a meal. They have blood banks these days. I happen to own a few. Before then, I learned when to stop before I killed someone."

His smug tone doesn't match the sweet boy next door I thought he was, but at the same time, he just got a hell of a lot sexier.

Stupid bad boy complex.

"Changers don't stop, they kill for fun," Frankie objects, his eyes narrowing in scrutiny.

"It's amazing you say that, considering the same was once said about witches and warlocks. You think you're the only ones who've evolved?"

Three girls and two more guys walk up to join him, all of them hiding their secret. Then one girl's eyes glow blue, making me sick.

"Night stalker," I shiver out.

"She's not going to hurt you. She's here to help," Thad says as he walks toward me. "Your mom isn't here - never was. But someone wanted the council to think she was."

"And we're just supposed to take you at your word?" Frankie scoffs.

"No, but a thousand souls really are tied to that tree. That's what the dark ones used to bless it. If you use your white magic on it, you'll release more hell on earth than Pandora's box ever thought about, and you'll have nothing in return."

"Where is she?" I interrupt, holding Frankie back when he starts to do something foolish.

Thad keeps a wary eye on Frankie for a moment before answering me.

"That, I don't know. I do know you're not going to find her this way, but I'll help you find her the right way."

I glance at the dark tree that seems to be taunting me right now, a silent plea for me to free the mayhem begging to wreak havoc, whispering its desires to me. I cut away before I get too entranced by the fucked up chaos living inside of it.

"How did you know?" I ask, suspicion oozing from my tone.

"About your mother's disappearance or the fact you're a witch?"

"Both."

He cracks his neck to the side, and then looks around before speaking.

"I'm here as a servant to... Drackus. If I can't help you, he'll get involved. No one from either side wants that," he almost whispers, making the others lower their eyes.

"My father?" I gasp.

Frankie takes a step back once he hears the name that has struck fear in so many for so long. Thad nods.

"Believe it or not, he's been keeping tabs on you since you were a child. He sent me to watch after you after he learned you had branched out on your own."

I'd be touched if my father wasn't a psychotic asshole with too much power for any one person to hold.

"Where do you suggest we start?"

"I suggest you let me take over the legwork from here. I didn't mean to get this involved, but now that I am, it's time to let us seek her out. I'll call you if I find anything."

He turns to walk off with his entourage, but I race to get in front of him.

"Hell no. She's my mother, and I want to be there."

He gives me a look filled with condescension, and I refrain from using my magic on his alpha ass.

"Alyssa, you're looking at old world relics and falling into obvious traps. You can't expect me to let you come. You have no idea the things your father would do to me if anything happens to you."

"Nothing will happen. Please. She's my mom. She's all I've got," I whimper, and his eyes soften, his arrogance slowly subsiding and fading into sympathy.

"I'm really, really going to regret this, but... fine."

Without thinking, I throw my arms around his neck and he staggers back lightly from the unexpected hug. Tears stroll down as the last couple of days full of exhaustion and overwhelming fear catch up with me.

I'm hugging a changer. So fucking stupid.

"Thank you," I murmur through my tears.

He sighs as he gently returns the embrace, and the he pulls free to walk over beside a tree. I gasp as he turns into a hawk, slipping out of his clothes, and then he shifts into an enormous white wolf in front of my eyes.

"You're gonna want to hold on tight," a guy says as he lifts me to be on top of the wolf - on top of Thad rather.

"Alyssa, I don't like this," Frankie murmurs hesitantly while looking around at the new assembly that certainly out numbers our sad little duo.

"It's better than going at this alone," I counter, while straddling the beast more comfortably.

I've never seen a wolf smile until now, and my mind flashes back to Kane calling him a wolf. He'd flip the hell out if he knew how literal that was.

"Can you keep up?" one of the guys teases to Frankie.

He looks at me, his eyes rolling. "Now that I'm not walking human style, yes."

Before I know it, Thad is racing through the woods with me strapped to his back. I lean over, making sure my head doesn't get taken off by any stray limbs and to avoid the bugs slapping my face as well.

Changers and night stalkers. I wonder who the lycans are.

Chapter Eight

"So, you'll be staying here," Thad murmurs while motioning to the shady motel in front of us. "I smelled night stalkers in the woods following our trail. They never found us, but they seemed pretty determined to catch up. You'll be safe here until I find out what they're after."

"You can smell them?" I murmur in disbelief.

He shrugs, though it's a poor attempt at not looking cocky.

"When they're using their speed and I'm in changed form, I can. If I know their scent, I can follow them any time, much like a lycan's ability."

"How did you stay in form so long with me on you?" I muse curiously. "Witches have a sour affect on changers."

He seems agitated with me but a hint of excitement sparks as well as he continues to play teacher.

"Again, old world rules. Things have changed. Your mom taught you a lot, but she didn't stay up to date. Your dad warned me of that. He said you'd be a little naïve and too trusting."

I should feel insulted, but I'm too tired to lash out. I just want a shower and a bed right now more than anything.

"Should I trust you?" I ask, arching an eyebrow, realizing that's a really stupid question. I repeat, I'm tired. No one thinks clearly when they've been awake for as long as I have.

"No, but then again, you don't really have a choice," he says while taking a step too close to me. "You shouldn't *trust* anyone right now."

I take a step back, but he just comes closer until his body has mine pinned against the wall, a daring grin forming on his lush lips.

"So, that guy the other morning... your boyfriend?" he asks while brushing away a wild blond strip of my tousled hair from my face.

Surely he's not trying to seduce me right now. Not looking like this.

"No," I answer, swallowing hard. "But maybe one day."

"So you like him?" he says while bending down, but before I can answer, his lips are pressed against mine, almost bruising them with his ferociously devouring kiss.

Everything on me heats up, but then Kane's face flashes through my mind, reminding me I want him to be my first. I sure as hell don't want a changer to be my first.

"Thad, I-"

He pulls back, his menacing smirk spreading, and then he shrugs.

"I'm sure your dad would probably skin me for that. I'll see you in a day or so. For now, just lie low. I'll call you if anything pops up." He turns to Frankie, who has just walked in and is fuming after witnessing the accidental kiss, and says, "You coming with us or staying here?"

He looks from me to Thad several times, but his shoulders finally drop.

"I suppose I have to come with you to make sure you're really here to help."

Thad smirks, and then he turns back to me before strolling his thumb over my lower lip.

"I'll see you soon. Next time, I won't hold back."

He walks away, leaving me shaken and feeling like a fool. I wipe the stupefied look off my face and head inside, ready to wash away the terrible last few days. My phone buzzes, and I look at it curiously until I see it's Kane.

"Hey," I murmur softly while turning on the bath.

"Alyssa, thank God. I've been worried to damn death. Where are you?" he breathlessly releases with relief.

I walk over to the window and peer out at the sign.

"Motel Lassier in Higdon, Canada. Don't ask. It's been a rough few days. It's good to hear your voice though."

And I mean that more than he realizes. After Thad's advance, I really miss my human. I felt gross before, but after kissing a changer... I just feel dirty.

"You have no idea how good it is to hear your voice. Are you okay? You mentioned going into the woods, and then I never heard back. Did you find your mom?"

I hold back my truly miserable emotion, and then I murmur, "No. We never found the cabin her friend told us about. I'm okay though."

"Did you run into any problems?"

Several.

"We had something a little... odd happen, but you'd think I was crazy," I murmur, not really able to completely lie to him the way I probably need to.

I almost want to tell him who I am and what I'm meant to become, but I'd scar him for life and take away his naïve bliss. It'd be selfish and illegal to tell him the truth.

"Try me," he says with sincere curiosity.

"It's crazy. Anyway, we're still tracking down my mom. Frankie and I met up with some... colleagues of his, and now I've been tossed in this motel to wait until they get back with info."

"They left you alone?"

He curses loudly, his anger spilling over. It makes me smile to hear his protective tone, a warming feeling spreading over my weary body.

"Yeah, but I'll be okay. I live alone, you know."

I expect a small chuckle, but I get silence.

"You there?" I ask, wondering if we've been disconnected.

"I can't believe he just ran off and left you alone," he murmurs while offering a few more spewed profanities.

"Well, I'm glad to have a minute to myself. I'm exhausted, I smell like days in the woods, and I look like hell. I'm going to take a long, hot bath, and then I'm going to get a full night of sleep. Believe me when I say I need sleep."

He sighs and then murmurs, "I'm sure you do. Call me later, okay?"

I smile bigger, feeling the butterflies attacking my stomach.

"You really care, don't you?" I ask, feeling my cheeks sting from the ridiculous smile I'm wearing.

"Very much. Does that mean you'll call me?"

His flirty tone, makes me wish he was here.

"Yeah. I'll call. Talk to you later."

"Bye, Alyssa."

I smile while hanging up, and then I head back to the bathtub that is eagerly awaiting my disgusting, tragically ragged body.

The water heats my skin almost too much, and I sigh in content as it rises to be up to my neck when I become fully submerged. I need this so, so badly.

I wake up to a pounding at the door, and I shiver as the water I'm in reminds me it has turned to nearly ice.

"Shit, hold on. I'm coming," I yell out.

Leaping out of the tub, I wrap up and ignore my chattering teeth while rushing to open the door. My jaw tries to hit the floor when I see Kane wrapping his arms around me and pulling me to his body.

"You're wet," he chuckles out, looking too damn good to be anything less than a hallucination, and I'm worried I'm still in the frigid water... dreaming - possibly drowning.

"You're... here," I murmur in breathless disbelief, blinking rapidly to make sure I haven't gone crazy.

His smile almost makes me lose my footing, and he scoops my soaked body up to walk farther into the room.

"I'm here. I took a plane to Washington last night when I hadn't heard from you. Then you told me you were here, alone, so I rented a car and drove like hell."

My eyes water. No one has ever done anything like this for me before.

Even though it's not safe for him to be here, I still want him with me.

He stands me up in the bathroom and hands me another towel.

"Thank you," I murmur as the first tear falls, and he wipes it away while bending down to kiss me.

"Dry off, and I'll go grab us a plate of food from the diner next door."

My stomach growls as if on cue, and he smiles. I skip telling him the part where I haven't had anything but beef jerky and water for a few days.

"Sounds nice."

He smiles, and then he ducks out, giving me a chance to panic as I rush around to start rifling through the few clothes I packed.

Damn. Not one sexy pair of underwear.

Since my wardrobe is lacking, I opt to go with a pair of pajama shorts, a long-sleeved, tight-fitted shirt, and no panties.

I dab on a little makeup, and then I quickly dry my hair, using a little bit of magic, but not so much that it's obvious. As soon as I spray myself down with some fruity fragrance, the door swings open to reveal Kane carrying a bag of food.

"So, I got us some breakfast for dinner because it was the only thing on the menu that looked promising."

"Sounds good," I murmur while walking into his view, and he smiles when he sees me.

"For the record, I knocked on five doors before I found you. The clerk wasn't very helpful."

I laugh a little while sitting down at the small table by the window.

"Considering you only had fifteen rooms to choose from, I don't think that task was too daunting."

He smiles, and then he pulls his chair closer to me while wrapping his arm around my back.

"I'm glad I'm finally seeing you again. I shouldn't have been missing you so much so soon," he softly confesses.

I instantly dissolve under his gaze, and then I take a deep breath, hoping I don't say anything stupid.

"I missed you, too."

His smile grows, and then he leans over to kiss my cheek before scooping a pile of eggs on his fork. He's human, but he's my hero right now. I didn't want to be here alone, and now I don't have to be.

"So how long are you staying?" I ask curiously.

"Until you find your mom."

My eyes widen a little. He can't be here for all that. We already have changers in our midst, and despite Thad's claim of clean-living, I'm not going to wave my human in front of his face.

"Um, I don't know how that will work out. It's been a little... hectic around here. Besides, I'm sure you've got a lot going on back home."

He shrugs, his grin growing.

"I don't have anything going on. You'd be surprised at how helpful I can be."

I don't feel like coming up with some fabulous lie right now. At this moment, I just want to enjoy him and pretend as though he really could protect me if he had to, though it would be the other way around.

"You're freezing," he says while rubbing the side of my arm, warming me so easily with his heated touch.

Mmm.

"Yeah, I spent too long in cold bathwater."

He laughs a little, and then he stands to grab a blanket from his stuff. He wraps it around my shoulders, and I breathe in his delicious scent that is drenching the blanket.

"Thanks. You're just full of things I need tonight."

"Just food and a blanket," he chirps obliviously.

"And you."

He looks at me, his face expressionless, and then he pulls me to his lips, filling me with his passionate release as I slide out of my chair and move to be straddling his lap. My hands clasp his hair as I pull him closer, and then his hot kiss starts trailing down my neck.

"Kane," I breathe, and he rips me up from the chair to carry me to the bed.

He drops me to it, and then falls between my parted legs as his heated breath and perfect lips ravage my neck and chest. Then he pulls back to stare me in the eyes I'm praying are just blue.

"This isn't why I came here. I want you to know that. Just tell me to stop and I will."

I laugh a little, and then I run my fingers through his hair. With all the drama going on, I just want a night in his arms, something to kill the worry that's eating me alive.

"I really don't think this is why you came all the way to Canada. If one of your friends knocks on the door or calls you though, I'll lose my cool."

He smirks, and then his lips find mine again.

"For the record," he murmurs against my lips, "I would kick someone's ass if they interrupted us right now."

I giggle lightly, but it ceases immediately as his daring tongue starts sliding down my body, trailing down my chest as he pulls my shirt up and over my head. He moans as he cups my bare breasts in his hands before finding my right nipple in his mouth.

My breaths become coarse, harsh, and needy as his tongue and mouth bring my back to an arch beneath him. I feel like we've had nothing but foreplay since we met.

"Kane, please," I hoarsely release, and his hands suddenly grip my ass with a fervent cling.

His mouth moves lower, finding the top of my shorts, while his breath heats my lower stomach. That glorious, expert tongue dips beneath my shorts, and then he pulls back to remove them fully.

"No panties?" he asks, seeming amused and turned on. "Are you trying to make sure I don't last long?"

I let a laugh escape while blushing, as he continues pulling down the shorts the rest of the way.

"Damn, you're too perfect to be real," he murmurs while staring down at me, making me feel a little exposed and vulnerable.

I'm not used to showing someone my bare body, but the way his eyes are looking at me, I'm on fire and I don't care what part of me he sees.

I feel my eyes trying to freak out and go crazy colors, so I shut them tight as his mouth finds its way back to my body. I gasp, spreading my legs wider and pulling him closer, and then his sweet, hot mouth finds that quivering junction between my legs - a place no one has ever gone before.

I gasp louder when I feel his tongue colliding with a spot I had no idea was so sensitive, and then my hands tangle in his hair as he greedily nips, sucks, and plays. Each flick of his incredible tongue pushes me closer to an edge I've never fallen off before.

"Oh… my… fuck," I gush out, and his pace only quickens, forcing a tightening in my lower abdomen.

My legs begin trembling before stiffening, and I arch my back slightly before his hands push my hips into place. Then he slips a finger inside me to push me over the edge, causing me to scream out his name involuntarily.

When he feels my whole body trembling, he smiles against me and slowly starts making his way back up, trailing his lips over my very sensitive skin.

"I love the way you want me," he breathes against my neck, making my whole body shiver.

My legs wrap around his waist as I free his erection with my greedy hands. He moans into my mouth as his lips return, and then I pull him to me, silently begging him to be my first and end my innocent drought.

He pulls his shirt over his head and tosses it to the floor, revealing his perfection fully. Then he jerks his pants off before returning to me. His hand skims over my sex as he guides himself to my opening, and then his lips cover mine as he surges in.

I cry out upon feeling the unexpected strike of pain shooting through me from his abrupt, brutal entry.

"Fuck, I'm sorry. What's wrong?" he worries, staying inside me and giving me a chance to acclimate to his size.

A tear falls from my eye as I shake my head.

"Sorry, I might should have mentioned I'm… um… I was…"

His eyes widen and he pulls out of me as his mouth falls open. He looks down, and then up again while shaking his head.

"You're a virgin?" he says, his face turning pale.

I blush feverishly, my bare body now feeling all the more exposed. The word *virgin* has never sounded so embarrassing or dirty before.

"I don't think I am anymore."

He grips his head as if he feels regret, and I pull a sheet to my body to cover my growing insecurities.

"Why didn't you tell me?"

I look away shamefully, and then I stare at the ground.

"I'm sorry. I didn't know it would matter. Do you want to leave?"

My heart feels heavy, painful, and foolish as I stare straight down. He tilts my chin up, sincerity in his eyes.

"Alyssa, I don't want to go. I just feel like a jerk because I didn't know. I wouldn't have been so… rough… if I had known. You're… it's just… you're twenty, and well, we sort of got close to doing this the first night we were together. I only assumed-"

"I was a slut?"

He laughs a little and shakes his head.

"No. Not a slut. I just assumed you had been with someone before."

I draw back, feeling all the more stupid as I pull my knees to my chest. I went from feeling like a woman to a small child, and I thought it was supposed to go the other way around.

"I'm sorry," I murmur, trying not to sound like the crying kid I am inside.

His body softens, his eyes now holding pity.

My first time ended after one fucking thrust. I wish I had just bit through the pain and ignored it.

"Alyssa, I'm not going to let this be the way you lost your virginity."

This is humiliating... mortifying actually.

"Don't patronize me, and ugh! Don't say that word."

He laughs as I cover my head up with a pillow, and I feel his hand slipping under the sheet to curl around my bare body, pulling me to him.

"Stop, Kane. You're right. I was stupid and I should have told you," I mumble into the pillow.

"Hey, no. That's not… Alyssa, I'm sorry. I would have liked to have known so I could have made it a little more special for you - not to mention gentle."

I shake my head, and then he removes the pillow from my face before his lips find mine. I try to pull back, but he pulls me tighter to him, refusing to let me recoil again.

"Kane, you don't have to-"

He cuts me off as he moves to be between my legs again, and his hot, demanding tongue slips inside my mouth to silence me more, rebuilding the fire. I never thought it possible to recover from that, but now I'm realizing there's nothing about him that can keep me away… even a botched first time.

"Alyssa, I want you like I've never wanted anything before," he murmurs against my lips, making me feel hot in all the right places as my hands begin to tangle in his hair. "I'm assuming you're not on birth control though."

My mind flashes back to my mother's spell she cast on me when I just hit puberty. It's better than any mortal birth control there is.

"I am."

His lips become more demanding, as does his tongue. He guides his firmness back to my opening. I tense up, and his hand slides down the curve of my ass to angle me differently.

"Relax, baby. I swear I won't hurt you again," he soothes, as his lips stroke slower, more gingerly across mine.

I just nod, but I don't really know how to relax. A calming sensation suddenly floods through me as I stare into his soft, warm, green eyes, and I feel my body relaxing as if on its own. His lips return to mine, making the calm all the better, as he guides himself back inside me.

This time, unlike the last, his thrust is gentle, slow, and not painful at all as he slides in to my deepest point, making me gasp in pleasure instead of pain. My legs slide up around his waist, giving him more depth, and he tugs at my back as he releases a delicious breath of his own pleasure.

"Damn, you feel so fucking good," he murmurs in a hoarse tone, his body claiming mine as he pulls out slowly and then glides back in, making me greedy and desperate for more.

My nails dig into his back as I pull him to me, and he steadily quickens his pace as my hips start rising to meet his. He grunts when he starts treating me like I'm stronger than a fragile piece of glass.

His slick thrusts are still nowhere as brutal as his first delivery, and now I sort of want that. I want to feel him claiming me the way he wants to.

Deliberately holding back, he finds a gentle rhythm that still forces my whole body to tingle. If I had known how incredible this could be, I might have turned into a slut long ago.

He holds onto me with more passion than I thought possible, and each thrust pushes me closer to the edge I'm desperate to fall off of... again. I grip him tighter as something stirs in me once more, and I feel a tear slipping out for a whole new reason as I cry out happily.

He shudders inside me, filling me with his warmth, as he lets out a low moan of pleasure before collapsing to my body and pulling me into his arms.

"You okay?" he asks so sincerely while kissing my forehead.

I'm frigging awesome.

"Definitely okay," I pant out, still unable to catch my breath after that incredible release.

"Is that a little more like you expected?"

"*So* much better."

He lets out a huff of a laugh, and I cringe.

Crap. I didn't mean to say that out loud.

"Good. That's what I want to hear."

He lightly kisses my lips, and then he pulls me up so my face is even with his as he slides my leg across his waist.

"I wish I had upgraded the room at least," he says somewhat humorously.

I let a laugh free, and then I roll my eyes.

"Single level motels don't usually have suites."

He chuckles lightly, and then he props up while staring down at me.

"Well, I'll see about rustling us up some champagne. There's got to be a store around here."

He's intent on making this special, but he doesn't realize how incredible it already is.

"I don't want you to leave right now. Just stay here, and we can do champagne another time."

He smiles so genuinely, as if I've said something wonderful, and then he pulls me closer to him.

"I can handle that."

My lips stroll over his collarbone, and his hand slides down to grip my ass, making me want more of his delicious body inside me.

"So... belated question... how old are you?" I muse, grimacing lightly for not even knowing that much about him before he plucked *all* the petals from my flower.

"Twenty-five... I think."

I pull back to stare at him with an arched brow. "You think?"

He laughs and then shrugs. "I told you we party a lot. Sometimes I forget things."

I shake my head, and a stupid smile spreads across my face.

"So, why didn't you tell me?" he asks curiously.

"Tell you what?"

"That you were a virgin."

My face glows red at this point. If I could hide under the covers all day, I would. He laughs a little at my embarrassment, but he refuses to let me hide.

"I didn't think you'd believe me, for one. Like you said, we almost did this that first night you were at my house. Also, I didn't want you to treat it like it was something sacred. Either you wouldn't have done anything with me, or you would have made me wait for the 'perfect place and time.' I didn't want to wait, and I didn't want to scare you off."

He smirks, and then he kisses the top of my head.

"Well, it'd be damn near impossible for you to scare me off, but I would have liked to plan out something better than a shady motel in the middle of nowhere. I wanted to plan out something better for our first time together, actually, without even knowing you were a virgin. You're too damn irresistible though."

I try my best not to giggle, but I do a little anyway. He strokes my cheek with his thumb, and then he slides over to start kissing my neck.

"For the record, I've never been one too concerned with the place or the decorations... It's always been about the *who*," I murmur softly, and I feel him smiling against my neck.

"That's good to know. Do you care if I'm your *who* for a while?"

The goofy grin that spreads over my face is insuppressible, and he rises up with a smile of his own as his lips lightly peck mine.

"I was hoping you'd ask that," I mutter while bringing my arms up around his neck and drawing him in for a deeper kiss.

His tongue invades my mouth once again, drawing forth that explosive heat, and then his erection grazes the insides of my thighs as he parts my legs.

"I'll be gentle," he murmurs against my mouth as he starts to slide in.

"Not too gentle. I'm not so fragile anymore," I utter with a vixen's intent, and he growls in the back of his throat as he surges in a little harder, while still showing a tender touch.

Mmm.

For the first time ever, I wake up in someone's arms, and I grin as I roll over and wrap my leg around Kane's body. He smiles down at me, looking rather alert, and I let out an involuntary giggle.

"Been up long?" I muse.

"A little while. I was going to go get us some breakfast, but I didn't want you to wake up without me."

My cheeks officially hurt. Apparently, once you have sex, you can't stop smiling like a complete goof.

"I'm glad you stayed."

"Me too," he murmurs softly while kissing my forehead.

"We can go out for breakfast," I say while sitting up.

"Definitely not. I want you to wear that sheet for a little while longer. I'll go grab us something, and when I get back, I'll distract you until Frankie gives you a call."

I smile lightly, and then I feel guilty. I'm in bed with a guy, enjoying myself, and who knows where my mother is.

"Sorry. I shouldn't have said it like that," he murmurs with a grimace.

"It's fine."

His fingers slip through my hair as he pulls me to him, and his soft lips comfort me, making me feel safe and wanted.

We're suddenly jarred apart, and I scream as the door to the motel swings open. Kane has somehow already jerked me behind him, ready to keep me safe - *ironically enough* - but we both exhale in relief when we see it's just Frankie.

"What the hell, Frankie?" I scold.

His lips have etched up in an are-you-kidding-me grin, and I roll my eyes as I pull the sheet to my body.

"Sorry, I didn't realize you had company, and I was just going to give you a little scare. Kane, right?" he asks with a devilish grin.

"Right," Kane says with his own sheepish grin, and then he turns to me. "I'll go get us some breakfast now."

"Thanks," I murmur, my cheeks burning.

Frankie lets out a teasing chuckle as Kane kisses my cheek, and then he climbs up from the bed with nothing but his boxers on before slipping on his jeans and shirt. He gives me a quick wink and then disappears out the door.

"Really?" Frankie says once the door shuts.

I plop down and pull the pillow over my head.

"Skip the embarrassing taunts, and tell me what's going on."

"Yes, ma'am," he snickers out, and I pull my head back out from under the pillow while using my magic to dress me under the sheet.

"So, from what I can tell, Calypso isn't in Canada. Just so you know, it's hard as hell to work with night stalkers, considering they're our worst natural enemy."

"Yeah, I know, but those night stalkers saved our lives. You'd know that if you had been conscious."

"Are you sure it was them?" he asks, his face turning more serious.

"I'm sure it had to be. It's not like there's a long list of blood drinkers coming to our aide. Anyway, what else did you find out about Mom?"

"Nothing much, kiddo. Whatever they're up to, they're covering their trail pretty damn good. Thad says he has some contacts that deal with light and dark. He's going to try and get a hold of them, see if they can help us out."

"Do you think he's really on our side?" I ask while emerging from under the sheet, my body now fully clothed.

"I think he has to be, otherwise Drackus will rip him to pieces."

Ah yes. He's Drackus's errand boy. I almost forgot about that. Just because he's on my dad's payroll doesn't mean he's necessarily on our side.

"My dad has ulterior motives anytime he helps out. I think we should watch Thad and the others closely - make sure they're not playing an angle while pulling the wool over our eyes."

Frankie thinks about that for a moment, weighing my words in his head.

"True, now back to pretty boy. Why's he in Canada?"

I smile involuntarily, blushing a little as well, and then I murmur, "He showed up and surprised me last night. He said he wanted to be here for me."

Frankie doesn't seem quite as jubilant about that as I am.

"As sweet as that is, how are we supposed to operate with a human amongst us?" he asks more seriously.

I frown. I know Frankie has a good point, but I can't just send Kane away.

"I'm still working on that. In the meantime, make sure no one does anything crazy in front of him. It's not like I can come with you anyway. All I do is slow you down. The council is supposed to call me when they have more information - though their information sucks. I'll play middle man, and then help out when and where I can - now that you have *real* immortals helping you out."

He shivers, a look of disgust climbing over his face.

"Changers and lycans I can handle, but night stalkers   yuk. You have no idea how hard it is not to lose my magic on them."

"I know. I hate night stalkers, too, but we need their help."

"I wouldn't do this for anyone but you and your mother, by the way."

I smile, knowing Frankie is beyond in love with Mom, and then I nod.

"I know."

Just then, my door opens again, and Thad steps inside.

"Well, look who's still in the bed," he says with a seductive tone and an animalistic twinkle in his eyes.

At least I'm clothed now.

"Yeah, yeah. Hey, Thad, there's a human here, and if any of your guys-"

"Chill. I already told you we don't eat fresh meat," he says dismissively with a wave of his hand. "Does this *person* know about us?"

"Hell no. It's-"

Kane interrupts as he walks in holding a bag full of diner food. He stops and stares in confusion at Thad.

"Ah, the boyfriend," Thad says with an eerie, menacing grin.

"The neighbor?" Kane murmurs in bemusement. "What the hell are you doing here?"

He almost looks angry or betrayed… or both.

Oh shit. Think. Think. Think.

"Thad was apparently hired by my dad to keep an eye on me after he found out I moved away from Mom. Then, when Mom went missing, my dad had Thad start playing private investigator."

Yay! That was the best lie ever! Though it's actually the truth with some omitted sections.

I'd pat myself on the back if I wouldn't look like an idiot.

"Your dad?" Kane asks curiously, his interest in Thad dissipating.

"Um, yeah," I murmur dismissively, and then I turn back to Thad and Frankie. "Call me when you've got something."

"I'll just come see you if we run across something," Thad adds menacingly, intentionally poking at the human he could easily take. "Until then, head to Chicago. I've already gotten you a ticket. We'll be there as soon as we can be."

I just nod and accept the plane ticket he proffers, and then he gives me a wink before disappearing out the door. Frankie watches him for a minute, and then he shakes his head.

"I still don't like that guy."

I let a laugh free, and then Kane adds, "I'm with you on that."

Frankie smirks, and then he pats me on the shoulder.

"Chin up, kid. You know I'll find her."

I force a smile through tight lips and hold back the tears.

"Thanks, Frankie."

Kane's arms wrap around me, making my head press against his chest, and for the first time in my life, I fall apart in front of someone. The onslaught of tears is unexpected, and now I can't stop as they pour out harder, soaking through his shirt.

I'm so embarrassed, but I can't help it. Kane coos as his lips stroke my head. Consoling me like a scared child, he scoops me up and carries me over to the bed.

"Thanks for looking after her. Make sure she doesn't miss the flight," Frankie says with a torn tone.

I know he hates leaving me, especially since I'm breaking, but at the same time, he knows he has to. I'm too slow to be of any real help.

"Don't worry. I've got her," Kane murmurs while pulling me closer, letting me sob freely.

Frankie finally leaves. I'm completely unable to shut off the floodgates right now.

"I'm sorry," I whimper as I continue to fall apart.

"Hey, no. Don't be sorry. You have every right to be upset, Alyssa."

I try to choke back some of it, finally regaining a little composure, and then I glace down at the ticket. I sigh when I see I've only got four hours to get my stuff and board.

"I should get ready," I say through my emotion.

He takes a deep breath, and then he lets me go so I can get up. I can't look at him now that I've turned into a weeping mess. Does losing your virginity also take away your strength?

We pull up to the airport, and I turn to give Kane a soft kiss as we head in.

"Thanks for bringing me. What time's your flight?" I ask, feeling lonely already.

"One," he says with a small smile.

"Same time then. At least you don't have to wait around to get home. Will you call me later?" I ask when we reach security.

"Well, I could, but that would be a little odd," he says with a bit of a smirk.

I get a little sick, wondering why he said that.

"What's *that* supposed to mean?" I ask, sounding a little offended, and he roars out a laugh while pulling me to him.

"It would be odd since I'm going to be with you," he snickers out.

"What? You're going to Chicago?" I gasp.

"Of course. You thought I came to Canada to see you for one night? I'm here for the duration, babe," he says with a sexy tone, making me blush.

We make it through the checks, and then he walks up to take my hand in his.

"So how is it you can just pick up and fly to Canada and Chicago? What is it you do exactly?"

"We really do know very little about each other, don't we?" he asks, a smile playing on his lips.

"You know more about me than I do you. I think it's time to level the playing field."

He lets a small chuckle free as we head to the lounge in front of the terminal.

"My roommates and I invested in several different things when we were younger, and now we turn a profit from those investments. It makes it easy to come and go as we please, spend as we want, and live comfortably."

I'm jealous.

"Okay, what about your parents? Or should I ask that?"

His lips tighten, and he takes a deep breath, letting me know I've rushed the getting-to-know-him process.

"They've been gone a while, but we were close at one time."

Oh I'm such an idiot.

"Kane, I'm sorry. I shouldn't have asked that."

He forces a smile and shakes his head while wrapping his arm around my shoulders.

"I made peace with it long ago. Your turn. I haven't asked about your dad because you've never mentioned him. Now that you have, I'm curious. Why isn't he here himself?"

Because he's a murderous son of a bitch who rarely goes anywhere, due to the fact he has more enemies than friends.

The last time my dad was in my life was the day the world almost turned to night forever. Fortunately, it was passed off as a meteor shower blocking the sun - at least that's the story the humans know. Mom got us out of there before he really lost it and endangered us both.

"He's not exactly the sort of person I want in my life. He's actually a bit of an asshole, and it's better if he doesn't get involved."

He tilts his head curiously, not really understanding my answer, and then he murmurs, "He can't be that bad if he's hired a private investigator."

He sent a blood thirsty changer and a group of night stalkers - my natural enemy - to be my aide. Yes, he's that bad.

"I wish I could say something nice about him, but the truth is, I barely know him. What I do know isn't exactly flattering. Let's just say there's a reason I don't talk about him very much."

"I hate to say this, but I don't even know your mom's name," he murmurs shamefully.

"Oh. It's... Callie. At least that's what most everyone calls her."

The humans anyway.

Calypso is a bit too unique to try and explain.

They start boarding our flight so we start walking up to hand in our tickets to the smiling woman happy to send us on our way.

"Any siblings?" I ask curiously.

"No. Deke and Zee are like my brothers though, and Sierra is like my sister."

A slight scowl spreads over my face as we find our seats, and he lets me have the window while climbing in beside me.

"And where does Amy fit in?"

He lets out a laugh while shaking his head.

"Amy was... well... *is* Sierra's fault. She took her in when Amy was struggling to find her way. She needed help, and Sierra has a lot in common with her."

I'm not crazy about the vague answer, but I won't press the issue.

"So are all those people you hang out with your roommates?"

He swats at the air as if he's batting down my question.

"Hell no. We've got a lot of friends, but it's just Zee, Deke, Amy, Sierra, and myself in the cabin. As you've seen, it's plenty big enough for more. It gets lonely living by yourself after a while."

"You're only twenty-five," I chuckle out.

He shrugs. "I don't like living by myself. What about you? How do you like it?"

It's not exactly as thrilling as I originally thought it would be, but it's better than living with a coven before I have to.

"It's creepy, but I won't ever tell my mom that... if we find her that is," I murmur on a sour note, my eyes watering again.

"We'll find her. Did the police ever find any sign of foul play?" he asks while running his fingers through my hair in an affectionate motion.

No, because they're not the ones looking for her.

"No. I'm sure she's just off being stupid. I still worry though."

He smiles and pulls my hand to his lips.

"I guess you didn't get to spend too much time home alone. I started stalking you almost as soon as you moved in," he says to return to our previous conversation, keeping me from crying.

I laugh, my tears fading, and then I lean into him.

"You're one stalker I look forward to seeing."

"Good, because I plan on seeing you as much as I can for as long as I can."

Butterflies ruffle my stomach, and his hand slides down my back.

"I like the sound of that," I murmur as I nestle into him.

"I hope so," he says as if to himself, and then my eyes become too heavy to hold open any longer.

Chapter Nine

"Any word?" I ask while rocking back and forth on the bed, wondering where Kane has been for so long.

"No. We're still looking. Are you in Arizona?" Frankie asks.

"Yeah, I've been to Chicago, Memphis, New York, and now Phoenix within five days. What's going on? Why am I changing locations so much?"

He exhales heavily, and then finally he murmurs, "I should have told you, but Thad worried you already had too much on your plate. Your house was ransacked, your work was trashed, and we're worried whoever has Calypso is after you, too."

My heart sinks to the floor and my head begins pounding, searching aimlessly for answers.

"Who would want me and why? I haven't lived long enough to have enemies."

"No, but your mom has. And let's not even get started about your dad's long list of enemies. The point is, we're trying to keep you safe. Is Kane still with you?"

I glance out the window, still seeing no sign of my human.

"Yeah, but I'm not sure how long he's going to want to stay with me if I'm constantly on the move. I've already told him he could go home, but he swears he's not leaving until I can go home."

"Well, I'm not sure how long that will be. Just sit tight. We'll figure this all out soon enough."

"I hope so," I mumble.

"Look, I've got to go. Thad says it's too dangerous to keep our cells on with so many dark users nearby. He's gone off with two of the night stalkers right now to speak in private with his contact. If they're looking for you, my calls could point them in the right direction. I'll try to call when I can."

I hang up, doing my best not to cry, and then I pace around the rental house Thad just happen to have handy, wondering where in the hell Kane has been for so long.

Great. I'm a nagging housewife.

The door opens, and I turn to see him walking in, his eyes seeming… off.

"You okay?" I ask curiously, but he doesn't answer.

Instead, he grabs me at the waist and tosses me to the bed, his lips pinning mine as his tongue invades.

Oh damn.

My greedy hands readily return the spontaneous gesture, but he doesn't taste right.

Then it hits me, and I get sick just before throwing my arms out, tossing the imposter across the room, using my magic.

"Who the hell are you?!" I blare, my whole body trembling as I force out my strength to hold him down.

He starts laughing ferociously loud, and then he releases his mask to reveal himself.

Thad.

"You asshole. I could have killed you!"

I drop my hold on him, and he laughs harder while rising to his feet.

"Chill out. It was just a spot of fun."

"A *spot* of fun?" I scoff. "I'll turn you into a *smear* of pain if you do that to me again."

He gives me a carefree wink and then stands to his feet, pretending to dust himself off.

"What are you doing here?" I grumble as my body continues to tremble from the adrenaline high.

"I came to show you these. I need you to tell me if you recognize any of these people."

He hands me a handful of pictures - surveillance type shots - and I carefully study the strangers' faces.

"No. Why?" I ask while handing them back to him.

"Because," he sighs, "supposedly these people were seen with your mother a few hours before she disappeared. From what I gather, your council isn't being very forthcoming with you either."

"What is *that* supposed to mean?"

He gives me a devilish grin before propping up on the back of the couch.

"I'll tell you if you kiss me like that again."

I really hate the fact I'm grinning right now, and I do my best to wipe it from my face.

"You're incorrigible."

"This I know. Now, the kiss?" he muses, playfully feigning impatience.

I walk over to him, and then I almost put my lips to his before shoving him over the couch, making him fall in a toppling motion. He starts laughing again as his back slaps the floor, and then he shakes his head while propping up.

"That's not a good way to ask for information."

"Perhaps I should call my dad and tell him you're trying to exploit me for sex."

He narrows his eyes, his smile lighter now. "Firstly, don't call your dad. He's fucking crazy. Secondly, it's a kiss… not sex… not yet, anyway."

I accidentally laugh, and he stands up to walk back around to where I am before he starts his explanation.

"The council sent you to Washington, where the dark users hold the root of their power. I found it suspicious to begin with, and then on top of that, they didn't tell you your mom had been receiving threats."

"Threats?" I prompt, expecting him to elaborate.

"Nothing deadly, they just kept saying she would get what was coming to her if she didn't return what was theirs."

That sounds deadly enough to me.

"What did she have?"

He shrugs, plopping down on the arm of my chair, and then he pulls out a bottle of red liquid I dare not watch him drink.

Blood.

"I don't know. I haven't found out that much. One thing is for certain though, your council is holding out." I hear the swishing of the liquid going from the bottle to his mouth, and I shiver in response.

"Not a fan of blood, love?" he teases.

"Not a fan of blood meals."

"Well, I need less blood than night stalkers if it makes you feel any better." *Not really.* "So I take it you have no idea what your mother was holding either?" he asks almost rhetorically.

"No. She didn't tell me anything about the politics or even the reality of our world. She always tried to bring out the sunny side of my fate, since I'm constantly at odds with magic. What about Frankie? Does he know anything?"

I just talked to him. Why didn't he tell me any of this?

"I haven't spoken with him yet. He's not exactly very *honest* with me, given the fact I'm a changer. I wanted to speak with you before he could coach you up. It's hard to help someone when they're holding back."

True, but I don't blame Frankie for not trusting any of them.

"Well, I'm not holding back. Apparently I know very little about my mother's life."

He sighs, frowning slightly, and then he stands up to walk to the door.

"If you think of anything, let me know. Also, watch your back. If anything goes wrong, head to your next safe house. No more hotels."

I glance at the heavy book of procedures he has drawn up. It's resting on my dresser, making me smile

"Thanks for the long list of places to go, by the way. How the hell do you have so many houses?"

He lets a laugh free, and then he shrugs.

"I've been around a while. One tends to accumulate. So, where's loverboy?"

"Out. I'm sure he's tired of changing places all the time."

"Then tell him to go home," he says with a devious grin. "If you don't like being alone, I can swing by and keep you company."

His boy-next-door persona was washed away the day I met him - well, since I met the real Thad. Now he's the wolfish bad boy who loves to tease me.

"I can't believe I thought you were such a sweet guy," I huff out with a bit of a grin.

"I'm a changer, baby. I can look like anyone… including a sweet guy," he teases, his menacing grin emphasizing his mischievous eyes.

"Change into someone leaving," I mumble playfully while ushering him out the door.

"It's been a long time since a girl kicked me out of one of my houses."

I laugh loudly, and he jerks me by the back of the head to push his lips against mine before disappearing out the door, leaving me scowling at his quickly fading back as he blurs out of sight.

Obviously he was watching me to know Kane is gone, so I quickly go to draw the curtains shut.

The door opens again, and Kane walks in, carrying… nothing. *Thad?*

"Hey," I murmur softly, not sure if this is Kane or Thad. "You've been gone a while."

He smiles as he walks over to me, and his arms slide around my waist as his lips find mine. He tastes so damn good, and I smile.

Mmm. Definitely Kane.

"Yeah," he says pulling back. "I decided to go for a run after I went into town. I was going to bring you back something nice to eat, but I thought we

111

could go out instead."

"Like a date?" I say too excitedly, quickly masking my giddiness with a more respectable composure.

"Yes," he snickers out while pulling me closer. "Like a date. Judging by your reaction, I'm assuming you've been wanting a date for a while."

I blush lightly while feigning nonchalance, making him laugh a little more.

"Go get ready, and I'll make us some reservations."

I tug at his hand, suddenly a little too turned on to simply walk away. I've never been this enthralled by anyone. At the same time, I feel guilty for dragging him around the country.

"Do you want to go home? I know you weren't expecting to be gone for so long, and I'm sure you didn't plan on living on the move."

He strums my lips with his, and then he shakes his head.

"I'm not leaving you. I'm perfectly fine bouncing around. Now, get ready, I'm taking you out."

I tug at his hand again, and he looks at me curiously.

"Actually, I sort of feel like ordering in now," I seductively release while leading him to the bed.

A smirk begins to play on his lips as he plays along, and he picks me up to gently toss me on the bed.

"Oh really?" he asks with a low, sizzling hot tone.

"Mm hm."

His lips find my neck, his teeth lightly grazing my skin as he sends the most delicious shivers all over my body. His hand slides between my legs, pushing aside the shorts as his finger rolls across my aroused center.

I moan lightly when his touch stimulates the insatiable beast inside me, and he starts pulling my shorts down slowly, drawing out the torture.

"I'm starting to think I've created a monster," he teases when my hand rubs across his erection.

"Maybe. Let's find out how vicious I can be."

He lets out a laugh, and then he pulls my shirt over my head just before his lips find my chest. I moan more, and then I rip his shirt over his head to offer me skin on skin.

His body still astounds me. Each line is carved by perfection's hand. It's surreal how amazing he is. *All of him.*

My hand slides under his jeans, finding his desire for me, and he moans as his lips find mine. He flips over, bringing me with him as I sit astride his gloriously perfect body.

I bend down, bringing my lips to his, and he grabs my ass to grind my center against his, making me all the hotter.

I start pulling at his pants as my lips start trailing down, and his breath hitches in his throat when he feels my lips on his perfect piece of firmness.

"Alyssa," he breathes in a hoarse whisper, making my head move a little faster as I take him deeper into my mouth.

Then suddenly I'm ripped up and his lips are crushing mine as he thrusts in from underneath. A loud breath falls through my lips in a grunt when he slams in a little harder, no longer taking it easy on me, and I sit up as his hands grip around my ass to aide my rhythm.

I pull his hands to my breasts, and he moans as his head falls back. I push against his chest for balance as his hips buck harder, pushing me to the edge, and then I cry out as I find that incredible release only he has ever given me.

He shudders inside me, releasing his force, and I fall forward to collapse against his chest. My ragged, tired breaths fall free as I work to steady my thudding heart, and his arms wrap around me as he kisses the side of my head.

"You're amazing," he murmurs with a breathless tone of his own.

"I've had an incredible teacher," I playfully retort, making his laughter break free in an expected spurt.

I rise up, a smile on my face, and then I kiss his neck. I tilt my head to the side when I see a faint scar - his lone imperfection. It's something I've never noticed before.

"Where'd you get this?" I ask while running my finger over it.

He tenses, and I feel like an ass for asking now. Apparently it's not something he likes to talk about.

"It happened a long time ago. It's not something I like to talk about though."

"Sorry," I murmur regretfully, and then he kisses my head, warming me through my hair.

"It's fine. We're still learning about each other. Right now, I want to learn what you look like in the shower."

I laugh a little, but I willingly cede to his request as he pulls me from the bed and leads me into the bathroom.

The bed is empty, and I start looking around the dark room for the warmth I'm missing.

"Kane?"

I'm met with silence, so I get up to start my search through the large home. Each turn is another empty room, no sign of the man who has seemed to abandon me in the middle of the night.

Then my eyes fall on a note, and my heart drops as I read it.

Alyssa,

I'm sorry. I had to head back home to take care of some business. I'll be back tomorrow, I swear. Please don't be mad.

Kane

I huff, and then I walk over to pick up my phone to call him. It rings for a while before going to voicemail, so I hang up.

Who leaves in the middle of the night without saying anything? *Someone with secrets.*

I can't be mad at him for having secrets though. It's not like I can ever tell him who or what I really am. This can just be fun while it lasts… as long as I don't fall in love.

A chill spreads through the air, and I move over to the window to see a shadow flashing from place to place.

I get sick when I see several pairs of glowing blue eyes in the distance, their bodies swiftly moving across the sands as they head toward me.

"Shit!"

I grab my phone and dial Thad as quickly as I can, praying he's still close by.

"Mmm, I love a late night call."

"Good, because I'd love a late night hero."

"What's going on?" he asks more seriously, slightly panicked.

"Night stalkers - at least twenty. Please tell me you're close by."

"I'll be there as fast as I can. There's a weapons room in the master. Press the lever above the fireplace disguised as the head of a sparrow. Shoot anything that gets too close with the silver gun. The bullets have been blessed by your kind."

Thank fuck.

The phone goes dead, and I rush over to the mantle to press the button, praying it will hurry up and open. My phone starts ringing just as it does, and I look down to see Kane's name.

Too late to talk now.

I'm actually glad he took off in the middle of the night now. The last thing I need to do is drag him into a centuries-old war. I rip two guns from the secret compartment, and then I start firing through the window while using my magic and scattering the shards of glass away from the frame for me to leap through it without getting ripped to shreds.

Hollow, shrill squeals erupt from the death-seeking, bloodthirsty bastards, and I force the power from my body to blow them back, praying Thad hurries the hell up.

"What the hell do you want from me?" I scream while spinning a circle of power around my body, a force strong enough to keep them away from me… for now.

"Just you," one hisses, fangs out, bloodlust in his eyes as he lunges at me, but the protective circle I've spun deflects his attacks, throwing him back.

"It's going to hurt worse next time," I bluff, knowing I'm not strong enough to keep this shit up against so many.

"Stupid witch." He snarls while climbing to his feet, and the headlights in the distance make my stomach tense up.

Please don't be Kane.

The lights disappear, but my distracted mindset has left me vulnerable. The eager bloodsuckers quickly take advantage. The stinging pain in my side knocks the wind out of me as I go sailing backwards.

I fall to my face, splitting my lip and making blood taint my taste. I cringe, feeling the grit sliding down my throat as I cough up the remnants of the intrusive earth.

"Bastard," I growl, barely defending myself from the next attack in time.

Then I grunt and wheeze when I feel a hand around my throat from behind, lifting me high into the air and turning me to face the glowing blues on the pretty face. As long as he's touching me, I can't use my fucking power.

"Now, where the hell is it?" he demands, his tone dark, ominous, and scary as hell.

"I… don't… know… what-"

A shrill screech rings out as a hawk zooms down from the sky, growing in size as it nears us. I scream as the talons grip my arms and rip me away from the monster who can't hold back my powers anymore.

I sling my arms out as the hawk carries me off, and I deliver one last blow to the vicious bastards below. I struggle against the piercing, sharp claws, and I look up at the hawk intent on getting us out of here.

"Too tight!" I squeal just as slithers of blood drip free from my arms. "They'll find me if I'm bleeding every-damn-where."

He can't answer in changed form, but he swoops low, almost slapping the ground before releasing me. My feet run to fight the built up momentum, and the hawk changes into the white wolf, his head motioning for me to hurry up.

I run and leap into the air, and he grows under me after I land on top. I hang on for dear life as he charges ahead, deep into the desert. The wind slaps me in the face, along with desert bugs, and the chill of the night creeps down to my bones, fighting against the heat of my adrenaline.

Everything around me turns into a blur, and I push my face into his back to warm me with his fur and keep the flying insects away from my gaping mouth.

Within minutes, we've lost them, and a car pulls around just as we come to an abrupt halt. I fall forward, but foreign hands grab me when one of the "friendly" night stalkers catches me, leaving me with an eerie feeling.

"Thanks," I murmur halfheartedly.

"Go! We have to go!" Thad urges as he leaps into the car, human and... *naked*.

Ah crap. Why does he have to look like *that* naked?

I climb in, my face glowing red, and keep my eyes focused anywhere but the naked man as another changer gasses the vehicle, surging away from the craziness behind.

"They'll track me down if I'm in my changed form for too long," Thad sighs while relaxing in his seat.

"You should... um... put something on. It's cold," I stammer, still refusing to look at him.

"Is that a dig at my *manhood?*" he chuckles out. "For the record, I'm not turned on by near death encounters."

My glowing red burns brighter as I bury my face in my hands.

"I didn't look at your *manhood*," I lie, and he *is* turned on.

He laughs lightly, and then I hear the rustle of his clothes being pulled on beside me. Turning to face him, I feel my face slowly fading back to its normal color.

"Where'd loverboy go this time?" he asks.

"He had some work to do back home. Speaking of which, can I borrow your phone? Mine was sort of left back at the house."

"Yeah." He relinquishes his phone.

I quickly dial Kane's number and start biting my nails as I anxiously await his answer, the tears trying to fall as I mull over what I need to say.

"Hello?" he asks curiously, not recognizing the number.

"Hey," I murmur in relief just to hear his voice.

"Alyssa? Whose phone are you using?" he worries. "Are you okay?"

I'm not even close to being okay.

"Yeah, I'm fine. There was a small problem back at the house, and I had to leave rather quickly. Thad came and got me. I was just worried about you."

"Shit. What happened?"

It'd be easier to tell him monsters are hunting me, because then he'd definitely stay away.

"Nothing you need to worry about. Look, Kane, this has gotten worse than I realized it would, and I don't think-"

"I know - it's a lot worse. I went by your house tonight to grab you some more clothes, and your place was trashed. Alyssa, I don't think your mom is with friends. I called a detective I know, and he's looking into the case for me. I'm on my way back right now. Where are you going?"

My breath shakily slides out, and everyone in the car tries to pretend they're not listening in.

"That's just it. Kane, I think it would be best if you stayed away from me until we find out what's going on."

"Hell no," he scoffs. "Tell me where you're going. I'll be there as soon as I can get a flight."

Tears start to drip, and Thad pats my leg as I try to gather some composure.

"Kane, I can't. I care about you too much. I don't know what's going on, but I won't let you be in the middle of it. I'm sorry, I really am."

"Alyssa, tell me where the hell you're going!" he demands, fear lying in the undertones of his voice.

"I'm sorry," I repeat in a whispered whimper while hanging up.

The phone starts ringing immediately, but I just stare blankly at the number I can't answer. I have to know what he's going to do though. Using my magic, I wave my hand over the phone to listen to the man who doesn't know I can hear him as the phone starts ringing again.

"Damn it. She won't fucking answer!" he blares to someone.

"Who do you think is after her?" Deke asks.

I'm sure they're all telling him to stay the hell away from me. As much as it kills me to think of, I hope he listens to them.

"I don't know, but she needs to be protected. She thinks *I* could get hurt."

Deke laughs, and I hear Kane cursing again as the phone lights up and rings once more.

"That's a rather nifty trick," Thad says, now realizing what I've done.

"It'll only work until he calls someone else," I murmur softly.

"What are you going to do?" Deke asks.

"I'm going to find her, and then I'm going to beat the fuck out of whoever is messing with her. I'm not going to leave her side again, and so help me, if you call for my help one more time with that fucking bitch, I'll never talk to you again."

Amy? His business was Amy?

My anger takes the place of my tears as fury runs through me.

"I'm sorry," Deke exasperates. "You're the only one who has any influence over her when she loses it. It's just… you and this Alyssa girl spending so much time together is making Amy crazy. Maybe it's good if she goes off on her own. Amy needs all of us, and it appears you're the one she needs the most."

It's nice to know this now. At least it makes this easier.

"Amy can go to hell for all I care. Sierra wanted a pet, she can train her. I'm not her fucking leash-handler anymore. In case you haven't noticed, I happen to give a damn about someone else who needs me a hell of a lot more than Amy. She's her own worst enemy, and Alyssa is just a fragile girl."

Fragile girl? Really?

I'll show him fragile the next time I see him… if I can even stand to be around him.

"Call the detective and find out what he knows," Kane urges.

"I can, but-"

"Fuck it. I'll call him myself."

Just like that, the conversation is lost when he apparently does call someone else, ending the bit of magical influence I had.

I hand the phone back to Thad, and he sighs as he puts it back in his pocket.

"I'm sorry you had to do that, but it's for the best," Thad murmurs sympathetically.

"As you heard, it sounds like it was the best for more than one reason."

I fight back the furious tears that try to fall. I can't believe I was so gullible, so stupid.

"I'm not sure what you mean. It's sounds like some psychotic girl has a fatal attraction to him, but he wants you."

It sounds like he'll always go running in to save her.

"I'd like to show him *fragile*," I grumble.

"Now that was a little funny. He just doesn't know any better. Mortal men think most girls are fragile," he chuckles out.

"Let's just get the hell out of here."

Chapter Ten

"It's been a week, and this bloody fool won't stop calling me. I've got to get my number changed," Thad exasperates while flopping down to my bed.

Kane's number is still flashing across the vibrating phone he tosses to me, but I push it away. I can't talk to him.

"He'll stop calling. Eventually *Amy* will need him again, and he'll forget all about me."

Thad rests his head on my lap as I flip through the pages of a magazine, and I look down to arch my eyebrow at him.

"Comfortable?" I ask sardonically.

"I would be if you ate a little more. Damn, your hipbones really jut out."

I laugh lightly, and then I roll my eyes.

"I'm on my back. It happens. Why are you in my room instead of tracking down my mother?"

"Crack the whip some other time. I've got to lie low here. I'm not very well liked in L.A. I'm letting the others run down the leads down there, while I crash here in the condo with you."

I put my magazine down, now that I'm a little intrigued and curious.

"What did you do to become *not so well liked?*" I muse.

"Long story. I've been around a while."

"Well, I'm about to change clothes, so I need you to *not* be around for a while," I tease while lifting my hips to knock his head from my lap.

"Why change?" he asks while sitting up and stretching.

"Because I have to go buy some more clothes. I'm sick of wearing the same stuff over and over, and I can't go out in my pajamas."

I motion to the short pajama set I've worn so much that the hems are starting to show their tattered signs of early aging.

"I happen to be fond of that little purple shirt I've seen you in a time or two," he says menacingly while bouncing his eyebrows up and down.

I let out a laugh, and then I start shuffling through my bag.

"Well, that purple shirt is spent. I'm sick of it, and I'll quite possibly trash it after I wear it one last time today."

He smirks, and then he licks his lips before winking at me.

"I should probably stick around. You might need some help."

I let out a laugh, and then I start pushing him out the door. Though he's sexy, he's not Kane. I wish I could stop thinking about him.

Once Thad is out, I stare at my new phone, wondering if I should at least let Kane know I'm okay. If I call him, I could at least listen to his voice... even after we hang up. I hate the fact he keeps leaving me to help Amy, but I miss him so much.

"I'll probably regret this."

I pick up the phone and dial his number quickly before I can talk myself out of it. It rings a few times, and then I sigh when I realize it's about to go to voicemail.

"Hello?" he says unexpectedly, again puzzled by a new number.

I sit there quietly, not sure what to say.

"Hey?" I finally strain out. "I was just calling to see how you're doing."

"Alyssa, shit. Where the hell are you? I've been worried to damn death."

He really does sound worried, tormented even.

"Sorry. It's been a long, busy week. Um, Kane, I think this goes without saying, but you know we're not together anymore. If you want to be with Amy-"

"Damn it, Alyssa. Stop with the Amy shit. I don't even fucking like her as a friend. As a matter of fact, I quite possibly hate her at this particular moment. Please tell me where you are, and don't you dare say we're not together."

I sigh out heavily, and then I glance out the window of the huge condominium to stare down at the small humans below, oblivious to the world of deadly beauties around them.

"I just called to see how you are. I've been worried my mom's shit was going to affect you since you've been with me."

"Alyssa, please tell me what's going on. My detective friend can't even find out anything about her. It's like she's not real or something. Are you in trouble? Are you in witness protection or something?" he asks, worrying all the more.

Oh how I wish it was something as mundane and human as that.

"Sort of. Look, don't worry. As long as you're safe, I'll be okay. For the record, I'm not as fragile as you think I am. I'll be fine."

Don't ask me where I heard that.

"Alyssa, you *are* fragile. You're a twenty-year-old girl. Please let me come be with you. I can help."

I wish that was true.

"Sorry, but it needs to be this way, and we *aren't* together. It's for the best. Maybe Amy is psycho, but she's probably better for you than me."

"Fuck! I'm so sick of hearing about her. I want you. Do you hear me? *You.*"

The butterflies ruffle in my stomach, and I lie back on the bed while pulling on my shirt.

"I want you, too, but things are just too complicated right now. I'd rather you just forget about me."

"Please don't make me beg," he hoarsely whispers, making my tears form.

I grip my hair and walk over to pull on my jeans, my heart sinking to the pits of my stomach as I stare woefully at the girl who has started to fall in love with a human she can never be with.

"Kane, I'm sorry. Listen, if-"

I scream when I see the scaly tail of ... *something*, dangling from the top of my shirt, and I start flailing around wildly to rid myself of the mystery varmint invading my cleavage. I leap onto the bed as a lizard thuds to the ground, and then I see it wink at me. The fucking lizard even laughs as it scurries out the door.

Thad!

"Alyssa!" Kane yells, as if he's been saying my name repeatedly, expecting an explanation for my panic.

"Sorry. I'm fine."

He breathes out a rattling breath, and I actually hear him collapse to a chair or something.

"What the hell just happened?"

"We've apparently got... pests," I grumble, scowling at the door which I know Thad is lurking behind.

Pests of the changer variety.

I need to remind Thad how much it hurts to be brought down by a witch.

"You damn near stopped my heart," he mumbles, his breaths still coming out in pained wisps.

"Sorry. I need to go. I've got to get some new clothes before we head off to some new, random destination."

"Alyssa, please tell me where to find you."

I hesitate to say no when all I want to do is just crumble, beg him to find me.

"I can't," I almost whisper.

Silence creeps through the phone as we both sit waiting for the other to cave. I can't give in though. I can't watch my world break him.

"I'd give anything to take that night back," he finally says, breaking the breathy suspense. "I'd tell Deke to fuck off and deal with shit on his own for once. I'd stay in bed, holding you to me as you curled around my body. There's not an inch of your body I wouldn't have explored by now, and there's no way I would ever leave you alone for anything again."

My tears finally start dripping, making me hate myself for falling for him. I knew better. As much as I want to be human, I'm not. Stringing him along was the worst mistake I could have made.

"But you already did. Kane, I'm not going to lie. I know you went back for Amy. There's apparently something going on, and I-"

"I swear it's not like that. Please let me come to you. I'll prove it."

"Let me finish." I sigh while gripping my head. "I don't know what the deal is between the two of you, but I don't want in the middle of it. I care about you too much too soon as it is. You probably did me a favor by disappearing into the night. I need to go. Please stop calling Thad's phone, and don't start calling mine."

He sits silently on the other end, and then I hear a harsh breath.

"L.A.?" he asks, making my heart slap my throat.

"What?" I release with a crackle, my mouth drying.

"You're in L.A.? I can be there in a few hours. Don't leave. We'll discuss this in person, and I'll show you how much I care about you."

"How do you know where I am?" I shiver as excitement and dread fills me at once.

"I just traced your phone. Money affords someone more than a nice house. I'll be there soon."

"Kane, don't. We're about to leave. Please stop this."

"Then call me when you get to where you're going, and I'll follow you then."

"No, I won't call, and I'm switching off my GPS. Just forget me."

"That's impossible. I'm coming to you whether you like it or not. Now, you can stay there, or I can come find you at your next place. You'll call me again, Alyssa. You want to be with me just like I want to be with you. Admit it. This chemistry between us isn't something people find everyday. I know better than anyone that it's not."

I swallow my heart back down, and then I shake my head.

"It's not something someone finds everyday, but it's also not good for you." *Or your life.* "I'm sorry, Kane. I won't be here when you come."

I hang up, quickly rushing into the room where Thad is packing.

"Yeah, I heard. Loverboy is persistent, I'll give him that."

I don't have time to be aggravated with the fact he was eavesdropping. Damn immortal hearing.

"We were going to leave tonight anyway, weren't we?"

"Yeah. No worries, pretty girl. Just grab your stuff, and we'll meet the others at the next rendezvous."

He offers me a wink, and then I narrow my eyes.

"I don't want to catch any more lizards down my shirt."

He starts laughing, and then he moves over to where I am, letting his thumb trail over my lips as he stares down at me.

"I would have gone for a snake, but I thought it'd be too much of a pun. Grab your stuff."

He kisses my forehead, and I roll my eyes while heading back to my room. I peek out to see him walking out the door, heading to the elevator, and I capitalize on the fact he's out of earshot. I wave my hand over the phone, using my magic once again.

"Are you really going after her again?" Amy bellows.

"Of course I am. Stay the hell out of my way and out of my life!" Kane berates, sounding furious.

There's silence for a minute, with the exception of drawers opening and shutting in the background.

"You really do hate me, don't you?" she whimpers, and I hear him sigh hard.

"Amy, I'm not the one for you. I've told you this countless times - even before Alyssa came into my life. I hope you get your shit under control, really, I do, but it's not my responsibility, it's yours. Acting out every time I'm with the girl I *want* to be with only pisses me off. Excuse me, I have to holler at Zee."

I hear his feet shuffling away, and I start to end my use of magic.

"Kane still mad?" asks Sierra, and I decide to be nosy and tune in instead of tuning out.

"Very. What's so special about some blond girl? Does he miss being a normal guy that much?" Amy scoffs.

Normal?

I suppose being insanely wealthy has its drawbacks. It'd be hard to appreciate the small things and know when someone actually likes you for you.

"Amy, he's right though. You can't keep doing this to him. He's not responsible for you. You're responsible for you. You'll find someone who loves you the way he loves Alyssa."

Loves? He doesn't love me. Slow down the wedding march, Sierra.

"He doesn't love her. He barely knows her," Amy snorts.

Bitch.

"He does, or he wouldn't be in a frenzy to find her. Just leave him in peace. He'll never forgive you if he loses Alyssa, and then you won't even have his friendship."

"If I wanted his friendship, I wouldn't have told him I love him."

She loves him? Shit.

"If he loved you, you wouldn't be sitting here scheming up ways to get him. You have to stop crossing that line. If you back off, he will eventually come around. Right now, you're on a slippery slope. Soon, you might not be able to stop from making a mistake that you'll have to live with after you've sobered up."

Sobered up? Drugs? Booze?

"I-"

"I need my phone," Kane murmurs, interrupting whatever Amy was going to say.

Crap. I want to hear more.

"Be careful, and call us when you find her. I'd like to know she's alright," Sierra murmurs genuinely.

"I will, in the meantime, stay on standby. I might need some help finding the sons of bitches after her."

"You know we'll help in any way we can. That's what family is for."

"Just… if she says… when I-"

"We'll accept her," Sierra says comfortingly, and I get sick.

When he what? What will I say?

"I think it's stupid, and I won't accept her, no matter how long she stays," Amy spews.

Stays?

"It doesn't matter if *you* accept her or not. You're the only one here whose opinion I don't give a fuck about," he growls, and then I lose the connection.

"No," I mumble, waving my hand over the phone, but nothing happens.

Shit. He must have called someone else, or they called him.

"Ready?" Thad calls from the living area, and I drop my head back momentarily while sighing in exasperation.

"Yeah."

Ready for my life to make sense.

The rough winds scrape across the house thought to be abandoned deep in the woods. Crackling out its strength, the fireplace warms the room.

I've gone from cold weather to hot weather so many times that I'm finally getting sick.

"You okay?" Thad asks as he sits down beside my shivering body.

"Yeah. I think I'm getting a cold."

"Can't you do a healing spell or something?"

I laugh in the middle of a sneeze while shaking my head.

"Sure, if I want to end up crippled for all eternity. Healing spells have to be done by very well practiced witches. Not even Frankie can pull off a healing spell. My mom is the only one I know to successfully do it without side effects."

"Did not know that," he murmurs while wrapping his arm around my shoulders, and I eye him suspiciously when he feels too close.

"I'm sick, not desperate."

He smirks, and then he leans over to my neck, making my breath hitch. I feel his breath on me, warming my skin, and the warmth suddenly travels through the rest of my body, relieving me of my chills.

"Wow," I murmur while wiping my nose with a tissue. "Any cure for the sniffles inside your breath?"

"Let's find out," he says before pressing his lips to mine, and I sneeze while laughing as he draws back with a look of disgust.

"I think you did that on purpose."

I shrug, feigning innocence, and he rolls his eyes while leaning back and letting his head rest against the couch. My phone buzzes, and he rolls his eyes.

"That boy never takes a hint, does he?" he grumbles under his breath.

I glance down, realizing it really is Kane... *again*, and then I put the phone back down.

"He'll forget me eventually," I strain out, trying not to show the truly devastated emotion teetering on the edge. "Can you give me a minute?"

"I'm exhausted. Please don't make me move," he groans while stretching out. "You can listen in. I swear I won't judge or comment."

He closes his eyes while breathing steadily, but I put the phone down instead of listening. Just hearing Kane's voice would probably make me cave and beg him to come risk his life just so I can have his arms around me.

Selfish bitch.

"Sorry to interrupt, but the warlock needs your help ciphering a code outside," one of the night stalkers murmurs.

"Tell him I'll be there in a minute, Rain."

Rain's eyes glow blue momentarily, as if he's taunting me, and then he smirks before walking out.

"Remind me why you have night stalkers in your party," I grumble, a chill spreading throughout me.

"Because they can subdue the dark users better than anyone. Not to mention, they're some of the strongest beings in existence. Why exactly are the two of you mortal enemies? I've never understood it."

I sigh out as all the stories my mother told me when I was growing up suddenly rattle around in my mind.

"They have the ability to hold us down, making our powers worthless. In the old days, they lived solely off our blood and essence. Draining a witch kills most blood-thirsters, but to a night stalker, we're worth fifty humans."

"How do you build up resentment over something that happened centuries ago when you're so young?" he chuckles out.

My lips tighten, and then I pull my shirt down to reveal a spot along my collarbone.

"What?" he says with a devious smirk. "Finally willing to let me show you what an *animal* I really can be?"

Though his witty little pun is humorous, I'm not exactly feeling the urge to laugh. With a heavy sigh, I wave my hand over the spot to reveal the blemish I masked long ago.

The red, savage scar reveals itself, and his eyes widen in disbelief.

"Bloody hell. When did that happen?" he gushes while running his finger along the mark.

I pull my hand back over it, making the skin pull smooth, and the scar vanishes once more. I let my collar pop back into place and turn to face him.

"It happened when I was seventeen. One day I went for a walk, but a night stalker had been tracking me, waiting for me to slip up and step out of the protective circle I was living in at the time - my overprotective mother's circle around our farmhouse coven.

"Obviously I didn't expect him, and he pinned me down, using his powers of subduing. My blood became his meal, and little by little, I felt my life slipping away. He fell between my legs, lifted my skirt, and all I could do was lie there, stunned by his hypnotism. I thought... For a minute, I worried he was going to do more than just feast on me, but he didn't get the chance.

"After he dug his fangs in the second time, my mother showed up. He got away, but it's doubtful he lived, considering the wounds he sustained. I spent three days in a healing room, barely surviving the attack after he drained me almost dry within minutes.

"So don't say it's something that happened centuries ago. Not everything has changed. You know as well as I do, night stalkers still love a good witch meal, they just clean up better than they used to."

"I thought that attack was just the rumor your father started in order for your mother and you to live freely. And I thought you were like eight or nine when it happened."

"No. I was ten the first time I was attacked, and that's when they told everyone Airis Devall had died." I pause, motioning to the other side of my neck. "It didn't scar like the last one. That night stalker's venom was weaker, meaning a smaller scar, and he met my father's wrath fairly quickly. He was a fool to even come into Drackus's home."

He lets out a heavy, harsh breath, and then his fingertips trail along my collarbone as he pulls my shirt back down. My breath hitches as his lips find the hidden scar, and he drags them across it on his way up to my neck.

I start to push him away, but he pulls back on his own.

"Just so you know, there's not a night stalker here brave enough to touch you with me around. They know what I'd do to them, and most of them remember how very ruthless I once was. You're safe."

I would smile if that didn't sound so morbid and a little… scary. Too bad a changer is nowhere nearly as strong as a night stalker. I would feel comforted if I knew he really could take on a night stalker as old and seasoned as Rain.

I lean into him, my eyes growing heavy, and then I shake my head.

"I'm stronger now. You haven't even seen all I can do because I'm scared I'll end up like my father. I hold back because I have to; not because I can't do more. I almost dread my immortality."

"Why?" he muses, his fingers strumming through my hair.

"Because I'll be even stronger. That's the real reason I don't like using magic. I'm afraid I won't know when I've gone too far… just like him."

He nods, his hand sliding down my back now, and it almost feels like he's trying to comfort me. In my wildest dreams, I never pictured a changer comforting me. Sadly enough, he's the closest thing I have to a friend right now, and I really need a friend.

"There are few things left in the world that scare me. I've seen hell try to rise above ground, but I lived through it. Your dad… honestly, he scares the shit out of me." *Well, the comfort is gone.* "But it's not because he's powerful; it's because he has no reservations about using his power against anyone who crosses him. The council may have condemned him to the lost lands, but you know as well as I do he can leave at any time - and does.

"He stays there most of the time though, never using his magic outside the fields, but only because he doesn't want to make things harder on your mother. He doesn't ever want her punished for anything he does, and they *would* use her against him."

"Don't make it sound as though he truly cares. The reason he stays put is because the only time the light and dark agree is when it comes to keeping him away. He's powerful -deadly powerful - but he's not invincible. I've seen it. I've seen him hurt. I was young, but I remember what happened."

His lips tighten, as if he wants to say more, but he decides against it. I still can't believe Drackus told someone I'm his daughter. They're all supposed to think that young girl died.

My phone buzzes to interrupt the awkward silence that has fallen, and I frown when I see Kane's name on the screen.

It finally stops, and Thad kisses the top of my head while standing up.

"Go ahead and spy. I'll go help the warlock."

I force a smile, though I know it's a poor attempt, and he gives me a wink before disappearing out the door. With a wave of my hand, Kane's voice comes through, making me miss him more than I thought possible.

"Still nothing," he says with frustration.

"This is ridiculous," Deke spews. "How the hell did they leave L.A. without leaving a bit of a trail? Are you sure this was the condo?"

"Positive. What about Sierra? Do you think she could pick up anything?"

Not unless she's a very gifted immortal.

Kane and his friends have no chance of finding us. Hell, I don't even know exactly where we are. I'm sick of keeping up.

"Doubtful. She's had that damn cold going around and it's fucked up her smell. We could ask Amy to help."

I get sick. Just the mention of her name makes me snarl.

"I'm not asking Amy for anything. I'll figure out something. Call around, see if you can find-"

His voice cuts out, meaning someone just called him since he was mid-sentence. I can't believe he's still looking for me. The problem is, I wish he'd find me.

If I tell him where I am, and he comes, I have to feel guilty for dragging him around and risking his life. If he finds me on his own, then I ... shit. I would still feel guilty. I have to keep him away.

Chapter Eleven

The moon casts its silvery glow through the window, making the hair on the back of my neck stand up. A full moon always makes me jittery. Night stalkers are so much stronger the brighter the moon is. And mortal witches are a coveted delicacy of theirs.

Looking out the window, I find Thad wrestling with a lycan, as if they're playing. It's all so frigging weird.

Then I feel a chill. It's not from outside either. I whip around to see the glowing blues in the corner as Rain stares at me.

"What the hell are you doing in my room?" I bark.

He smiles, his fangs sliding back in as he shrugs.

"Thad wanted me to see if you felt like training?"

Training?

"I don't train yet. I'm still mortal. Now get out of my room."

Within a blink, his hands are on me, restraining me. I gasp, but no air enters my lungs as his eyes penetrate mine, locking me into place and proving he's older than he looks as he uses the ancient power.

"I thought Thad was lying. He said you were already immortal, but I knew better."

I would scream if my lips would move, but he's frozen me, leaving me to his mercy as my stiff body protests my futile attempts to move.

"Unfortunately for you, that means wonders for me. Your father... let's say he's owed this."

His fangs slither out, slowly drawing out the building dread in the pit of my stomach. A tear breaks free to roll down my cheek, my only release of terror as he hovers over my body, his gaze leaving me defenseless... leaving me his prey.

"Damn," he says while pulling a lock of my hair to his face and breathing it in. "You smell so good… so strong."

I've only ever suffered this frozen state of terror twice, and I almost died both times. This time, there's not a healing room or a group of witches capable of the spells it would take to bring me back.

"Your father thought it funny to kill the woman I had turned - the woman I loved. He said he had to remind me who was in charge. I think it's time I show him what happens when you take someone from somebody - you lose someone you love, too."

Just as his chilled breath finds my neck, the door bursts open, and the cold blooded bastard is yanked off of me and thrown out the window as Thad walks toward me.

"Are you okay?" he growls, his eyes not moving off the night stalker who is still trying to figure out what just happened.

I just nod while grabbing my throat, checking for punctures, and then he drops into a hawk and zooms out the window. I wobble up and gaze out to see him changing into a tiger - a white, beautiful tighter - before leaping onto the back of Rain, his teeth shredding the skin of the stalking asshole.

"Kick his ass, Thad," one of the girl changers cheers.

"What the hell is going on?" one of the night stalkers interjects, and then the chatter rises to urge on the brutal fight.

"Alyssa?" Frankie murmurs while stepping into my room. "What the hell?"

I don't answer as I stare out and wince when the night stalker digs his fangs into Thad's shoulder, and red stains the white fur. He roars out his pain, changing into a white, majestic lion, and suddenly the fight shifts again as he takes over.

The night stalker wails into the darkness, and though he's stronger at night, Thad's apparently older, more in control, and one hell of a force to be reckoned with. The lion roars louder, and suddenly red paints the white snow under their bodies as the night stalker goes limp - a chew toy for the fierce kitty with a bad temper.

"Shit. Did he just kill a night stalker?" Frankie gasps in disbelief.

"Yeah," I almost whisper, feeling my whole body growing a little numb from the adrenaline overload.

"He's stronger than any changer I've ever seen to take on a night stalker under the full moon. That's when they're at their damn strongest."

"I know," I murmur, still stunned as the lion shifts into Thad, and then he limps toward the house.

I rush out of the bedroom and into the living room just as he comes in, and a girl offers him a towel to cover up his... bare lower half.

He takes it, but he doesn't wrap up before collapsing to the chair, his shoulder bleeding profusely as he wearily pants his painful breaths.

"Thad," I murmur guiltily while kneeling down to examine the terrible gash.

"I'll be fine. I just need some blood, some sleep, and some solid food," he strains out.

"I'll get the blood," one girl chirps, disappearing seconds later.

The others disperse, and one begins clanking pans to start cooking him something. I cover up his lower half with a blanket that had been tossed across the back of the couch.

"A naked man's body really bothers you, doesn't it?" he jokes, but then he winces when his laughter proves to hurt.

I grimace while shaking my head.

"I can't believe you survived a night stalker under the full moon... under any moon for that matter," I murmur softly, ignoring his comment.

"I told you I wouldn't let someone touch you and get away with it. If I hadn't gone all day without blood, I wouldn't have even gotten a scratch."

"Why'd you go all day without blood?" I ask as one girl brings him a bottle full of it.

He rises up slowly, wincing the whole way, and then he starts sipping. After a few guzzles, he pulls it back from his lips to answer me.

"Drinking blood under a full moon makes me a lot stronger, but it also keeps me up all night. I prefer to sleep... unless I have a reason to be up all night," he says, ending on a menacing note.

I let a ghost of a smile free, and then I stand to my feet.

"I'm going to go get you some clothes," I say while walking toward his room.

"Just shorts please. I'll be burning up all night now that I'm drinking this with that out there," he says, pointing at the full moon glowing through the window.

I nod, and then disappear into the room. After I grab him some shorts, I decide to change myself. I feel creepy now that I've been almost violated by the night stalker.

When I walk into my room, I shiver. The damn broken window has let all of nature's chill settle inside.

"Crap."

I start to use my magic to reassemble the shattered pieces when a shadow appears around me. Nausea strikes, but before I can scream for help, a hand clamps over my mouth, and we evaporate into the wind.

Blurs, streaks, and glimpses of the world pass me by as we travel through the forest. Dizziness rules me, and my heart feels like it's going to explode. Tears are stripped from my eyes by the winds, and every second I'm a part of the air, I feel closer to death.

Finally, I feel the ground beneath me as I crash to it, being freed from whatever dark user just took me.

I rock up to my knees, and then I expel the contents of my stomach as the dizziness starts to feel more like drunkenness.

"It'll pass. I know how to carry people through the planes without killing them," a voice says from behind.

I try to focus in on it, but I can't see the face. The images and colors are so distorted that I feel like I'm trying to see a face at the end of a Kaleidoscope.

"Who are you?" I choke out before hurling out more liquid.

I hear the chatter of the leaves as the unseen dark one walks around, circling me, as he watches me in my humbled state.

"Someone who doesn't feel like being framed for the disappearance of your mother," the guy's smooth voice says, and the shadow moves to my side.

I feel a hand on my back, and then my sickness subsides before clarity comes to life. My body stabilizes, bringing me back to normal.

I whip around, falling back to my ass, and then I scammer backwards.

"Calm down," he says, his dark hair a little longer, tousled by the wind in a sexy sort of way.

Damn bad boys.

"Calm down? You've got to be kidding me," I scoff, praying my voice is loud enough to reach Thad or Frankie. Then I recognize him - the eyebrow ring, the dark hair, the mysterious beauty. Oh shit. "You're the guy from the diner. You sat in the corner and used the free Wifi."

He smirks, running his hand through his hair. "I was keeping an eye on you. It would have seemed odd if I just sat there drinking coffee."

"Keeping an eye on me? You had to have heard that night stalker threatening me that night, yet you did nothing. You were probably hoping he'd drain me dry, or you were planning to kill me yourself before Frankie and Kane showed up."

Shit. I shouldn't have said Kane's name aloud. *Damn it.*

His head drops back and he releases an exasperated sigh.

"I wouldn't have let him touch you. I stayed until closing, and then I watched to make sure you made it back to your home, untouched. If I wanted you dead, I've had ample opportunity to kill you. I'm here as a friend, for now. My people are not responsible for your mother's disappearance, so you need to call off your flock of killers."

Say huh?

"My flock of killers?" I ask in bemusement. "I don't have a flock of killers, and I don't believe you don't have my mother. You're the only ones with a true vendetta and the resources to take someone as strong as she is."

He snorts derisively. "Your mother has pissed off a lot of immortals. That's what happens when you're a strong witch - you make enemies. Your killers are attacking innocent dark users."

I let out an incredulous laugh while standing to my feet, readying myself to fight.

"Innocent dark users? That's an oxymoron if I've ever heard one."

His eyes narrow when he takes offense, and I silently start reminding myself I'm still not immortal. I'm an idiot to provoke him.

"Don't be such a fool. Dark users are no different from you, except we harness black magic and live of our own free will. Not everyone who joins dark are vicious killers. Most of us just don't like the rules set up by the hypocritical light council. They think they rule you once you've chosen light, and yet they might as well be dark themselves. They'll condemn you to death for breaking the rules, but they'll abandon you when you need them most. Tell me I'm wrong."

He has me there. The light council isn't what it was designed to be, but that doesn't make me trust a dark user.

"If not you, then who?"

"Who has your mother? I don't know, but I would know if her disappearance was related to my kind. No one wants to pick a fight with you or your father. You're not far from your immortality, and we're not the only ones afraid of what you'll be able to do. Have you ever thought this might not be about your mother at all, but you instead?"

"Me?" I squeak, an overwhelming surge of questions burning through me. "Why would they go after someone as powerful as my mother when I'm still not changed? And how the fuck do you know who my father is?"

"I have my ways of knowing things, though I can't believe he'd give you access to these killing machines destroying my people right now. Whoever this is went after your mother because if they swooped in and took you, your father would surely get involved. Whoever this is could be using her as a means to get to you without alerting your father of their true intentions."

I shake my head as sense comes to me. "No, they want something my mother has. A group of night stalkers attacked me, and one of them wanted to know where *it* is. I assumed they were working with you."

This time he lets out a mocking laugh.

"Our people don't work with night stalkers, at least not on sanctioned missions. If one of our kind is involved, they're not aligned with the dark council. I can assure you of that. As for the things your mother protects, there's a long list. She's the strongest of the light, so they've tasked her with a great deal of their possessions. However, you might want to consider the black diamond of Roth."

"The what?"

"It's a powerful gem that can destroy or create. In the hands of the wrong user - light or dark - it could easily suck all the life from the world. The gem was too powerful to be entrusted to anyone else. Even we agreed with that."

His soft blue eyes are almost convincing. His tall, lean body moves closer, and my breath catches in my throat as his true beauty is shown under the full streak of light cast by the moon.

"Your mother is also respected by our people. You should know that we'd never seek to cause her harm when unprovoked."

I force myself to counter, though his beauty still calls for my attention.

"Your *people* tried to kill me when I was-"

"In our domain, near our root of power?" he interrupts, sounding condescending and bitter. "They were protecting our tree just as you would yours. You even demolished many of our men for doing so."

I take a step back, bringing my wandering eyes back up to meet his.

"That wasn't us. A band of night stalkers and lycans stepped in and saved us."

He tilts his head, and then he glances toward the house I can no longer see.

"They're coming for you. Call off your killers, and I swear you won't have any further problem from my people."

"I don't have killers. The people up there are looking for my mom, not chasing you down."

"Not them," he murmurs. "There's a group of twenty or more night stalkers who've been shredding us apart."

I gasp, suddenly realizing who he's talking about.

"Those are the same ones who attacked me," I almost whisper.

Again his head tilts, and then he kneels in front of me as the ground begins to sweep around us. Suddenly, an image appears, as if he's opened up a mirror to another place, and I gasp in awe as I stare down at the power.

"Is this them?" he asks while moving back.

I kneel and stare at the imagery - the horror show playing. Savage night stalkers rip apart dark users with effortless ease. They're fast enough to keep up with the evaporating warlocks and witches.

"Yes. That one is the one who wanted me to tell him where-"

"Alyssa!" Frankie screams from the distance.

The dark user glances that way, and then he turns back to me.

"It appears we have a common enemy then. You'll hear from me soon."

He walks away, and before I know it, he's dust in the air.

"Down here," I call as I stare in the direction of my nighttime captor who is now gone.

I turn back to view the image again, but it's gone as well. The vacant ground rests peacefully, showing no proof of the fight it once shed light on.

Suddenly Frankie is beside me, materializing as he throws his arms around me and jolts me forward.

"What the hell happened?"

I pull back, staring once more at the empty, silent woods ahead as I step out of Frankie's hold completely.

"A dark user robbed me from the room, showed me proof the same people are attacking them, and then he disappeared."

"A dark user?" Thad growls as he joins us, his shoulder already healing.

"I'm fine, Thad. You should be resting," I murmur while walking over to him.

At least he's wearing something over his bare... um... manhood now.

"You're not *fine* if you were just taken by a dark user."

His hand snakes around my waist, and he starts leading me back toward the house, looking over his shoulder the whole time. Right now, I don't know if I want to tell them about the black diamond of... whatever.

None of them will believe it until they see what I saw, and we don't have that kind of magic. I'll just wait on him to show up... again.

The glare of the sun promises to melt the snow, but the frigid, white blanket refuses to go without a fight. I smirk as I see it sweating, the melting pieces trickling down, but there's so much of it. There's not a chance it'll all melt.

"What are you doing? Watching the snow?" Thad chuckles as he sits down beside me on the porch steps.

I sip my coffee and then nod.

"This is the longest we've stayed in one spot, and I've finally had time to get bored. Where're the others?"

"Out, running down leads. I'm yours for the day it seems. Let's cure that boredom," he says menacingly.

"What's that?" I ask, motioning to the coin he wears on a chain and ignoring his scandalous comment.

He looks down, running his fingers over it before palming it.

"It's something I'm supposed to keep safe."

"For what exactly?"

He shrugs, dropping it back to his chest while leaning back.

"I don't know. It was just given to me by someone special - someone powerful - and she told me to keep it safe until it found its way into the right hands."

That's vague.

"Whose hands are the right hands?"

"That... I don't know. I assume the answer will reveal itself in time."

Riddles and mysteries. I hate our world.

His shoulder draws my attention. In just two days time, it's completely healed - no proof of his scrape with the night stalker.

"How are you not freezing with just a tank and shorts on?" I ask.

He shrugs, and then he leans farther back to prop up on his elbows.

"My metabolism burns quicker than yours. I have to eat more frequently, drink more, and... well, have blood of course. It's enough to warm me up in the coldest of places. I admit, heated spots are a bitch."

I laugh a little, and then I touch his healed shoulder with the tip of my fingers.

"It's a good thing you don't scar after immortality. That would have been a bitch," I murmur jokingly.

His eyes are suddenly burning into mine as his hand rises up to catch mine on his shoulder. I'm worried about what's about to happen, but then Frankie materializes in front of us.

"Hey," I murmur in surprise, meeting his eyes which don't seeming very approving

"We should talk," he says very seriously, and I look at Thad who rolls his eyes while releasing my hand.

"You're going to have to trust me sometime, warlock," Thad mumbles as he stands to his feet.

"I just want to talk to Alyssa, alone. Nothing pertaining to the case, of course."

"Sure," Thad grumbles. "I need to go flex my muscles anyhow. I have to make sure the perimeter is safe. I'll see you in a bit, pretty girl."

He bends and takes my hand before pressing his lips to the back of it. I blush, and then he turns into a hawk, dropping his clothes in a puddle at my feet before flying off into the trees.

Frankie rolls his eyes as he takes a seat beside me, and I listen as the hawk's screeches become too distant to hear any longer.

"You have to stop getting so close to him," Frankie murmurs in a near whisper.

"Frankie, he just saved my life the other night. Not to mention the battle in the woods where he saved us both while you slept."

"Have you asked him about that?" he muses, his eyebrow arching.

"No, but just because it hasn't come up. What's wrong?"

He sighs out loudly, and then he steeples his hands in front of his face while staring straight ahead into the woods.

"I don't know. This just all... it's so odd. They've already proven to be dangerous. Rain could have killed you."

"But he didn't because Thad tore him to pieces."

He turns to me, his eyes a little worried, as he murmurs, "Exactly. A changer took down a centuries old night stalker under the full moon. Thad shouldn't be that strong, no matter how old he is. The moon fuels a night stalker's strength. The fuller the moon, the stronger the bloodsucker. It scares me, Alyssa. And the way you've been looking at him scares me even more."

"The way I've been looking at him?" I chuckle out, my cheeks blushing.

"Yeah. You act like a schoolgirl with a crush every time he's close lately. Ever think that's a little odd, considering you're head-over-heels for a human?"

Kane's face flashes through my mind, and seriousness takes the place of my humor.

"Kane's safer if he's not with me. As for Thad, it's called hormones… normal hormones. He's sexy, and he has that hero appeal. Sex never fazed me before, but now that I've had it… well… it's like socks."

I blush deeper, staring away from the man I've always viewed as a father figure. This is definitely not a conversation to be having with him.

"Socks?" he asks, seeming amused. "How is sex like socks?"

I laugh a little, my crimson burn stinging my cheeks a little more.

"Well, if you lived your whole life without socks, your feet would be just fine. You wouldn't know the difference. But, once you've had socks and felt their comfort in hard shoes, warmth in cold weather, and softness against the harsh floor, then you become a little spoiled, and you notice when they're gone. You want socks again… *a lot*."

He roars out his laughter, his seriousness broken, and then he shakes his head.

"Honestly, only you could forever ruin the idea of sex."

"This is gross," I murmur awkwardly. "I can't talk about sex with you."

I stand up, and he laughs louder while following me into the house.

"I thought we were discussing *socks*."

"Ha," I mumble, not looking behind me to find his mocking face. "I need a real drink and a change of subject."

"Fine, then let's discuss your aunt."

"Aunt Hilly?" I ask while whipping around. "What about her?"

"She's coming to help us."

"I thought she was working undercover on some big immortal case."

"She was, but when she found out about your mother's disappearance, she dropped the ruse, and now she's on her way to join us. She's not as strong as Calypso, but she'll be some serious help - trustworthy help."

"We can trust Thad, too," I murmur with a little agitation.

"Then why haven't you told him what the dark user said?" he asks, his eyes narrowing.

"Because Thad thinks I'm naïve. He'd probably go after him just to prove he was trying to play me. I want this guy to come back, tell me more. I believed him, and none of you ever listen to me."

"I just think-"

"Exactly," I grumble. "*You* think, but you never listen. Just forget it. I'm going to my room, reading, and shutting all of this out. Let me know when there's something I can do to help get my mom back."

Storming by him, I huff as I head into my room, slamming the door behind me. No one thinks I'm mature enough for all of this, and here I am throwing a tantrum. I hate old magic.

I stare at the phone in my hand, Kane's name slowly fading as the buzzing stops. Taking a deep breath, I wave my hand over it to bring it to life.

"We'll find her. Maybe if you-"

"Just stop. Stop trying to comfort me, Deke. I appreciate it, but it's pointless. She doesn't know how dangerous this world can be, and it's starting to scare the hell out of me. I wish she'd just let me know she's okay."

I frown, realizing the depth of his concern for me, and suddenly I feel extremely guilty for all the scandalous thoughts I've had about Thad. It's like I can't help myself though, and that scares me. I know it's in part because of the change I'm not far from - my immortality. I've been warned of the hormonal overload that comes with that.

"I could call that friend of mine. He's never failed in finding someone for me before," Deke says, interrupting my own private thoughts.

"He's too dangerous. He's a loose cannon, and he might hurt her. I'll find her on my own. Did you come up with anything on Callie Coldwell or is it just an alias?"

My stomach sinks. I've always called myself Coldwell because, though Devall is my true surname, it had to die with the ten-year-old girl they knew as Drackus's daughter. It's easier to conceal myself with my mother's first surname.

She's been married so much her name has changed too many times to count. Coldwell, her maiden name, is barely recognized.

"Callie Coldwell exists, but not the one you want. I'm coming up with the same dead ends the detective did. If they're in witness protection, Alyssa might not even be her real name."

It isn't.

I feel like such a bitch for lying to him, but it's always been important to conceal my identity. I haven't heard anyone call me Airis in so long that it's as if Alyssa really is my name.

"I don't care what her damn name is. I just care about her."

With a sigh, I type in a text, and I stare at it, wondering if I should send it or not.

I'm okay. I miss you, but I hope you're moving on. I'd never forgive myself if anything happened to you.

Pressing send, I hold my breath and listen in.

"It's her," he gasps.

He pauses briefly, and then Deke impatiently prompts him to share.

"What? What is it?"

"She said she's okay. See if you can ping where that just came from."

Shit.

I didn't think about him being able to trace me from a damn text.

Now I'll have to listen until I know if he can track me down. He can't come to this place, not with so many of them now here... *helping*. Not now that I know they can't all be trusted.

My encounter with Rain shook me up, and now more than ever, I realize how dangerous my life can be to someone as human as Kane.

"Frankie, I messed up," I mumble, and he materializes in the room, proving I was right to believe he was listening in on me.

"What?"

"I sent Kane a text to tell him I'm okay because he was worried about me. Now he's trying to trace me from it."

He sighs, and then he takes my phone from my hand.

"I'll make him think you're at home," he says, waving his hand over the phone. "Better yet, I'll send him back to his house."

I smile, though it's forced. Part of me wants Kane here so badly it hurts, but the realistic side of me knows he'll be killed in my world.

I listen in, waiting for Deke's response.

"Got her. She's in... what the hell?"

"What?" Kane prompts, and Frankie smiles before giving me a wink and vanishing from the room.

"She's at our place," Deke gushes in bemusement.

"Call Sierra. Find her."

It doesn't take long for Deke to fill that request.

"Hey, it's Deke. Alyssa's phone is saying she's at our house... I swear that's what it says. Go check."

I wish I could hear her side of the damn conversation. I'll have to wait on immortality for that luxury though. I can only hear when they're closer, and for some reason, Kane and his friends keep their phones really low.

"This doesn't make any sense," Deke says, apparently still talking to the girl looking for me.

"Fuck. I'll just go home and see if I can track her down. If she's in the area, I'll find her," Kane huffs. "Let's go."

The conversation cuts out when he dials someone else, and I drop my phone while sighing in relief.

At least he's still safe.

"Just to be clear, this tastes like bark," Frankie grumbles, tossing his toast down to his plate.

I laugh lightly as Thad glares at him.

"It's wheat bread. You're such a spoiled brat."

They've done nothing but bicker these past few days, and it's gone from annoying to humorous.

A wave of air rushes me, filling me with the scent of jasmine, and my eyes widen with Frankie's as we both murmur in unison, "Hilly."

Rushing out the door, I stumble down the stairs, falling to my face in the cold, unforgiving snow.

Aunt Hilly laughs as she comes to help me up, her bright, blond hair glistening under the radiant streaks of sun.

"There's my girl," she says while wrapping me up in her arms. "I've missed you so much, Airis."

That name sounds so odd to hear.

"Oh, I'm so glad you're here."

She holds me tighter, and then she looks around at our unusual allies.

"I almost didn't believe Frankie when he told me what company you were keeping."

I follow her gaze, unsure if I believe it myself.

"Well, the company we're keeping is the only company that would offer us help. Light or not, they're our only chance of finding Mom."

She sighs, and then her fingers run through my hair that has grown even blonder.

"You're less than a year away from your change now. I can tell. Have you found a coven yet?" she asks, her eyes studying my new color of hair.

"Um… actually… I have a house."

"Good. Where and with whom?"

"It's in Pine Shore, and it's… just me."

Her eyes try to pop out of her head as she gapes at me in disbelief. Finally, she bursts out laughing.

"You almost had me," she chuckles out. "If you didn't have the most overprotective mother there is, I'd believe you."

I don't laugh, and Frankie walks over to join us.

"She's not kidding, Hilly. Calypso fought her on it, but Alyssa is living alone… for now."

For good, unless *I* decide to live with someone.

Her mouth falls back open, and then she gapes at me once more.

"Do you have any idea how dangerous that is?" she scolds.

"It's dangerous to live with a coven too. I've heard the horror stories," I murmur dismissively while walking away. "One dispute could result in an eternal rivalry. One like Mom and Shay had."

"Shay had that coming, and so what if there are rivalries. It's far safer than going it alone. Your coven becomes your chosen family. You've had a coven your whole life. You don't know how to live alone."

I turn to face her, and I pull out my phone while shaking my head.

"Do you want to know what Mom's coven - her family - said when I asked for their help?"

I hand her the phone to show her the texts I just recently received after asking them for help the day Mom disappeared.

"Let me read them aloud. I have them memorized," I snark. "*Sorry, dear. It's too risky.* That's from Amelia. *I wish I could help, but I'm working on a spell right now.*

151

Keep me posted, love Semara. Oh and this one is great. *I'm sorry I can't help, but I'm on my honeymoon right now.* That's from Kenshaw, her best friend.

"A coven is worthless," I sum up, a scoffed breath following.

Her eyes soften, and she shakes her head while reading over the words herself.

"Foolish, selfish witches."

"Foolish, selfish bitches if you ask me."

Frankie interjects, "The point is, Alyssa has chosen to live alone, and there's no law stating she can't."

"I've never been fond of that name change," she huffs, staring at me a little harder.

"Well, Airis is a hard name to explain to people, since she's supposed to have died ten years ago. Come in and we'll catch you up," I murmur while happily avoiding anymore of her scolding lectures.

"Well, I have a friend who is undercover in a dark user realm, so I asked him to do some digging around for me," Aunt Hilly whispers.

"And?" I prompt.

She frowns and plops back against the headboard of my bed.

"He hasn't contacted me yet. Hopefully I'll hear from him soon."

I sigh out, agitated by the true lack of information we have.

"With the new moon coming, we might have a chance to find these night stalkers and take them down," Frankie interjects while peeking out of my room to see if our company is still lingering.

"Doubtful. They'll lie low with the sky not offering them an extra burst of strength," Hilly adds.

"Well, I'm sick of talking about it. I just want to take a hot bath and unwind."

"Be careful. Water is our natural enemy," Aunt Hilly murmurs as I stand up.

"Lately I think everything is our natural enemy," I exasperate. "Besides, I've not obtained immortality yet. I can die any old way."

She frowns, and I head away to close the door to the bathroom. It's odd how witches were once burned at stakes, hanged, or even shot, when the only mortal thing that can kill them is water. For some reason, humans just never thought to drown us.

I hope no one is trying to drown Mom. She's strong, but not even she can over come it if they hold her under for too long. It's our secret though. Only witches know, and it's not like they tell anyone outside of our realm.

As long as mystery boy was telling the truth, a dark user doesn't have her, and therefore they won't know to try to drown her. They want something from her though, so she's safe until they have it regardless.

My phone buzzes, and my heart flutters when I see Kane's name pop up. Using the trick Frankie showed me, I wave my hand over it to jam his tracing device as I finally answer it.

"You're not moving on if you're still calling me," I murmur, happy I'm doing something to keep him safe.

"Alyssa, I've been all over the place looking for you. Where are you, baby?"

His voice is weak, tired even. He sounds as though he hasn't slept in days.

"I'm somewhere you don't need to be."

"I just want to be with you. I know this sounds completely crazy, but I really miss you. Please let me come be with you."

With Hilly here, there's no chance he won't get a glimpse of magic. With night stalkers willing to attack me, there's no chance he'd make it out alive.

"I wish you could, but it's just not sa-"

"Don't say it. I'm sick of hearing that bullshit. You have no idea how much I want to be there keeping *you* safe. Stop worrying about me. I swear to you I'm perfectly capable of handling anything you have going on."

He'd flip the hell out if he saw someone shift into a hawk or a wolf, or if he saw a night stalker's fangs emerge. Not to mention if he saw what I could do.

Our fridge is stocked with blood, and the men here have no modesty - Thad especially. I've seen more naked men these past couple of weeks than I've seen in my life - though I have been rather sheltered.

"I wish you could be here, really I do. I miss you, too, but I can't risk it. Kane, please stop calling. Please move on. Treat me like some bad dream, and shake me like a bad habit."

"Alyssa, please stop saying that shit. I'm tired of hearing it. I just want you. You're the best bad habit I've ever had." I laugh lightly, and I almost hear his smile. "I miss that sound."

Sighing I murmur, "I miss you making me smile. This is pathetic. We barely know each other, Kane. I shouldn't be... you shouldn't be... *we* shouldn't be acting like this."

"You know as well as I do this is something incredible. Alyssa, please tell me where you ar-"

He stops, and I smirk. He thought he was going to be sly and track me again. More than likely he wasn't going to tell me he knew where I was this time, since I bolted the last time.

"Something wrong?" I muse, my smile spreading.

"How does it say you're at my house when you're most likely not even in town? How are you doing that?" he grumbles, disappointment falling in his tone.

"You have your gadgets, I have mine," I murmur while pulling up my hand like a gun and blowing the tip of my finger like it's the barrel.

"Damn it. I should have known the last time."

"I need to go," I mumble, my eyes glancing toward the clock.

"Please don't. If you won't let me be there with you, at least talk to me for a minute. I've missed your voice."

His voice is so soothing, so relaxing, and so amazing. Instead of hanging up like I know I should, I just climb into the tub that has filled with warm water and lie back.

"Okay. Talk to me... but not about coming here."

He pauses for a minute, more than likely a little stunned that I'm not fighting him about talking.

"I can do that. How about a date... soon? We never did get to go out."

I smile as I think back to that night, and then I frown.

"I knew you were getting tired of being pulled around that day. You stayed gone for so long, and then you took off. I'm sorry I tried to keep you out with me."

"Alyssa," he exasperates. "I told you I'd give anything to have that day back. I had stuff to take care of."

"Tell me about Amy," I blurt out after hearing about the *stuff* he had to take care of. "Why does she think the two of you belong together, and why do all of your roommates seem to want the union to happen?"

"How do you-"

"I'm smart. I figure things out. You wanted to talk, and this is me talking."

He sighs louder, but his desperation shines when he finally answers.

"It's a long story. Amy was a loner with a lot of severe issues when Sierra found her. She has a problem Sierra understands. I just happened to be in the wrong place at the wrong time, and she was in a place where she would fall for anyone who was nice to her.

"After a long, stressful week, I came home, and she was here... with Sierra. All I fucking did was tell her she had a place with us if she needed somewhere to stay. She took a kind gesture and turned it into something more. Since then, I've had to deal with being the object of her obsession. Now your turn. Are you and Thad doing anything?"

His jealous turn of conversation catches me off guard.

"If I said yes, would you move on?" I ask, though it still aches to think of.

"No. I'd just rip his head off his shoulders before using it for a soccer ball."

I laugh a little. It's cute to hear him so jealous.

"No, we're not doing *anything*." *Though Thad doesn't give up easily.* "He's just helping me search for Mom. Your turn. Why aren't you into Amy? She's cute enough."

"Cute enough?" he chuckles out.

Well, I'm not going to say she's hot because he'd probably start paying her the attention I really don't want him to.

"Yeah, cute enough."

"Alyssa, she's not my type."

"You like blonds, eh?" I tease.

"I like you. Other than that, I've never been into blonds. Amy just isn't... she's annoying as hell. You're the first girl I've ever felt like I was going crazy over."

A goofy, pathetic grins spreads across my face as I close my eyes and relax in the tub.

"You're good at this," I tease.

He lets a light, somewhat sad laugh free.

"Apparently I'm not too good or you'd let me be with you right now."

Frowning, I start to counter, but a breeze in the air pops my eyes open, and I squeal as I see the dark user staring down at my naked body, his brow arched and a faint smile playing on his lips.

"What's wrong?" Kane worries.

I narrow my eyes while sinking lower in the bubbles as I stare into the eyes of the guy from the other day.

"Just more pests. Can I call you later?" I ask, forcing the dark user to smirk more.

"*Will* you call me?" he sighs.

"I will, I promise. Just get some rest. You sound tired."

I hang up before he can say anything else, and then I stare expectantly at the unannounced visitor in my bathroom.

"How did you get in here?"

He takes a seat on the sink, and keeping his voice low, he says, "You should put a protection spell around the house if you don't want me popping in."

"I can't. We've got dark ones here… well, blood drinkers. My magic is light, meaning they'd be locked out."

"You mean killers?" he leads.

"You're one to talk," I scoff. "The last I checked, dark users are just as vicious as night stalkers."

"We're not all vicious, just as you're not all angels. Don't get it twisted. Now, dry off and come with me," he says while handing me the towel I had hanging up.

My eyebrow arches, and then I mutter, "Why?"

"Because I'm going to prove to you *our* dark users do not have your mother, and then we'll help each other find the monsters after both of us."

He looks harmless, but so does a squirrel right before it tries to rip your fingers off once you get too close.

"Why should I trust you?" I murmur softly.

He leans over, his eyes shifting to be darker, and then he lets a deviously sexy grin free.

"Because I could have killed you more times than you know by now."

The knot that instantly forms in my throat is too large to swallow, and my voice becomes rasp, harsh, and strained when I counter, "That's not exactly making me want to trust you."

"No, but the fact you're still breathing should make you want to trust me. Now come before the others realize I'm here."

I'm so fucking stupid.

"Fine, turn around."

He grins a little more, and then he stands to turn his back to me as I quickly climb out of the tub, sloshing water everywhere before I wrap up in my towel .

"You'll need these," he says, and suddenly a pair of pants and a red shirt appear in the room.

"Thanks," I murmur, but before I can reach for them, they're on my body.

Great. He's a pervert in reverse - dressing me against my will.

"Sorry, but there's not really a lot of time. Your changer friend will be coming in any minute."

"How do you know that?" I muse while stepping over to him.

"Because I heard him talking to one of the others. He told him he was going to see if you needed anything from town. Just go to the door, tell him to get you something random, and then say you're tired."

Instantly, there's a knock at my door. Heading away from someone I fear almost as much as night stalkers, I make my way to the door, unsure of whether or not it's smart to send away a strong ally so I can sneak out with a known enemy.

"Hey," I murmur as Thad pops into my room.

"Wow, you look good. Did you finally manage to get some new clothes?" he asks, his curiosity now a little piqued.

"Um," I mumble, looking down and then up, "I just forgot I had this. What's up?"

"I have to go into town. You need anything, or would you like to come with me?" he says almost suggestively. "I know you've been wanting to do some shopping."

Crap. I finally get the chance to refurnish my wardrobe, and Mr. Dangerous shows up, wanting to prove his peoples' innocence.

"I would, but I'm actually exhausted right now. I didn't sleep too good last night. Could you get me some chocolate while you're out?"

"Yeah, no problem. You feeling okay? You look a little flushed."

His hand cups my chin to tilt my head up, and I nod against his touch.

"I'm fine. I just talked to Kane a little while ago. I guess it sort of... well..."

"You miss the human?"

"Yeah."

At least it's the truth.

He looks a little disappointed, possibly wounded, but he nods in acceptance.

"I'll get you some chocolate, and I'll grab you some socks, too. Frankie said you need some."

My face heats up instantly, and he tilts his head curiously as I squirm.

"Something wrong?" he asks, seeming amused.

"Nothing. Tell Frankie I'm going to kick his ass."

He smiles, seeming confused and intrigued, but he doesn't say much else before disappearing out the door. I turn around, and in a blink, Mr. Dangerous is staring into my eyes, taking my breath with his startling closeness.

"Stop doing that," I whisper breathlessly.

He smirks, and then his arms wrap around my waist, making me feel the edge of regret before we're suddenly blurring out of the room, everything passing me too quickly. I feel dizzy, sick, and oh... damn... I'm...

Chapter Twelve

My eyes are too heavy to open at first, but a distant dripping sound leaves me with the taste of dread, forcing me to summon the strength to wake.

I gasp for air as I surge forth, and I look around, surprised by my surroundings. I expected a dank, dark dungeon, but this is a beautiful room with one flaw - a leaky faucet in the gloriously gold bathroom adjacent to me.

The sleek, white walls are lined with gold satin fabric along the edges. The sheer gold curtains flow in the wind from the balcony doors that have been left open, offering an airy, sensual feel.

Where the hell am I?

"Hey," a soft voice from behind prompts, and I whip my head around to meet his eyes.

It's him. The dark user I so foolishly trusted.

"Where-"

"You're in the council's ward. It's a castle veiled from the mortal world. You okay?"

I grip my head that seems to still want to spin, but other than that, I feel fine.

"Yeah. Why did I-"

"I was worried your conscious state couldn't handle the vaporized pace for the distance I had to carry you, so I rendered you unconscious instead. Sorry, but it was the best way to keep you from dying during the intense travel. This is one of our healing rooms. The council wants to speak to you now."

I swallow hard, suddenly feeling like a lamb spread across a sacrificial altar.

"The Dark Council?" I barely break out in a whisper.

"Yes," he chuckles out. "The Dark Council," he continues, a melodramatic tone carrying out a mock eerie delivery.

"This isn't funny. I'm light. This is suicide."

"Chill out. I wouldn't have brought you if I felt you were in any danger. As I told you before, this is simply a declaration of innocence."

"Fine. Where do I need to go?"

He takes my hand in his, and I follow him, my legs still wobbly. He steadies me by wrapping his arm around my waist, and I ignore his dark beauty as we step through the threshold together.

"You ever going to tell me your name, or should I stick with Mr. Dangerous?"

"Mr. Dangerous?" he asks with amusement. "This coming from a girl bunking with changers and night stalkers?"

Rolling my eyes, I murmur, "I don't mingle with the night stalkers… ever. They creep me out even worse than your kind."

"Ouch," he says teasingly. "And here I was thinking we were starting to get along."

"Your name?" I grumble.

"Fine, but don't mention me to your father, please."

"I don't speak to him… ever."

He seems to relax, making it obvious my father really does scare the hell out of him. Of course, Drackus scares the hell out of everyone… including me.

"It's Gage. For now, that's all you need to know. When you go before the council, they're going to expect you to make eye contact. Otherwise it'll seem as though you're being dishonest."

That's the complete opposite of the light council.

"Well, they can kiss my ass if they're worried about my honesty. I didn't come here to prove my innocence, and you can take me home right now if that's what this is about."

"This is a two-way meeting. I'm just asking you to show my people the same respect I've shown you."

"The same respect you've shown me?" I ask incredulously. "You've kidnapped me once already, and now I've been led here under false pretenses. What respect have you shown me?"

He looks at me, his eyes showing more seriousness. "More than one of your kind would have shown me."

This is so fucked up.

The way he talks, you'd think my kind was dark and his kind was light.

"Well, *your kind* has been trying to abolish mine for centuries. If it was up to you, we would-"

"Just drop it. It's obvious we'll have to agree to disagree, for you feel all dark users view things the same. It never occurred to you that some of our kind happen to respect all forms of life simply because you're a biased, spoiled brat with some naïve notion the world is only layered in black and white."

I rip free from his grip and glare at him, my eyes going crazy with their random shades.

"Whoa," he says while backing up. "What the hell is up with your eyes?"

"I'm pissed, that's what's up. You brought me here, and you've done nothing but bash the light, yet you feel as though I have no right to do the same to the dark. Your kind *are* vicious, unforgiving, and merciless monsters with a need for blood. You're no different from a night stalker, other than the fact you don't shed blood to survive!"

He sighs, exasperation oozing from his stance, and then he grips his head as his dark hair falls over his hand. Finally, he looks up while steepling his hands in front of his face.

"Let's just do this, and see if we can at least *try* to get along for five damn minutes. If they see us bickering like this, they'll never agree to uniting in an effort to track down our stalkers - the real threat out there."

"I never said I wanted to unite. In fact, I'm ready to go home. Screw this. I've got enough on my plate with my mom missing. I hope the gang of night stalkers find you and the rest of your kind and rips you all apart."

I turn to storm off, knowing I can't escape if he chooses to force me to stay. My whole body burns with fury, adrenaline, and fear. I don't know what the hell I was thinking when I agreed to go with him.

When I turn around, I expect to find him right on my heels, but he's gone. The hallway is empty, and a breeze stirs as a door to the outside blows open.

With a heavy breath, I turn toward it and rush outside before he has the chance to change his mind.

Great. Lost in the damn *woods. Stupid, stupid, stupid girl. Why in the hell did you trust a dark user?*

If I had never gone with him, I wouldn't have spent the last five hours wandering aimlessly in no man's land. I'm cold, hungry, and freaking the hell out every time the wind blows too loud.

Great, I'm Frankie.

I hear a crack, and my body whips around to look for where it came from. I sigh in relief as a fox scurries out of a burrow and hustles deep into the woods. When I turn back around, my breath leaves my throat as a strong hand clamps around it, stealing my ability to use my magic.

Night stalker. It's the same frigging one from Phoenix.

My mouth falls open as strained wheezes emerge from my throat, and the few breaths of air I struggle to get are painful. With what little mobility I have, I look around to see the other fanged, blue-eyed beauties ready to show me their monstrous side.

"Where the fuck is it, witch?!"

I shake my head - what little bit I can - to answer when the only sound to escape through my lips is a strained squeak.

Slivers of night's black drapes are disrupted by the random streaks of moonlight, the glowing beauty only fueling these deadly assholes' strength.

"Tell me where it fucking is!" he blares, his spit finding my face and giving me the urge to gag when I can't wipe it away.

"Pl..eeaas..ee," I gurgle out, mindlessly begging for my life with that one word.

Then suddenly I'm released when the night stalker is launched backwards by some invisible force.

Oh thank you, Frankie.

I throw my arms out, sending out my own attack as several of the others fall to their backs, digging up the once dormant ground. Between dodging their desperate hands and fighting off their lunges, my eyes scour the surface for Frankie, but with all the blurring nonsense, I can't find him.

"Get me the hell out of here!" I plead, my attacks still coming out fluently.

The ground shakes beneath me as all of the night stalkers are tossed back at once, and my breath leaves when arms appear around me, vaporizing me with the invisible savior I now know isn't Frankie.

Frankie can't vaporize me.

I turn my body as we move too fast, and my legs wrap around a waist as I cling on for dear life. The dizziness and nausea sets in, but before I have to vomit, I feel the seat of a car and the slamming of a door.

Gage pops in beside me, and the little black car we're in suddenly charges into the night, racing through the winding roads.

Shit, shit, shit. He saved me. Now what?

His eyes study the road, but his ghost of a smile tells me he's waiting for some form of gratitude. He's enjoying this far too much. After I blasted his entire race for being nothing but dark - hence the name *dark users* - he saved me.

"Thank you," I mumble, quickly looking away as soon as his smile tries to twitch up more.

"I'm sorry, what did you say? My vicious, unforgiving, and merciless killer ears couldn't hear."

Crap. Jackass.

"I said, thank you. You saved my life," I humbly mumble, choking on crow. I refuse to look at him, but I can feel his taunting smile.

"You're welcome. Now, can you accept the fact things are not black and white? You obviously think a changer can be good, and they really do kill for blood."

This time I turn to eye him suspiciously.

"You've been spying on me, haven't you?"

He shrugs, not finding that to be the invasion of privacy I do.

"I've had to. You apparently trust anyone with a pretty smile, and there are a lot of pretty smiles with deadly fangs behind them. If you're to be of any use to me, you have to stay alive."

Crossing my arms over my chest, I glare at him.

"I don't trust every pretty smile. I don't trust yours," I growl, and his eyes light up as he turns to me with his far too sexy smirk, as if he's mocking me.

I hate hot immortals... all immortal males.

"Despite my title as a dark user, you came out with me tonight, and you didn't even know my name. You trusted my smile, you just didn't like it when I told you the truth."

If I knew it would do a bit of good, I'd slap him for that.

"You just barked at me earlier, calling me naïve, spoiled... and . and something else. I think you're just as judgmental as I am. And, I never *trusted* you. I'm just desperate to find my mother. Thad has been there for me enough to prove himself."

He lets a laugh out, and then he shakes his head.

"You barely know the guy. *Thad* just tells you what you want to hear, and he constantly flirts with you, flashing his *pretty smile* for you to dissolve when you see it. If you're not naïve, then please tell me what you are."

Asshole - him, not me.

I refuse to say anything else. He's just going to twist my words around no matter what I say.

Instead of *poking the bear*, I simply sit there quietly as we drive around a mountainside. It's obvious he was just waiting for me to need his help. We're nowhere near the cabin I was in, and he was there to save me the second I screamed for help.

"Where are we exactly?"

"About a ten hour drive from where you were. I'd vaporize you and carry you with me, but after having done that not too long ago, it would quite possibly kill you. Besides, it's exhausting to travel long distances too frequently that way."

This is just weird. I'm living with changers and night stalkers, and now I'm riding with a dark user.

"Did I get you into trouble with the dark council?"

He huffs out a touch of laughter and then shakes his head.

"Not at all. They couldn't believe you made it that far before backing out. Your council wouldn't listen to you anyhow. It was purely for your benefit to know the truth so you'd stop chasing down dead ends that all lead to us."

"Okay, okay. Fine. So if those night stalkers aren't with you, who are they with?"

"They're sure as hell not with me, but I don't know who they're working for. It's obviously someone of magic, otherwise they couldn't use the black diamond of Roth. If it's someone dark, they're keeping themselves distanced from the council. If it's someone light, they're doing the same. Keep an eye out for someone who might have recently dropped off the grid. They would have had high clearance to even know who the keeper was."

"And what happens if I find out something? How do I get a hold of you?"

"Don't worry," he says with a small smile. "I'll be checking in."

"I'm not sure if that's a warning or a threat," I dryly joke, and he lets out a laugh, proving he's not as stern-faced as he pretends to be.

"It's simply a promise. If you need me, you can always send up a message flare with the right chant, and it'll call me to you."

"Really?" I muse, considering I've never heard of such.

He bursts out laughing, mockery in his roaring release, and then he shakes his head as my cheeks burn red.

"No. Don't be ridiculous. You can call me. I've already programmed my number in your phone. It's under *Vicious One.*"

I slouch down, now that I've revealed how truly gullible I am, and I face the window while scrolling through my phone to see *Gage Saber* as part of my contacts, though he didn't literally program it the way he claimed.

Hmm. Saber? It's a fitting surname, considering this alliance could very well be a double-edged sword.

"You're right. You did program it under *Vicious One.*"

He chuckles lightly while rolling his eyes, and I let my eyes fall heavy, exhausted from the day of unexpected craze.

Waking up in my bed, I quickly glance around at the room. Frankie is asleep on the floor, and I nudge him to see him startle awake.

"Shit, you scared the hell out of us," he gushes while reaching up to jerk me in his arms.

"What happened?" I muse, not remembering anything after falling asleep in the car with Gage.

"We spent most of the day looking for you, and then suddenly you were just in your bed, as if you had appeared out of nowhere. When I tried to wake you, you wouldn't budge. I realized it was a sleeper spell, one that just has to take its course and wear off naturally. Who took you? Was it that guy again?"

Knowing Frankie would storm the castle and fight Gage to the end over this, I shake my head.

"I don't think so. I'm fine now. Where's Aunt Hilly?"

"She's with the others in the living room. You want to talk to her? She's been worried."

"Um, actually, I think I'll just get some more rest. As crazy as it sounds, I'm still a little tired."

And I don't want to deal with Aunt Hilly.

"Well, tomorrow we're taking you back home," he bluntly adds, surprising the shit out of me.

"What? Why?"

"Because it's obvious you aren't safe here. You can't cast a protection spell here because of all the bloodsuckers coming and going at random. It'd be a hassle to unlock the spell for all the new ones who are only here for small spurts at a time. And as bad as I hate to say it, you would be safer in your own house. I'll help cast the spell, only it won't just be against dark, it'll be against everyone. No one will be able to come or go without your direct consent. Understood? That means no strangers, no matter how friendly they seem."

"Understood," I grumble, feeling like the child everyone keeps accusing me of being.

Sighing, I collapse back down to the bed, and I think of how impossible it will be to keep Kane safe once he knows I'm back. I only thought he was relentless before.

Chapter Thirteen

"Call me if you need anything. I'll be here as soon as possible," Frankie says while kissing my forehead.

"Where's Aunt Hilly?" I muse, looking around outside.

"She went on ahead to start calling in some favors - get a few more light ones helping us out."

"Ah. Well, then I guess I'm on my own now," I sigh out, and Frankie smirks as his eyes cut toward the side of my house.

"Um, you might want to lift the spell for one person before he knocks himself out," he whispers, his tone almost too low for even me to hear.

I look over to see Kane pulling himself over the porch railing on his hasty way toward me. His arms are around me and pulling me into the air before I even have a chance to say anything.

Kane can come in.

I feel the magic working, thankfully, before Kane's lips cover mine and we abandon Frankie on the front porch while heading inside.

"Damn I've missed you. Why didn't you call me?" he breathes against my lips while squeezing me almost too tightly.

"Sorry, it's been crazy," I murmur while wrapping my legs around his waist, my lips devouring him with a hunger I didn't realize I had.

He pulls back with a breathless rattle, and his forehead presses against mine as he keeps me strapped to his waist.

"I hope you know, you're never leaving my sight again."

I smile, though it's forced. I wish it was true. I wish I could spend my life in his arms, but I know soon it won't be possible at all. Being with a human is completely forbidden once you're immortal.

"Well, how about we start with tonight and see where that leads?" I chuckle out, though the weight of reality still rests on my shoulders.

"Tonight's a good start," he says with an adorable grin, and then he starts carrying me toward the bedroom.

"How did you know I was here?" I muse before I slip onto the bed, and suddenly I don't really give a damn anymore when he falls between my legs.

"I was on my way to the diner, and I ran into Thad. Needless to say, I knew if he was here, you were here. I didn't give him a chance to object either."

I smile as his lips reclaim mine, and my legs slide up to be fully nested around his waist. His hands feel so incredibly familiar, though he should still be a stranger. His breath is heaven's grace as he fills me full of his life with each kiss.

My shirt starts slipping over my head, and I surrender completely, giving myself to him without pause, though I shouldn't. I can't help it though.

His lips slide down my chest, and my breath catches in my throat when his touch burns through me, awakening the desire I've forced to lie in hiding for far too long.

"I love it when you do that," I murmur as his lips stroll over my neck, nipping at it as he pulls the skin between his teeth.

Something I should loathe actually turns me on when it's him doing it.

"Do you?" he murmurs softly while moving to the other side and repeating the arousing action.

"Mm hmm."

I feel his smile against my neck as he starts lowering himself against me, his lips still owning me as my pliant body folds to his will. My hips start to rock against his, giving me a chance to feel his erection digging into the front of my pants that he decides to pull off of me in one swift motion.

"Damn. I can't believe I forgot how fucking perfect you are," he breathes in exaltation.

"I think you should look in the mirror," I giggle out. "Your scale for perfection should be much higher if you get to look at this everyday."

I rip his shirt off, and then his body slides against mine, his lips pulling me in closer as my hips rise to meet his.

"Kane," I mumble against his lips, "this is probably not a good idea. You shouldn't be around me. My life is... complicated, and I-"

"Forget it. You're mine," he interrupts, and then his lips crush mine, silencing me for good, except for the moans rising from my throat.

"Completely yours," I utter involuntarily, scaring the hell out of myself, and suddenly he backs away.

Crap. I just scared the hell out of him, too.

"Sorry," I murmur with embarrassment. "I got carried away."

I keep my eyes low, refusing to look at him. Before I know it, he slams my body back against the bed, his weight crushing against me as his carnal desire becomes almost overwhelming.

I gasp as he surges in, not even knowing when or how his pants came off as I fully offer myself to him. His tongue dances and plays with mine, as his rough, fervent need calls to the beast within me I didn't know existed.

His body moves vigorously between my legs as his breaths become rasp, desperate, and fully engulfed in our heat. My body flames in a way I can't even explain, my insides burning as his body claims mine.

The sounds exuding from both of us only intensify the already hellacious, exquisite pace, and then his delicious mouth finds mine again, drawing out my few, harsh breaths as a tear springs free from my eye, and my body goes stiff - my toes curling, my fingers gripping, and my eyes rolling back in my head.

Then I'm limp in his arms as he thrusts in one last time and holds himself at the deepest point, finding his release. He pulls me to him as he falls to the bed, and I nestle against him as he kisses my cheek, making me feel so warm, wanted, and... perfect.

"Say it again," he murmurs softly, pulling me closer as he does.

"Say what?" I muse while running my lips over his collarbone as my leg slides around his waist.

"Say you're mine."

My heart flutters, and I get a little sick. I wish it wasn't true, but I really am his - his to do with as he pleases despite all the heartbreak I'll be forced to endure when my immortality comes.

"I'm yours," I utter, and his lips fall on mine very possessively as he breathes me in.

Kane makes my bed look so damn good, and I feel somewhat like a creepy, lurking stalker just standing here, watching him while sipping my coffee. His glorious, bare body is only slightly hidden by the sheet as he rests on his back.

His smooth, even breaths are almost hypnotic, and those mouthwatering hip lines peeking out from under the sheet are drool-worthy.

His eyes flutter open, and he smirks when he catches my obvious gawking.

"Taking in the view?" he teases while pulling his arms behind his head, giving my eyes an even tastier treat.

I smile behind my coffee, careful not to giggle, and then I nod.

"It's not everyday my bed looks this good."

He lets a laugh free while shaking his head, and he stands up, his body sleek and perfect under the glow of the sun peeking through the window behind him.

"I wasn't kidding about not letting you out of my sight," he murmurs while coming to wrap his arms around my waist, pressing his bare perfection against me.

"I figured as much," I mutter with a goofy, ridiculous grin.

"I'm going to take a shower. You coming?" he says, a salacious grin spreading over his face.

"I would, but I just had one." I motion to my damp hair.

His lips pucker in an exaggerated, sexy pout, forcing a giggle out of me despite my attempts to restrain the degrading sound.

My arms slide around his neck as his lips press against mine. His breath shouldn't taste this good after just waking up. I'm starting to worry I've already fallen harder for him than I should.

"I won't be long, and then we can head to my place," he murmurs while pulling back.

Remembering Frankie and Thad pretty much forbid me to leave, I grimace.

"I should probably stay here in case one of the guys shows up to-"

"Absolutely not," he murmurs dismissively in interruption while walking away.

I tilt my head, admiring the nakedness of his body from behind as she struts into my bathroom.

Following him, I grumble, "No offense, but I'd like to steer clear of Amy as well."

At least that's not a lie.

He turns the water on, and I hop up on the sink as he tests it to see how long it will take to heat up. He shakes his hand to dry it on his way back to me.

"Amy is simply a roommate. Don't start this nonsense again. You're coming with me. I'll change, and we'll go out to eat. We can do whatever you want to all day."

I smirk, genius striking, and then I murmur, "Then we'll skip going to your place, stay here, and order in."

His eyes swirl with scandalous thoughts as a devilish grin plays on his lips, but then he frowns.

"As much as I would love that - and I would love that - I want to take you out. We've yet to have a real date, and I... I'm ready for this to feel like something more."

My coffee cup finds a place to rest behind me as he kisses me in a completely different way. For the first time, it's not a kiss full of passion, desire, and unkempt carnal need. It's something so much more, a depth I can't fully understand so soon.

His forehead rests against mine as he withdraws from the kiss, and against all of Frankie's demanded rules, I murmur, "Okay."

He smiles triumphantly, and then he steps away to head into the shower. Watching his body drenching under the cascading shower through the transparent curtain sends chills through my body, and the lustful devil inside commands my attention.

Without thinking, worrying about tomorrow, or even worrying about the next hour, I drop my clothes to the ground and follow him in, surprising him.

My eyes fall upon his hard body, and a sinful smirk plays on my lips as I take him in. His wet arms wrap around me, pulling me under the rainfall with him, and our lips become as entangled as our bodies.

The gathering awkward tension between Amy and me is only mounting the longer I sit here in the den, while Kane speaks with Deke and Zee. Sierra keeps coming up with short bursts of conversation, but neither Amy nor I care to speak for longer than necessary.

Hurry the hell up, Kane.

I hear the oblivious boys laughing about something mundane as the three of us sit quietly. Sierra shifts uncomfortably as she struggles to find a new topic.

"So, the moon is crazy bright tonight," she murmurs, her eyes glancing through the window.

Great. The brighter the moon, the stronger the vamps.

Although it's a small sliver of a moon, it is bright.

"Yeah," I murmur softly, feeling the uneasiness of the reality they don't know exists.

"Sure is," Amy mumbles while flipping another page on the book she's merely pretending to read.

"Well I'm glad you're back. It's nice to see Kane doing more than obsessing about finding you," Deke chirps as the three boys join our tense room.

Finally.

Kane's arms wrap around me and pull me to him as he sits down beside me, and I willingly nestle into him, paying no attention to the fuming black-haired girl trying not to be obvious with her dagger-throwing glare.

"You ready, babe?" he asks while kissing the side of my head.

Hell yes. Get me the fuck out of here.

"If you are," I murmur casually, trying not to show him how completely out of place I feel.

"Hallow's Ball is in two months," Zee randomly inserts as he sifts through the mail, obviously finding an invitation of some sort. "It's hard to believe Halloween is so close."

"Hallow's Ball?" I muse, happy someone is talking about something other than the moon.

"It's a local thing. Every year they throw a big masquerade ball at one of the prominent homes. You want to go?" Kane asks while running his fingers through my hair.

"That's two months away," Amy scoffs, not enjoying his future planning.

"And?" Kane growls, his tone more threatening than his word.

She looks down, huffing as she does. Apparently he's warned her not to say anything, and now he's reminding her. It just makes me feel all the more uncomfortable.

Zee walks by her, patting her shoulder as he does, and Deke's lips tighten as he too takes notice of her sullen stance.

"We'll see," I mumble, suddenly feeling like the girl everyone wishes would just go away.

It's obvious they want him with her, and I certainly know this thing between us can never actually work.

"It's up to you. I'd like to take you. I've never gone with a date before," Kane murmurs softly, pretending not to notice the sudden uncomfortable shift in the room.

"I think we should get going. Nothing in this town stays open too late in the off season," I say with a strained sense of nonchalance.

He finally acknowledges my discomfort, and his lips thin into a knowing line. I look away, feeling all the more insecure as his friends cast their disapproving stares to their roommate.

Standing, I wave at everyone, feigning dignity, and I walk out without waiting on Kane. Once the fresh air hits me, I fight to keep my composure. With the wind rustling in the trees, and the lake fighting with the shore, I can't hear them, even with my amplified hearing.

I know he's probably scolding them for not making me feel comfortable, but that's only going to make it worse.

"Out of all the creatures on the planet, humans are the most complex," a smooth voice murmurs from my side, forcing me to shriek a little.

"Damn you. Can't you ever just call ahead," I gripe while glaring at Gage who has appeared on the railing beside me.

"Sorry," he snickers out. "I didn't mean to startle you."

I don't believe that one little bit.

"Sure you didn't. What are you doing here? Did you find out something?" I ask hopefully, my eyes glancing through the windows to make sure Kane isn't coming out yet.

"Unfortunately, no, but I wanted to check out this town of yours. An associate of mine told me a vicious pack of lycans lives here. He also said he sensed my kind and night stalkers here. I was worried about you, and I see I was right to worry."

"What does that mean?"

"You're standing alone on a deck, your mind is completely distracted, and there's not a spell you can cast to keep yourself safe in the open like this. You should be in your house. The spell Frankie cast was strong. It even kept me out."

My brow arches as I eye him suspiciously.

"You tried to break into my house? I think we should discuss boundaries."

He smirks, and then his eyes flash to the inside of the house as Kane shakes his head and starts walking to the door.

"I suppose we'll discuss them another time. Go out tonight, but don't make a habit of this. I'll keep an eye on you."

Before I can say anything, he vaporizes and rides off on the wind. I'm not sure how I feel about a dark user looking out for me.

"I'm sorry about that," Kane murmurs while joining me outside, and I turn around to face him, still wondering just how closely Gage has been watching me.

He got one hell of a show last night.

My cheeks blush, but I shrug at Kane, not giving him any insight to my inner turmoil.

"Nothing to be sorry about besides making me wait so long on food. I'm starving."

He smiles, though he knows I'm simply downplaying the obvious distaste his roommates have for me.

"The guys and Sierra have no problem with you. I want you to know that. They feel sorry for Amy, but they do like you. I swear."

"Sure," I murmur, not meaning for it to sound as sardonic as it does.

"Alyss-"

"It's fine, Kane. Really, I get it. I don't have friends like that, but I've been around others that do."

His fingers interlock with mine as we start descending the staircase, and I try to shake off the lingering uncertainties plaguing my every step.

"Do you have any friends?" he asks.

Trying to find a way to not make myself sound pathetic and unloved, I choose my words carefully.

"Frankie… though he's more of a father figure than a friend. I suppose I've sort of started considering Thad a friend, but I wouldn't go so far as to room with him."

"I wouldn't allow that," he quickly inserts, sounding possessive and jealous once more.

My eyebrows cock up in surprise and defiance.

"You really wouldn't have a say in the matter. You live with two other girls, and well… You can't say they're *both* like sisters. I've met Amy."

Though my tone is joking, the context is somewhat serious. He shouldn't get all worked up about Thad when he lives with Amy.

"Does it bother you?" he asks, seeming authentically perplexed.

"You living with Amy?"

He nods.

It royally pisses me off.

"Not really. It's your life, your choice. It's none of my business who you live with."

He winces, and then his grip on my hand loosens.

"So it does bother you, but you refuse to be honest with me."

"Reading minds now?"

"Believe me, I wish I could read minds. It'd make life so much easier," he grumbles, making me laugh a little. "Since I can't read minds, you have to be honest with me. I'll kick her out."

My eyes widen. As much as I would love to see him kick her ass out of the house, it's not just his house. It's obvious the others care about her, and they were all friends before I came around. I can't be that girl.

"Don't be so dramatic. I'm fine. I was simply saying you don't have any room to talk. I wasn't trying to stir you up."

"I wouldn't let you live with Thad unless I was there to beat the hell out of him every time he made a pass."

I let a laugh out, and through my snickers, I mutter, "How do you know he's ever made a pass at me?"

He rolls his eyes, seeming insulted by the fact I even asked that question.

"Because I know how incredibly gorgeous you look. I also know how he looks at you. I fucking hate it."

His jealously is adorable, and Thad definitely tries shit. He makes it hard to be a good girl, but I managed to keep my pants up even with my hormones on the fritz.

"I lived with Thad since we split up in Phoenix, and nothing happened."

Well, other than the times he caught me by surprise with his devilishly soft lips. No sex though.

I think I'll keep all of Thad's sneak attacks to myself. Kane looks as though he's ready to combust as it is.

He sighs out, obviously not enjoying this conversation any longer. I kept him at my house until nightfall, but that was all I could wrangle him to stay indoors. I wish I could tell him how incredibly dangerous this all is - walking around in the open.

I knew this town was crawling with immortals, and then Gage confirmed it. It's amazing at the gravitational pull we all seem to have to each other - even though most of us are forever engaged in blood wars.

I dread that part of my future. Right now, there's not a whole lot I'm looking forward to as far as immortality is concerned.

"Are you okay?" Kane asks as a single tear rolls down my cheek.

"Yeah," I murmur while wiping the wet drop away, trying to be discreet.

"I'm sorry. This was stupid. I don't know what I was thinking. With your mom missing, a date is probably the last thing you have on your mind."

With my mom missing, everything is on my mind... especially what will happen when I become the new target. As the daughter of Drackus Devall, there's a world full of vicious revenge-seekers just like Rain. Apparently my secret identity isn't as secretive as I thought.

"It's fine. I'm just-"

"Let's go back. We can just curl up in the bed, watch a movie, eat some burnt popcorn... anything you want."

I laugh lightly, though it mingles with a sniffle. Then another tear slips free as I nod appreciatively.

"That sounds great actually."

"Do you care to stay at my place tonight? I have some stuff to do - work related - and all my things are there."

Crap.

It's not like I can tell him *no.* That would raise too many questions I can't answer.

"Sure," I murmur as my mind races to remember the protection spell.

I'll just cast one around his place. That would actually make me feel better anyhow. I can't cast the one Frankie did on my place because they constantly have friends over, but I can cast one to protect against dark users and blood drinkers of all varieties.

"So no friends at all, besides Thad?" he asks, sneering a little as he changes the subject on our way back to the house. "How is that even possible?"

My attempt to not sound pathetic apparently failed - miserably.

"Well I did, once, but we grew apart."

"Oh? Tell me about her and why you stopped being friends," he murmurs softly, obviously trying to distract my mind from my mother.

"Well, *h*is name was Chaz. Our mothers used to be really good friends, but they had a falling out. Shay, Chaz's mom, ended up leaving our co... um... I

180

mean our town. She and Mom haven't spoken since.

Chaz was adopted, and considering his birth parents were rather ruthless, cold, and cruel, he felt like Shay was not only the mother who took him in, but she was also his saving grace. Devoutly loyal to her, he thought it would be best if he and I stopped talking since it would cause conflict."

"What did they fight about?" he asks curiously.

"What do women usually fight about? A man."

"Ah," he says with a small smile. "So who won the guy in the end?"

Sighing, I mumble, "My mother, but he was no prize. He was a total creep, and she kicked him to the curb when she found him peeping in on me while I was dressing."

I shudder slightly, and his arm slides around my shoulders in response.

"Did Shay and your mother ever make amends… since she found out he was a creep, I mean?"

"No. I doubt Mom ever gave her the satisfaction of knowing. She's prideful like that. She has *horrible* taste in men, and that includes my father. Everyone in our community warned her to stay away from my father, but she was stubborn and in love. She kept their divorce a secret for years just so she wouldn't hear the I-told-you-so speeches."

He lets a small smile free, and I offer a weak grin of my own. I'm not used to so much sharing.

"So, did your Mom ever remarry?"

If he knew my mother, he'd realize I find that question to be rhetorical.

"Many, many, many times," I release with exaggerated exasperation while rolling my eyes and he lets out a laugh.

Not to mention the hundreds of times she was married long before dear old Dad.

"Do you ever talk to your father? I mean, he sent help to aide you in finding your mother."

From an outside perspective, I can see how that would seem like a sweet gesture. Unfortunately, I know Drackus Devall.

"One thing about my dad, he's calculated. If he's helping us, there's something in it for him."

"What could he possibly have to gain?" he muses, seeming genuinely interested in my fucked up family.

Power, release from his solitude confinement, the black diamond of Roth for himself... the list goes on and on.

"I don't know, but Dra... um, Dad doesn't do anything out of the goodness of his heart."

Because it's too dark to ever hold a speck of light.

"And I thought I had family drama," he chuckles out.

My eyebrows perk up, my interest very piqued.

"I thought you said your parents had passed."

"I was referring to my current family - Zee, Deke, Sierra-"

"And Amy," I grumble, my nose wrinkling as her name slips through my lips.

"Alyssa, Amy is just-"

"A roommate. Got it. So, how did you all meet?" I ask, trying to keep myself from sounding possessively jealous.

"That's a long story I'll fill you in on at another time," he murmurs softly while kissing my forehead.

He opens the door to his home for me, and I sigh as I walk in.

"Back so soon?" Deke asks as he walks through with a plate of spaghetti, a noodle slurping through his lips.

"We decided to spend the night inside instead."

"Cool. The girls cooked a big pot of spaghetti, and the meatballs are pretty badass."

Kane smirks as the sloppy boy holds the plate up and pulls another noodle to his lips before slurping it in as well.

I guess we were gone longer than I realized.

"Thanks. You're making me *real* hungry," Kane says sardonically.

Deke chuckles before walking into the den. My skin crawls as a chill spreads through the air, and I remember I have to cast the protection spell.

"Um, can I use your bathroom? I want to check my makeup."

"You look perfect, baby."

His soft voice is velvet in my ears, making me warm in so many ways.

"You're sweet, but I feel like my mascara is running. I'll be right back."

He pulls me to him, and his lips graze mine softly before releasing me to rush away. The masculine bedroom makes me smile on my way to the bathroom, and I shut and lock the door quickly while waving my hand over the mirror.

A flickering flame appears in the glass, and I draw a circle around it. Though my circle is merely smudges made by my fingers, it'll have to work.

Next I pull the safety pin from the hem of my dress, and I prick my finger with the sharp, stinging point. With a small wince, I force the blood out of the tiny opening, and I dab it into the center of the flame.

"Protect this home, let no dark pass through. Thresholds be strong, protection be true."

Chanting it softly three more times, I open my eyes back up to see the flame coming to life and sparking against my blood, accepting my magic. With a small flash, it disappears, taking my drop of blood with it as the veins of the house pump with a newfound will.

I walk out, heading back to the kitchen, and I smile when I see Kane light on his feet as he makes us two plates of food. I stifle a laugh as he pretends to bow to a dishtowel, the finale to his dancing number.

"Do you always dance when you're getting dinner ready?" I tease, and his cheeks blush a little.

"You weren't supposed to see that," he grumbles, an embarrassed smile playing on lips as his disheveled hair sweeps over his brow just barely.

I giggle slightly, fueling his embarrassment, and then he shakes his head. Our light moment is brought to an abrupt halt as Amy walks in from… the basement? That's really the only place that door could go.

"Hey," she says, smiling too big when she sees Kane.

Then her eyes land on me, and her face falls, disappointment tainting her darker brown eyes. They almost look black right now.

"Hey," Kane murmurs with an icy shot, the air bitten by the instant frost in his breath.

She glances at me again, and then she rolls her eyes before heading to the side door.

"Tell the others I'm going out for a run if they ask."

"You should invite Sierra if you're going for a run. You shouldn't be out by yourself," Kane murmurs without looking at her.

My heart cracks a little upon hearing his concern for her. I shouldn't be such a bitch, but I want him to be callous and cold.

"I'll behave, if that's what you're worried about," she almost whispers.

Behave? As in she won't go meet any guys? Why would Kane care?

"Hey guys," Sierra chirps while joining us. "What's up?

"Amy is going for a run. I told her to ask you to go with her," Kane says in a warmer tone, his eyes not giving Amy the attention she desperately wants.

"Sure," she murmurs.

Amy huffs as Sierra slips on a pair of shoes. I tilt my head curiously at the odd choice of footwear, considering tennis shoes would be better than boots. As soon as Amy jerks the door open, she slams into an invisible force, and her body falls backwards before she slams into the ground.

"What the fuck?" she spews, and my eyes try to pop out of my head.

Shit. I messed up the spell. Fucking shit!

Sierra bursts out laughing, and Kane turns while trying to stifle his own laughter.

"Did you forget you have to walk through the doorway and not the glass beside it?" Sierra teases, motioning to the glass she thinks Amy ran into.

"I *did* walk through the damn doorway, or I tried to. I swear something threw me back."

Shit! Think.

Spell I cast, please come back. I rescind you now, cease your attack.

Chanting it in my head over and over, I begin to get nervous the spell won't lift. Discreetly pulling the pin from my hem once more, I prick my finger to draw out my blood.

Kane's eyes fall on me as I pull my finger into my mouth to swallow my own blood, sealing the recanted spell's banishment.

"You okay?" he asks me, as Sierra continues to laugh at the fuming girl still on the ground.

"Yeah, just a splinter," I lie.

The small bit of metallic bitterness rattles around in my mouth.

"I swear!" Amy blares. "Look for yourself!"

My stomach knots up as Sierra walks toward the door. Kane has lost interest in the spectacle as he comes to draw my finger from my mouth and pulls it into his hand. I look around him, trying not to be obvious as I nervously await the results of my recanted spell.

Sierra playfully leaps through the doorway and lands on the deck, her laughter roaring louder. I breathe out a heavy sigh of relief.

"You lying klutz," she teases, her mocking laughter only growing.

Amy grumbles under her breath while pulling herself up, and then she hesitantly checks the doorway before trying to walk out once more.

"I swear I'm not that damn crazy," she gripes, her eyes studying the doorway.

"It must be out now," Kane says, drawing my attention back to him as carefully examines my finger. "We don't have a lot of first-aide here, but I can get you a paper towel or something for the bleeding."

Amy and Sierra walk off, though Amy continues to look behind her, and I visibly relax.

"It'll be fine. It just stings a little."

He smirks, his eyes still on my barely bleeding finger, and then he draws it into his mouth. My breath catches in my throat as he sucks the tip of my finger with his deliciously soft lips, and, without thinking, I part my legs for him to step between them, feeling completely aroused, beguiled, and lost in his touch.

His eyes close as he draws my finger in more, and suddenly I'm rushed with an overwhelming desire to rip his clothes from his body as he grips me tighter to him. He finally releases my finger from his lips, and I'm almost left with a painful ache after the withdrawal.

"Damn. What was that?" I mutter breathlessly, but he doesn't answer.

Instead, he jerks me up from the stool where I'm sitting, and he pulls me to him as he carries me away, promising this night just got a hell of a lot better. His lips claim mine with a bruising force, and the fire courses through my veins as every bit of me throbs to feel him inside my body like I never have before.

Ignoring the snickers of Zee and Deke, Kane slams the door to his room once we're inside. He drops me to the bed as he pulls his shirt over his head, and he stares down hungrily at me, making my heart race almost too fast.

"Kane," I murmur as the ache inside me grows, and he jerks me to him so my legs slide around his waist.

"I really like this dress," he murmurs as he bends down, his feet still on the floor.

The high bed places my center at a perfect angle to feel his erection through his jeans, making me hurt to feel his touch all the more. His fingers skim my sex through the lacy underwear, and my head tilts back as the sensation travels in a forceful tingle all the way up and down my body.

Then he slides my underwear to the side to feel the promise of the wet arousal waiting for him

"Fuck," he says in an exhaled breath, his own head falling back.

I gasp as his fingers work their magic, making my body contort and wriggle beneath his touch as ecstasy fills me. His head comes back down, and those perfectly green eyes find mine, making me want to say to hell with this torture he calls foreplay.

"Please," I murmur, surprised by how much it sounds like I'm begging.

"Please what?" he murmurs, feigning coyness.

"Fuck me."

The low growl in his throat proves he liked my crude, blunt answer. The panties slide down my legs, leaving a damp trail from my inner thigh to my ankle, and he tosses them to the ground.

I rise up, desperate to get out of my dress, but he pushes me back down to the bed.

Hovering over me, he murmurs, "Leave it on."

My body heats all the more, making me feel as though the fire is about to become real as he drops his pants to the floor and jerks me to him by the bend of my knees.

I'm not used to him being this rough, but something tells me this is how he normally is. I've been painfully aware that my newness to… sex… was giving him pause, but tonight he's not holding back

With one swift motion, he throws himself inside me, making me snap forward from the abrupt, incredible entry.

"Damn, you feel so good," he murmurs while stilling himself and leaning down to kiss my lips.

"I'm pretty sure I'm molded to you since you're the only person I've ever been with… like this," I mumble while blushing.

His body starts moving against me, and the air from my lungs gets sucked out when I forget to breathe. Looking up at him as he shows my body no mercy is almost too much to bear.

I hurl myself up, and his arms wrap around me as he lifts me from the bed and forces me against the wall, his relentless rhythm pushing me closer to the brink. I moan out in a gasping shriek, and his grunted growls grow louder when it comes close to being his undoing.

His lips find the curve of my neck just above the edge of my collarbone, and then I feel his teeth bearing down, forcing out my moans all the more. Getting bitten in my world is something you don't want to do, but with him - a human - it's incredible.

Feeling my excitement, his rhythm quickens even more, becoming exquisitely punishing, and driving me that much closer to my peak. My whole body becomes almost languid as I near that moment he's pounding me to.

His name becomes a screaming burst of ecstasy from my lips as I fall over the edge in the most surreal, mind-blowing release I've felt yet.

He grunts harder as he thrusts into me once, twice more, and then he pulls back, releasing my skin from his teeth while still holding my legs around his waist.

"Sorry," he murmurs with his eyes shut.

"For?" I muse, chuckling lightly.

"For being so rough," he murmurs while collapsing to the bed behind him, dragging me with him.

I fall on top of him, and then I nestle into the crook of his neck, kissing it lightly.

"I happened to like you being *so rough.*"

He lets out a laugh, but still his eyes stay shut. He pulls me closer, his fingers trailing up my back as he kisses my forehead.

"Are you going to keep your eyes closed all night?"

He smiles, and then they open, offering me a view of his emerald perfection.

"I just needed to compose myself."

"Why? You want to go for round two?"

He laughs at my poking joke, and then he shakes his head.

"That would be more like round nine today."

I giggle lightly, and then I start kissing his neck again.

"I'm sorry about that," he says while pointing to the place where his teeth had been.

"Don't be. It felt… good." *Ironically enough.*

Smiling, his lips find mine, and he turns me over to be on my back.

"You have to wear a dress all the time now. You know that, don't you?"

I giggle louder, sounding more like a fool with every chuckle, and then my fingers tangle in his hair.

"I might just do that."

His eyebrows bounce up and down for a moment, and then a knock at the door interrupts our naked humor.

"What?" Kane groans while I roll my eyes at the intrusion.

"Sorry to disturb your reunion, but Amy and Sierra just called. They said we might have a situation to worry about in town. You coming with?" Deke calls.

"No, but I'll be out in a second."

"What *situation?*" I grumble.

Obviously Amy is still trying to act out to gain his attention.

"Nothing for you to worry about. I'll be right back. Don't move, and don't you dare take off that dress."

I stare down at the blue, wrinkled mess of a dress that once looked much better.

"I think it needs to be replaced by something that doesn't say look-at-what-I've-been-doing."

He laughs lightly before kissing my forehead, and then he stands up to quickly pull on his pants.

"Stay," he says again, making me laugh.

"I'll be right here."

He smirks, and then he disappears out the door. Almost instantly, there's a shadow in the room, and I hold back a squeal as Gage materializes in front of me.

"Pervert!" I yell in a whisper while gripping my dress and pulling it tight around my legs.

He stifles a laugh, and then he shakes his head.

"I looked away," he whispers back, and then he motions for me to follow him out onto the balcony.

"You looked away?" I grumble as he shuts the glass door. "You knew what we were doing?"

"Close the curtains next time. You might also want to invest in an iron," he teases while motioning to my thoroughly fucked dress.

I roll my eyes, and then his eyes narrow.

"Shit. What'd he do to you?" he almost growls while examining me a little closer.

I flip my hair down, bringing it over the mark I still haven't seen, and then I push away his scrutiny.

"Nothing I didn't thoroughly enjoy. Why are you materializing in the bedroom?"

He leans up, his eyes still studying the spot where Kane left his mark, though it's not visible with my hair blocking the view.

"I was wondering how long you were planning to stay. I need to head into town. I've got a source who spotted a couple of lycans roaming free. I want to find out if they're friend or foe."

"Um… Foe, obviously."

"Don't be so judgmental. You were running with lycans just last week."

"I wasn't running with lycans. I was grasping at straws and taking help where I could get it. Just because I tolerated them doesn't mean I doubted their dark core for one damn second."

"Just like me?" he asks, his eyes narrowing. "You still think the worst of me."

Breathing out heavily, I ignore his statement.

"It looks like I'm spending the night, but don't worry. I'll be on alert."

"If you're staying the night, cast a protection spell. It was far too easy for me to get in."

I suddenly feel a little inept.

"I tried," I mumble. "I did something wrong. When one of the girls tried to leave, it threw her backwards. Can you... um... help me?"

He lets out a laugh, making my embarrassment grow. What witch can't cast a simple protection spell?

Me.

"I would, but I have dark magic. My protection spell could injure you, even fuck with your white magic, if I tried casting it on your behalf. I'll just stick around. I can call a friend to go check out the lycans."

"The hairless beasts you mean."

He frowns while shaking his head in disapproval my tart remark.

"It's fine," I continue. "You don't have to hang around. Besides, I'm not sure I like you listening in on our... moments together."

My face blushes, and he chuckles a little more.

"Fortunately, I can't hear *your moments*."

What? Immortals have hearing unparalleled by anything else on the planet.

"So your weakness is your hearing?"

"Not in the least. This house is apparently very well insulated. I can't hear a word when the doors are shut. It's pretty nice actually. I don't have to hear all the mushy stuff. I'll stick around. I'll cast an awake spell so I don't drift off."

"You don't have to do that-"

"Believe it or not, I would like to see you still breathing in the morning. No one else is going to be keeping you safe. Your human sure as hell can't If

191

you're going to be foolish enough to sleep without a protection spell, then I'll stay vigilant."

I grip my head, feeling so... confused.

"That's ridiculous. You should just-"

He clamps his hand over my mouth just as Kane's voice comes into sound. It seems as though they're standing on the front deck.

"Just call me if it gets too rough," he says.

"No prob. We'll see you in a bit," Deke chirps, and then he and Zee start jogging away from the house.

Kane starts to walk back in just as Gage releases his hold over my mouth. Like the true klutz I am, I stumble forward, almost flipping over the rail before Gage can pull me back. Unfortunately, I squeal like a fool.

"Alyssa?" Kane asks curiously, the deck creaking under his feet as he starts toward the edge to see me.

"Um, yeah. Hey," I ramble out, and then I start swatting at Gage, trying to make him leave.

He shrugs innocently, and then I shove him with all my strength - and a little magic - to force him over the railing. He vaporizes and reappears in the tree across from me, stifling a grin.

I scowl at him, ready to knock him out of the tree just as Kane comes into view.

"What are you doing?" he asks quizzically while pushing his hands in his pockets and staring up at me.

Trying to ditch a dark user.

"Um... nothing. I just felt like some fresh air. Everything okay with Amy?" I ask, the bitterness clearly in my tone.

He frowns, and then leans against the side of the house.

"It's not like that... at all. I'll be right up to convince you."

I almost want to smile, but I'm sick of Amy and her needy ways. He disappears around the corner, and Gage reappears on the balcony with me the second the front door clicks shut.

"You've got to get out of here."

"I didn't even tell you what I came to say," he retorts innocently.

"What?"

"I wanted to ask you if you knew any of these people."

He hands me a stack of photos, but no one looks familiar.

"No. None." Then something hits me, making my stomach queasy. The earlier conversation with Kane has suddenly rattled around in my brain with an obvious jerk. "Shay."

"Huh?" he says while studying the beastly man in the top picture in my hand. "He looks more like a Hoss or a Goliath to me."

"No, dumbass. Shay Myers. She's a witch from my old coven. She's got a grudge against my mom."

His face turns more serious, and then he evaporates from the balcony. I look through the glass to see the door opening, and the far too sexy man walking toward me with a salacious grin as he opens the door.

"I love a pretty girl under the moonlight," he playfully murmurs, making me blush despite the fact it was meant to be *corny* funny.

I hate the moonlight.

Then he frowns as he dusts my hair away.

"What's wrong?"

His lips thin as he studies that damn spot.

"I shouldn't have done that. I almost brought blood."

I give him my best vixen's smile, which is very unrehearsed and probably pathetic.

"It's not like it hurts, and it felt damn good at the time. Stop taking away all the sparkle."

His eyebrow cocks up on one side, and he lets a slight grin free.

"Sparkle?"

"Yes. Sparkle."

He lets a laugh free, and then he pulls me against him.

"How about we go *sparkle* in bed. I've got a little work to do, but it can wait."

"I do love your bed."

"I do love that you love my bed."

With that, he scoops up me and my very wrinkled dress while walking back inside. I might not be able to stay his for long, but for now, I can enjoy my human.

Chapter Fourteen

"Did you find Shay or the lycans?" I ask Gage, holding my phone to my ear with one hand while my other holds my fresh cup of coffee. I sit down on the end of Kane's bed.

"My friend lost the lycans. I found Shay, but she's not the one who took your mom. In fact, she has started her own search for her."

"It could be a cover-up. It's not like she's dumb enough to just say, 'Yes. I did it.' She could be-"

"I know. I thought the same thing, but she didn't tell me she started her own search. Of course, she didn't actually tell me much at all, considering she sniffed out my dark magic right away.

"I had to do some deep digging. She apparently doesn't want anyone, especially your mother, knowing she's trying to help. Remind me to never get involved with two light witches, by the way."

"Why's that?"

He feigns a shivering breath, mocking a dramatic sense of fear.

"Because you girls are absolutely vicious. Did you know your mother turned her into a fox for three weeks - until the spell ran dry?"

"Yes," I grumble. "She lifted the spell though. Mom's spells run longer than the average witch's. She just didn't want anyone to know she felt guilty, so she waited until the usual time the spell ran dry."

"So are you still at your human's house?"

"Yeah, he's outside right now. His roommates just left, and he's on the phone, talking business. So you really think Shay is innocent? It would have been foolish for her to do this too soon, but now she has waited long enough to douse suspicion."

"I really don't think it's her. She shoveled out a hunk of cash to hire some trackers in an effort to find your mother. These guys are the best in the business, and I know for a fact they don't work cheap. She also paid them to keep their mouths shut and told them if they found her, to bring her home and never tell her it was she who hired their services."

"So how did you find out?"

"I'm dark magic," he says casually. "We don't play by your rules. *I* can make almost anyone talk."

"If you're talking about casting a truth spell, those are dangerous and unpredictable. Not to mention, that magic is hard to master, even for the oldest of magic wielders."

"Are you trying to get me to hint at my age?" he teases.

I smile involuntarily, and then I flop down on the bed.

"No, but now that you mention it-"

"Not a chance, light girl."

I laugh softly while shaking my head, and then I stand to walk back to the sliding glass door. A foolish grin spreads over my face when I see Kane standing by the lake, his soft, dark hair whipping in the wind as he chats on his phone.

"How'd you sleep?" Gage asks, making it sound as though he actually gives a damn.

I turn away, sighing deeply.

"Like shit. I stayed awake most of the night because I was worried to damn death about those night stalkers finding us. I'm going to convince him to stay at my place the rest of the day... and tonight."

"The day won't be as bad. Night stalkers are fools if they choose to attack under the sun when a witch is stronger. Keep your ass at home tonight though."

The door shuts, letting me know Kane is back inside.

"I will. Call me if you have anything."

"Of course."

I put the phone down just as Kane joins me in the room, and his arms slide around my waist as his sweet, perfect smile forms.

"You feel like a movie and dinner here tonight?"

Smiling like a fool, I murmur, "Not here. Let's go back to my place."

His smile falls, and then he moves a piece of hair from my face.

"You don't feel comfortable here?"

Shrugging, I say, "Amy is here, but she's not at my place."

His head falls back as a sigh of exasperation falls between his lips.

"Baby, she's nothing to me. How many times do I have to tell you that?"

You can't say it enough.

"It's not about that. I just feel like I have to hide out in your room when she's here, and it's… tensing. I'm tired, exhausted actually. I kept worrying I was going to wake up and find her hovering over me with a butcher knife."

He starts laughing, showing his amusement, and then his lips lightly stroke mine.

"Sorry. I don't want you feeling uncomfortable in my home. My other roommates find you pretty fantastic."

Sure they do. As long as they think I'm a temporary play toy… which… unfortunately, that's what I have to be.

With that sobering thought of reality, I back away, fighting back my tears as I turn to head into the bathroom.

"What's wrong?"

"Nothing. I just need to head home and get some stuff done. I also need to shower, change… that sort of thing. I'll catch up with you later."

I start pulling on my shoes, and his arms wrap around me from behind. His lips press against the back of my head, and a tear slips free. I let it slide down my face so he doesn't see me wiping it away.

"I'm coming with you. We'll stay at your place until you're comfortable here, but I really don't like you being in that house alone."

My house is much safer than this one.

"Why? Is it haunted?" I tease, trying not to reveal the emotion truly choking me.

"Something like that." The way he says it is almost chilling, as if he really believes there's a dark entity lurking in the shadows of my home.

"You're scaring me a little."

His eyes tilt up, and he forces a smile. "Don't be scared. I can swear to you no harm would ever come to you. Not as long as I'm around."

I wish I was completely human - not destined to walk an immortal life among the real darkness lurking within the heavy shadows he only thinks he fears. It would be so easy to feel safe in his arms. Though I do feel safety within his warmth, I know he could never save me from the real monsters that walk the streets in search of my blood, my power, my... life.

"It's just... I knew the people who lived there before you, and the woman who lived there before them. That house has a bad rep. I'd prefer it if you stayed with me more and there less," he continues.

His aura is buzzing with fear and anxiety right now. I usually can't feel or see a human's rattling aura because my power is so dormant, but I can see his right now. It's dark - scary dark. It's as though he's tormented by something he fears.

"Want to talk about it?" I pry while sitting down on his bed.

"They were just-" He pauses, uncertainty flashing through his normally gloriously untainted eyes, and then he sits next to me. "A while back - a long, long while back - a woman lived there who did less than savory things in that home. After she left, the ones who moved in suffered in ways I never want to see you suffer. It's a... it's just not a safe place."

I've been there for a while now, and I've never felt any darkness in the walls. Frankie is an expert on such things, and he never noticed anything either. I know my mother would have sensed it immediately and shooed me out before we unpacked the first box.

Maybe Kane is a victim of urban legends and dark gossip.

"Well, I can assure you no jaded spirits are there. They would have been run out by the numerous fits I've thrown while living there."

My attempt at humor is met with solemn silence. It's apparent he's holding back, and this really does have him scared.

"What sort of unsavory acts?" I prod, looking for insight to his adamant stance on my home.

"Dark stuff. Weird stuff. I'd sound like a complete idiot if I tried to explain it. You'd run out of here thinking I'm crazy."

He forces a smile again, but his eyes betray him. They tell me he's not at all comfortable, and the truth of his fear remains embedded in the undertones.

"Like witchcraft?" I ask, trying not to smile.

So, so many young humans toy with things they can never even attempt to understand. Some skilled users tap into a tiny fraction of our power, but never enough to turn the heads of the council.

If he's scared of witches, then this poor guy picked the wrong girl to stalk.

He lets out a touch of laughter finally, and then he shakes his head.

"No, not witchcraft. Look, let's drop this. Stay with me and let me make you feel better. I want you to distance yourself from that place until I know for sure she's not coming back."

"She?"

He turns to me, his lips tightening as though he just slipped up.

"The woman who originally owned it. I need to know that she's not going to return."

He's definitely creeping me out right now. His nervous, fearful energy is spilling out of him and eating at me. It's been a while since I felt my inner witch responding so strongly to something. I usually keep a lid on all my powers, but

I'm emotionally drained right now.

"Don't worry. I'm tougher than I look." I can handle a human witch toying with powers she can never fully understand.

"Stay with me?" His eyes are heartbreaking, soft, and so very sincere.

After a long pause, I murmur, "I'll stay."

Chapter Fifteen

"It's been a month, Frankie. I've been back here for a month, and you're no closer to finding my mother now than you were when I left you. I think it's time I called Drackus. If I ask for his help, he won't refuse me. He's probably sitting on the edge of his seat in anticipation for such. Sadistic bastard."

"Don't even think about it. If Drackus gets involved, he'll slaughter more than we can save. He'll bring us no closer to Calypso either. Before he's done, we'll have lost every trail we thought we had."

Sighing heavily, I lean back against Kane's headboard. I can hear him loudly arguing with Zee about who just won their stupid game. The constant clicking of remote controls is giving me a migraine.

After basically living with him for a month, I've decided men are boys until they die. I wish I wasn't so completely enthralled by him. I don't see how they can hear to argue over the roaring TV they have cranked up to full blast. Not even immortals have that good of hearing.

"Just tell me what to do, Frankie. My hope is running thin."

His exasperated sigh follows my words as he thinks almost loud enough for me to hear his thoughts.

"I don't know, Alyssa. I really don't know. We're heading to the Old Shot right now. It's a night stalker bar on the north end of town. Thad is going to shake down some of their men, see if they give us anything."

I sit up immediately, a prickling sense of fear spreading as I walk out onto the balcony and shut the glass door behind me.

"You can't go to a night stalker bar. One whiff of your blood and they'll be all over you."

"That's not how it works, Alyssa. They'll never know I'm a warlock. They can't smell it in our blood. They don't even know what they're drinking unless they've tasted us before. Don't give them more credit than they deserve. I'll keep my identity a complete secret. Don't worry. How are things with loverboy? Did your spell ever cast correctly?"

Should I tell Frankie I'm a poor excuse for a witch and can't cast a simple protection spell without locking everyone in or out? Should I tell him about all the times I've tried and failed this past month after he fought me on the decision to stay with Kane? I don't think so.

"No problems. Just worry about finding Mom."

"I miss you, kiddo. Keep your chin up. I'll call you if we find out anything."

"I miss you, too, Frankie."

I hang up as the weight of my mother's disappearance bears down on me without remorse. Just as I'm about to go back in, Gage is suddenly right in front of me, scaring the hell out of me.

"Sheesh! Stop doing that shit," I gripe while ineffectively slapping his immortal body.

He chuckles, playfully swatting at my pathetic swings. The dark user has been on my nerves for a while, but he's hung around and watched my back. I'm not too crazy about the fact he bought the house directly beside Kane's, but at least he's not sleeping in the trees.

"Sorry," he lies. There's not an ounce of a genuine apology in his tone.

"Sure you are," I mumble while glancing through the glass window.

"Relax. Pretty boy and his buddies are engulfed in a game of Grand Theft... something or another. He's not coming in any time soon. Mortals."

I let a small smirk free, but my inner turmoil instantly banishes it. He starts to say something when I finally notice the metal ring in his lip. Without thinking, my thumb brushes over it.

He almost shivers under my touch, which offends me.

"Don't like a light user touching you?" I scoff, trying not to sound as insulted as I feel.

I pull away and lean against the railing to stare away from him. He lets a laugh free and leans up beside me.

"It just caught me off guard. You like?" he asks while motioning to the steel circle.

I'd never tell him that he's the kind of guy who is sexy enough to pull it off. I refuse to feed the immortal male ego. He knows it looks good though, and it's obvious he realizes I think so.

"It's fine."

"You know I can read all the colors around you right now," he pokes, making me squirm. "You should guard your aura better."

"Did you come to try and make fun of me, or did you have something of any relevance to say?"

My patience has run thin, and I'm sick of his usual frustrating openings.

"I just sent your hound a message to check out the Old Shot. An informant of mine assured me there was a lead worth tracking down. I was coming to find out if your light warlock had told you yet."

"He told me. I don't like him going into a night stalker bar, but he assured me there was no way for them to know who or what he is."

He casts his gaze behind him once, checking for anyone who might be listening in, and then he turns his attention back to me.

"Shouldn't be. So, you look tired. Haven't been sleeping much?"

That's the stupidest question I've ever heard.

"My mother has been missing for over a month and a half now. How would you sleep?"

"Just fine," he says with an unaffected shrug.

I'm almost shocked, which I shouldn't be.

"That's cold, even for a dark user."

He pulls a pen from his jacket and starts scratching something down on a piece of paper.

"What are you doing?" I muse while trying to look at what he's writing.

"Keeping tabs of all the hurtful things you say about my kind versus all the hurtful things I say about yours. So far, you're way out in front. Who's the bad guy?"

He smirks as I roll my eyes.

"Fine. What's the deal with your mother?"

He puts his paper back in his pocket, and then he turns his attention to the ground below.

"You'll figure it out eventually, for now, let's focus on the other reason I'm here. Are you feeling stir crazy?" he asks while looking at me once again. "I've noticed human boy doesn't let you out of his sight very much."

Stir crazy? No. But it would be nice to get out of the remote-control-clicking environment for a while.

"What do you have in mind?" I ask, my suspension radar on high alert.

His menacing smile is quickly banished, but I had a chance to catch a glimpse of it. I still don't know if I trust Gage... never mind. I know I don't trust Gage. Though he's kept a watchful eye, dark users can't be trusted.

"There're a couple of night stalkers I want to take out. Believe me when I say you don't want to know what they've done. Their council should be the ones eliminating them, but they're not here to do so."

The blood in my veins turns to ice from his bomb drop.

"Are you crazy? A night stalker is our biggest enemy. They'll freeze you stiff and draw out your life."

Idiocy apparently haunts every male - immortal and human alike.

"Believe me, if you knew the details of what they did to their latest, underage victims, you wouldn't be so quick to turn tail and run. They need to be taken care of, and this won't be the first time I've taken them out.

"Night stalkers are allowed to kill with discretion. I don't like it, but it's the way of our world. These didn't use discretion, and they sure as hell didn't show mercy. Since their council refuses to clean up the mess, my council has approved my request to do so with no objection from the bloodsucking rulers. I've got some friends coming in for the job. Problem is, I need one little thing."

Crap. I know where this is going.

"Bait." My huffed answer almost makes him smile. "Fine. Where and when? And no vaporizing me from place to place."

He pulls my hand in his to look at my watch. He doesn't shiver the way he did only moments ago when I tried to touch him. The moon is faint tonight, just a small sliver. It's a good night for hunting night stalkers.

"Meet me at my place in five minutes. I'll fill you in on the plan, and then I'll *drive* us there. I promise, no vaporizing."

I frown a little at the spontaneous timing. I quickly glance through the glass door to see if Kane has returned.

"Fine. I'll see you shortly."

I turn to see Gage has already disappeared, leaving me talking to his leftover scent. Rolling my eyes, I head back into the house to tell Kane... something.

"Hey," he says as soon as I join him and Zee in the living area.

"Hey. Can you pause it for a second?"

"Sure, babe."

Without hesitation he halts the game, and I take his hand in mine to lead him back to the room - away from the unwanted listeners.

Amy is flipping through a magazine, pretending as though she hasn't been sitting in there to stare at my man this entire time. Sierra and Deke are curled up on a chair together, their lips entangled. I'm almost jealous.

He shuts the door behind him, his body tensing as if he's worried. "Everything okay?"

"Um... yeah. I just need to get out of here for a little while. I think I'm getting a little... stir crazy."

I suck at lying.

"Sure. Let me tell the guys I'm heading out."

I grab his hand, realizing I didn't clarify what I meant.

"I need some time to myself. I'll be back in a little while."

His eyes drop, suddenly a sense of guilt in them.

"I've made you feel trapped, haven't I? I'm sorry. I didn't mean to pretty much strong-arm you into living with me."

Now I feel guilty for making him feel guilty. Good grief. What a vicious little circle.

"It's not that. I'm just... I just need to walk around for a while. I spoke to Frankie, and they still don't have any leads on my mother. It's just a little much for one night."

As much as I hate using my mother's disappearance in my lie, it really will be therapeutic to kick some night stalker ass. *If* Gage is right about his foolproof plan.

He sighs as he nods. "Couldn't it wait until daylight? I don't like the thought of you being alone in the dark."

Now I know why I'm so utterly lost in this beautiful man. I've never known someone to be so thoughtful and sweet for no reason.

"I'll be fine. I promise I won't be too long."

He sighs while shifting uncomfortably, fighting the urge to beg me to stay.

"Well, take your phone. If you run into any problems, call me. Where will you be?"

"Um, I'm not sure. I might go to the diner, check in with Wade and some of the others."

He pulls my hand in his, holding it gently.

"Okay. Just... be careful. A lot of girls have been popping up missing lately. I don't like you going out in the dark."

If he knew what was actually out there, he'd really be against me going out into the dark.

"Thanks."

I lean up to kiss his cheek, but he turns and catches my lips. It's been so long since I've given into his delicious fire. This thing with my mother has forced me to disengage, feeling guilty for losing myself in him.

His breath tastes incredible in my mouth, and I love the way his body feels pressed against mine. He pulls me tighter, feeling the weeks of pent up frustration. Before I know what's happening, he jerks me up, and my legs wrap around his waist.

"Clear your head tomorrow. Stay with me tonight," he murmurs against my lips.

I groan instead of moaning, realizing by now Gage has already started growing impatient with me. If another girl falls prey at the hands of the merciless simply because I selfishly became lost in the throes, I'll hate myself.

"When I get back, we'll finish this. The diner will close before I can get there if I stay here right now."

He doesn't stop his perfect kisses. Instead, his hunger for me only intensifies in a devouring motion. The intoxicating sounds coming from him make my whole body tingle in ways I've almost forgotten.

Oh damn. I hate you right now, Gage.

"Kane, stop. Just let me go. I'll be back," I mutter grudgingly.

He groans, obviously not wanting to release me, but he does so very reluctantly, letting me stand on my own again.

"Fine. I'll see you soon. Hopefully really soon," he grumbles while adjusting his pants.

I chuckle lightly as he gives me a playful scowl, and then he kisses my lips one last time before walking back out to the crazy living room scene where the music is blaring and drinks are underway. I notice there are now a few new houseguests hanging out. How long were we in here?

Gage is gong to kick my ass.

Pulling out my purse, I find a vial of scent masker to drown out any trail. If one of the night stalkers escapes, I don't want to lead them back to my beautiful human. I'd never let anyone touch him, but I don't invite danger to follow me either.

When I walk out, my eyes fall on Kane in the far corner talking to Deke. They're whispering amongst the blaring music, which I obviously find a little odd. At least I think they're whispering. With this terribly obnoxious music, who knows?

A girl with store-bought blond hair drops her arms around Kane's waist and leans into him. Who the hell is she?

Without a pause, he slips her arms out from around him and dismisses her with barely a wave. Breathing out in relief, I pass the sulking fake-blond and walk over to Kane.

He smiles the second he sees me, and he doesn't waste any time pulling me into his arms.

"You guys can fill a house pretty quickly," I murmur, my eyes tossing back to the cheap blond whose eyes are on me right now, sizing me up.

As if Amy's obsession with Kane wasn't bad enough. Great.

"I told you we party. You just haven't had the chance to see it lately. The guys felt like getting their buzz on tonight though. You sure you won't just stay? I wouldn't mind seeing you slur a little."

I let a small laugh free and shake my head.

"Maybe I'll take you up on that when I get back. Don't let too many blonds rub up on you while I'm gone."

His bottom lip folds between his teeth just before he leans down to pick me up and pulls me against him. Those luscious lips find mine again, and he smiles behind the kiss.

"I've only got eyes for one blond."

Amy snorts derisively as she walks by, letting it be known she just overheard that comment. I roll my eyes, and pull back from his tempting offer to stay.

"I hope that means you're not thinking about some brunettes."

Amy's short black hair shakes as she tosses her head around to glare at me. I'm pretty sure she couldn't have heard that, but the timing is rather coincidental.

"No worries. You're the only girl that has ever held my attention, and that's not going to change. Hurry back. I don't want to spend the night around a bunch of drunken people without my girl to hold."

A goofy grin spreads across my lips, and I give him one last kiss before withdrawing completely.

"I'll be back soon, and I expect to be held all night."

"No arguments here."

He gives me a wink as I head out the door, and through the glass, I watch him resume his private conversation with Deke who never said a word to me. They seem so serious, and Sierra seems to notice it as well. I watch her approach, and instantly they loop her in.

I'm almost jealous of how close they all seem to be, because I feel like such an outsider. It's for the best though. In less than a year, Kane won't be able to be mine anymore.

A shuffle of people scurry past me on their way into the noise box of a house. It's crazy how soundproofed it is. It's obvious now why they had it soundproofed. They never cut the volume low on anything.

I down the vial of scent masker before attempting the stairs. My face distorts into a medley of disgusted expressions as the slimy, tart liquid slides down my throat. I always forget how terribly horrid this stuff is.

Feeling it start to strip me of my scent, I sprint down the steps and cover the distance to Gage's house. I knock, but his home is soundproofed too. An immortal thing.

The lights are on, and the entire house is covered in windows just like

Kane's. A small fluttering of butterflies hit me when I see Gage's shirtless body in the room just ahead.

His back is turned as he talks to someone on the phone. I notice the tattoos on his back - various symbols, mostly magical. I shouldn't find it sexy, but I'll be damned if I don't.

Finally, I ring the doorbell to keep from staring at yet another guy I can't be with. Gage's back stays turned as the door opens on its on.

"We'll be there shortly. See you then."

He puts his phone in his pocket and turns to face me with a small smile.

"You've taken a scent masker already I see. I was going to offer you some."

My eyes accidentally stray to his ripped body. There's not a flaw on his muscled physique. He's so lean... I wasn't expecting such definition.

"Yeah," I bumble out like a stammering fool. "I didn't want to risk leading them to Kane."

Gage is tall, almost as tall as Kane. Without my high-heels, I feel so short in comparison. Even with my heels, I still just reach his chin. Without them, I barely meet his chest.

"Uncomfortable?"

My eyes pop up from their forbidden journey over his salacious contours. Immortals shouldn't be allowed to be this eternally hot. I hate immortals.

"Huh?" I ask, feeling more than a little foolish.

"I was asking if you're uncomfortable. Again, your colors are all over the place."

Damn warlocks.

"I'm fine. I was just curious as to why you have so many symbols tattooed all over you."

It's obviously a rather transparent lie to cover my drooling fiasco. I never realized how *woman* I was until these past several weeks.

He lets a small laugh out, and then he pulls a shirt from the back of the chair to put on. I'm relieved when he finally covers himself up.

"I'm a member of the Somage. I run into some pretty unsavory creatures, so in order to avoid possessions, summons, and various other precarious situations, I took on the protective symbols. It's saved my ass more than once."

Somage?

"I thought the Somage were just an urban legend."

He smirks and then shrugs.

"We like it that way. We can only erase memories for short intervals, so it's a daily struggle to keep the fey world a secret when some creatures refuse to abide by the rules. We take out the ruthless and careless killers who could potentially become exposure threats, and we put down the wild, bloodthirsty bloodsuckers of all kinds if they lose control. We're just a group of dark users trying to take care of the *big bads*. What exactly do the light users do to keep people safe?"

His rhetorical question seeps sarcasm as he pulls on a thin, hooded jacket.

"I get it. I realize the light tends to-"

"Tends to worry about their own hide and not give a damn about anything else going on in the world? Glad we agree on that."

Jackass.

"So, is this where you pull out your score pad and mark where you've just insulted the light?"

He lets a snicker out, and then he shakes his head.

"This is the part where I give you some makeup lessons."

Question marks form in my head and swirl around in circles.

"Makeup lessons?"

He smirks as he walks over to me, and I feel his dark magic roaming through my body as something changes. It steals my breath with its invasive touch, and I almost feel the need to go on the defense when it's suddenly over.

"Easy girl. Don't be going to battle just yet. Your scent is gone for a few hours, but your appearance could still give away your identity. Take a look."

I walk by him and gasp when I see the red hair, bright green eyes, and unfamiliar face.

"How did you... we can't-"

"We can for short periods of time. It'll last for three hours at most. You won't be able to do it again for several weeks though. Magic is a beautifully tricky thing like that. Let's get going."

He ushers me out the door, and I follow him down the stairs of the deck to his garage.

"Don't have an inside access?" I ask.

"To my garage? Of course I do. I just didn't want to drag your through my house and give you a chance to get comfortable. The way you were looking at me... I was worried I was about to get unwrapped like a Christmas present while we were merely in the living room."

My cheeks flush upon hearing his teasing comment. I cut my eyes away as he opens the door. He laughs ridiculously hard, and then I hear a familiar voice behind us.

"Nothing?" Kane asks with disbelief, and without thinking, I whip around.

Gage walks over to me just as Sierra, Deke, and Kane come into view.

"Nothing. It's as though... I don't know. There's just nothing."

"What's going on?" Gage pipes up, and my heart leaps into my throat.

I'm going to kick his ass for this.

Kane walks toward us, not recognizing me at all as his eyes barely give me a second glance. What's he doing leaving his party? What are they looking for?

"Sorry. I didn't realize anyone was living here. I didn't mean to appear as though we were trespassing."

He sounds so formal, polite, and... oddly different.

"I just moved in a few weeks ago. My girl and I were about to go grab a bite to eat, and we heard voices."

I could slap him right now. I really hope he's reading the vibrant red of anger my aura is flashing at him.

He smirks, letting me know he has seen my fuming red colors lighting up like a neon sign.

"Sorry to have bothered you. I was just checking up on something. I won't hold you up. Welcome to the neighborhood."

Kane turns to jog off once Gage thanks him, and I watch as the three of them head into the woods - a shortcut to town.

"Seriously?" I slap Gage across the stomach, instantly regretting that foolish move when I pull back my throbbing hand.

"What?" he asks, feigning innocence. "We need to meet up with the guys. They've lured the night stalkers toward the edge of town - the deepest section of the woods that stretch on for miles. You, my little redhead, will be in the center, smelling like a virgin."

"I'm not-"

He rolls his eyes while cutting me off. "Believe me, I know. I live next door, and well... there was that one time-"

"Oh shit." I had completely forgotten about Gage being just outside during one of my bedroom romps. "I hate you."

He laughs harder as we hop in his very sleek, black sports car. It definitely suits a bad boy dark user.

"Chill," he teases while cranking the purring engine and throwing it in reverse. My head jolts from the unnecessary force, and he skids around to slam it into gear. The tires squeal with me as he continues. "The virgin blood is something we have in stock. Donated to us, of course. Many people enjoy helping our cause. It'll be strong enough to lure them to you. We use just tiny drops to represent a true wound. Their victims have all been virgins."

I still don't know the gruesome details, nor do I want to.

"Just don't let them get a hold of my witch blood. They'll never stop."

My breath catches when his hand is suddenly on mine.

"I wouldn't do anything if I thought you'd be at risk. We've pulled this trap more times than one can count. Never once has there been anything go wrong."

His hand moves back to the wheel as he skirts around a curve, making my whole body tense up. I'm starting to wish I had just let him vaporize me.

"Some of us are still mortal, you know."

He simply laughs at my aggravated remark, never slowing his hasty, dangerous, bat-out-of-hell driving.

Note to self, immortal drivers are bad for my health.

I'm relieved when he skids to a halt on the dirt drive next to the lake. The dark woods promise to carry mischief to anyone who enters. I climb out and instantly shiver upon seeing nothing but the leery darkness beyond the edge.

Gage climbs out, and I gasp when I see his masked face along with his drawn hood. He looks just as scary as anything I'll see out there.

"Always cautious. It's important to conceal our identities in case something goes wrong."

"That's encouraging," I grumble.

"No worries. Like I said, just cautious."

I follow him, wondering why I ever agreed to this. He moves with stealth through the forest that seems to go on forever. Finally, we stop. The silence is only interrupted by the scurrying night creatures who are curious about our imposing arrival.

"Okay, you'll be waiting here. Cade, one of my friends, just sent a text saying the night stalkers are on the way. I've got a few guys already out here."

I look around, but no one or nothing stands out.

"I don't see anything."

He nods, a small smile forming. "That's the point. I'll be out of sight too, but don't you dare think I'm very far away. When a night stalker is hunting for blood, they can sense our immortal veins. That's why you're here, and that's why we'll be hanging back. If something feels off, just scream my name. It'll make for good practice."

The devious wink he gives me after his seductive ending makes my cheeks flush. I roll my eyes, feeling completely idiotic.

"I believe you were the one who bashed Thad for flirting with me, when you've now done it quite a bit lately."

He smiles, his eyes lowering bashfully, and then he shrugs.

"Well, I prefer to think of it as us being a little less defensive around each other. Don't let it go to your head. I need to go get into place."

I think I just made a dark user blush. Didn't even know that was possible.

He starts to turn away, and I grab his arm as the reality of the situation sets in.

"Don't let them touch me. If they-"

"They won't get close enough," he says in interruption. "Even if they did, they won't be using their subduing powers against a witch because they'll just think you're a pretty little mortal girl lost in the woods. Just think of yourself as Little Red Riding Hood facing off with the Big Bad Wolf."

The problem is, I've heard the dark version of that fable - not just the bubblegum tale where Little Red Riding Hood comes out unscathed.

I shiver slightly, and then murmur, "These aren't the kind of villains that waste time on some evil monologue. They go straight for the kill without wasting time."

His eyes soften before the heat of his touch finds my arm in a comforting motion.

"Don't worry. I swear I'll get you out of here if anything was to go wrong. You're in good hands, Red."

He gives me a wink, and then he vaporizes to disappear into the darkness. In all my life, I never thought I'd be playing bait for night stalkers while my rescue lay in the hands of a dark user.

I'm either incredibly stupid or insanely brave. I'm not betting on the latter of the two.

I hear the rustle of the limbs, and I take a steady breath to calm my rampaging nerves. In an effort to play the part, I start playing the prey. I just hope I don't play the prey too well.

"Is anyone out there? Please, someone?" The fear in my voice is authentic, for I'm scared out of my frigging mind right now.

I'm sure they can hear my mortal heartbeat pounding against my chest as it tries to explode from the anticipation. Then I see them - glowing eyes in the distance. They keep fading in and out of sight as they start toying with me.

"Hello? Someone? Anyone?" My voice breaks this time. The squeaky pitch exuded is unintentional, but it still goes with my character.

Little Red Riding Hood only had one damn wolf to worry about. I've counted five sets of glowing eyes so far, and there were only supposed to be three. Already this plan is amiss.

Gage, you better not fuck this up.

I almost wish he could read minds right now. I'd tell him I changed my mind, and get me the hell out of this sacrificial placement.

"A lost lamb?" an eerie voice pronounces, but it's alone. Where are the other four?

"Can you help me? I don't know how, but I got turned around," I murmur to the vacant, dark air, trying to find the place where the voice came from.

My breath is stolen as the glowing blue eyes suddenly find mine - directly in front of me. I would gasp, but the painful air is trapped deep in my lungs, refusing to budge.

"Pretty girl," he breathes, playing with me all the more. "Let's see how pretty you scream."

I do scream. I can't help it. When at last the sound finds my lungs, I can't stop screeching a terrified shriek, praying the action is about to go down.

He wasn't supposed to touch me, but his hand is clamping my mouth just before my back slams the tree. Just when I think the game is over, he's flying backwards and crushing the tree behind him, causing the giant oak to creak, crack, and crash.

"Fucking trap!" another voice screeches, and within a blink, the five start rushing away.

Four others from Gage's mystery, masked brigade come into sight and start aiding in Gage's attempt to keep the night stalkers from fleeing.

I breathe out in relief as they are thrown back toward the circle the guys have prepared. Slumping down against the tree, I silently watch, my heart still pounding. Though I want to help, it's best not to reveal to them I'm a witch with mortal blood still coursing through my veins.

Blue balls of energy shoot free from Gage's hands, striking the snarling bloodsuckers. I cringe when I see the dark blood shooting free, and I'm forced to turn my head when the gruesome sights become unbearable.

Then I hear Gage shouting, "Now!"

I look up in time to see one of the guys slamming down a stone to complete a circle. A red, almost blinding light shoots into the sky from the circle, shedding light on all the curious forest creatures that instantly take cover.

I've only ever heard of trap nets such as this. I've never actually seen one for myself. It's incredible.

The night stalkers scramble around, but as soon as one of them tries to leap out, they're slammed back into the circle from the magic hidden inside the stones.

"Don't bother," Gage says as he runs a hand through his dark hair, pushing it away from his face after the ruffling fight. He quickly pulls his hood back down, though now it seems pointless.

At least his face is still well hidden.

The night stalker who had me pinned doesn't seem very frazzled, or even worried about the situation. That scares the shit out of me. How can someone remain calm while facing imminent death?

"You have no idea who you're messing with," the night stalker snarls, his tone threatening.

"Don't I?" Gage taunts. "You're Isolis, leader of this coven. I admit we were just expecting two to be following your lead. I didn't realize you could find four to follow you on a single kill."

Isolis's eyes cut toward me, and he gives me a dark grin that makes my skin prickle from head to toe.

"Is that a fact?" he asks while turning back to Gage. "Do you always use live bait for your traps, or was I a special condition?"

Gage lets out a sardonic huff of a laugh, and then he shakes his head, his mask still covering his identity.

"You're not special in any way. Let's talk about the sacrificial rituals you've been performing on the girls you've slaughtered and left for dead, leaving a few breaths in their lungs. That's not very discreet or humane of you, both of which are required by your kind in order to keep peace. Now, tell me why you've been performing the rituals."

Isolis just laughs - a deep, throaty, genuine laugh of amusement. Though I can't see Gage's face, I'm sure he's not too thrilled by the reaction.

"Something funny, Isolis? I don't think you quite realize how severe the consequences you're facing are. Tell me what these rituals were intended to do, and you won't die by fire. Deny me, and I'll make sure you feel the same pain those girls did before you left them gasping for their last breaths."

Isolis's laughter tapers off as his eyes grow darker with intent, his night stalker blues burning a glowing hue. A small, secretive smirk plays on his lips as he pulls his hands behind his back.

"Boy, you have no idea what's coming. There's more power at play than you can even fathom. Just be warned, the Somage don't have a lot of friends. Your faces may be hidden, your scents may be covered, but your voices remain the same. We'll find you, and it won't be pretty when we do. Remember this moment when I'm ripping your heart out through your throat."

If ever there was a scarier threat, I've never heard it. Gage seems cool, unaffected, as though he's heard this all too many times. I'm shaking like a leaf on a tree in the middle of a windstorm.

"I'm standing on the outside of this circle right now, while you're facing your last few breaths. Don't think you scare me. You're low on the food chain compared to what I've dealt with. Just another snake in the grass waiting to get his head chopped off - that's all you are to me," Gage murmurs, his tone equally as terrifying.

With all the time we've spent together this past month, I've almost forgotten the dark roots he bears. That's something I should remember before getting too close.

Isolis turns to face me, and my stomach slaps my throat when he gives me a devious wink, warning me something big is about to happen.

"Maybe you'd be right... if I hadn't been expecting a trap," he says, and as soon as those words release, the woods thunder with a sudden attack.

I scream as lycans and night stalkers crash through the trees. At least ten have joined our party, and they're out for blood. We set a trap alright - our own fucking trap.

The time for holding back is over. With this many, I'll have to reveal my power.

Gage starts whirling blue orbs of energy while using his telekinesis to shove them away. If they touch him, his fight is over. They'll use their subduing power to restrain him, hold him... kill him.

The other members of his masked brigade fight off as many as they can, but one screams out as he's brought down. His mask is ripped free by a night stalker who relishes the terror he's stricken before devouring him, forcing me to cut my eyes away.

I screech as one nears the circle, but while I'm busy hesitating, he has time to rip a stone up and free the other five. Now we're all the more outnumbered, and I have no choice.

Before I can release the first bit of magic, death's grip is at my throat.

"Pretty girl, you've been a bad, bad girl," Isolis murmurs with malice lighting up in his eyes. "Mortal dolls such as yourself should never agree to help those weaker than me."

I can't see the fight raging on. I don't know who's hurt, dead, or dying. All I can see are the glowing blue eyes in front of me, dulling down to a deep brown color. Golden flecks sprinkle along the rims of his chocolates, and his strong, chiseled jaw clenches as he breathes me in.

He's a beast, seeming even taller than he did the first time he held my life in his hands. I can still feel my power inside me, stirring. Gage was right, he has no clue I'm a witch, so he doesn't know he has to fight against me.

I hear a strangled release, and I know it's Gage. He's hurt, and I can't see how bad. It's now or never.

Just as Isolis starts to go for the kill, I put my hands on his arms that are holding my shoulders. Forcing enough volts out to kill a herd of elephants, I shock the fuck out of him and send him flying backwards.

The look on his face is pretty frigging priceless as the high fills me. My father's power is toxic, inebriating. I shouldn't have used it, but desperate times call for incredibly stupid measures.

Isolis stands as several more men surround me, their attention drawn to the mortal witch whose blood they're now desperate to taste.

With a devilishly wry grin, I pull the power forth, my silver orbs circling my hands as I step toward them without fear.

"Holy... shit," one of them releases in disbelief.

Little Red Riding Hood has a dark little secret. *Oops.*

My silver orbs glow brighter, swelling to be much larger as they continue to swirl around my hands. With one gloriously cathartic release, I sling them forth. The two orbs split, turning into four and striking a lycan and three night stalkers in the chest.

Their screaming yelps ring like music to my ears, proving the intoxicating dark power is starting to take me deeper into its clutches. I can't pull back though. We'll never survive if I do.

The fire blazes from the earth to join the next set of silver streaking beauties, and the screams heard are delighting my sadistic side as my roaring inferno grabs more lives of the dark.

Gage is suddenly beside me, slinging me to the ground before a night stalker's surprise attack can succeed, and then he jumps up to resume his attacks. Just as the high takes me over, a scream surges through my lips.

I feel the fangs bared, crunching against the curve of my neck, as the fire of the bite brings me to tears. Gage flings his blue orbs, but a lycan sideswipes him and sends him barreling across the forest.

More glowing blue eyes and new lycans join the party, making death a reality. Then something happens that I wasn't prepared to see.

The new deadly beauties leap into the fight, but they're not attacking us, they're attacking Isolis's men.

I look up just as Isolis is about to take another bite out of me, but he's thrown back as one of the newest night stalkers grabs him up and launches him back. I cry out in pain when my dark hero lifts me up, but relief isn't anywhere inside me.

The red hair I'm wearing stains with an even darker red as my blood flows freely. The face of my newest captor is hidden beneath a black mask just like Gage's. His gray hoodie covers his head, and his glowing blues check me over.

I'm starting to worry we've just stepped into a turf war, but then I realize the other numbers dwindling. The night stalker holding me feels so familiar to the touch, as if I know him. His scent is gone, just like mine. Apparently, everyone decided to be incognito tonight. Not that a scent really matters to me. I can't identify a scent or track it.

The night stalker holding me nods to the lycans of his group, and then one of his other night stalker friends whistles twice to signal some sort of attack formation. With grace and effortless poise, the two lycans jump into the circle, and they shred several of the night stalkers attacking our few men.

Isolis is gone - nowhere at all to be seen. Now one Devil has left, handing the keys to the gates of hell to another.

Gage runs over, but he stops as he stares eye-to-eye with the night stalker holding me. He pulls free a blue orb, poised to strike, but the night stalker gently places me on the ground at his feet.

Gage kneels, his eyes never leaving the foe playing friend, until suddenly they're all gone as quickly as they came.

"What the fuck just happened?" one of Gage's friends asks.

"Your guess is as good as mine. Don't question good fortune. Let's get the hell out of here for now. Grab Jesse. He'll need a proper burial."

I cringe as I glance in the direction of their fallen comrade. His dark hair shades his lifeless eyes. I didn't know him, but I'm sure Gage and he were close enough for his death to sting the dark user.

"Are you okay?" I ask softly.

"Me? I'm immortal. You... Alyssa, I'm so sorry. I swear to you nothing like this has ever happened before."

He had no idea I meant emotionally okay. He just lost a member of his group.

"You-"

"Shit. You're losing a lot of blood. I need to get you back to my place and get you cleaned up."

Before I can argue, I feel the wind against me. Either he forgot he drove, or the fanged demon left one hell of a mark behind which has prompted a hasty retreat.

Though the pain is excruciating, I grit through it. It's not like I haven't felt it before. Within a few deep breaths, we're back at his house. I look down to see the blood has covered my arm.

Damn it.

Dizziness is always a reminder as to why I shouldn't let him vaporize me, but right now I've got to focus on the more important things.

"My blood, it'll leave a trail."

"Every drop that fell was soaked up by the earth. Care to explain how that happened? While you're at it, how about telling me how a mortal holds energy in the palm of her hand, when some century-old beings can't even do such a thing."

I was *really* hoping to avoid this conversation.

"Are you saying you're over a century old? You used energy as well."

He smirks as he places me on his bed, and then he tugs his mask off to reveal the face I'm getting far too used to seeing. I take a moment to drink in my surroundings. It's a neutral colored scheme. Given the fact he's a dark user, I was expecting something a little more... gothic?

There's nothing dark at all about his room. In fact, it's actually a light, cozy sort of atmosphere. The taupe walls mingle with the splashes of red art. No personal pictures adorn the space, but there are plenty of wild, enthralling sculptures and paintings.

He takes interest in my bemused facial expression just before he rips my sleeve off my shoulder to reveal the severity of the wound I refuse to look at. He flinches, and guilt shades his eyes as he pulls out medical supplies.

"Let me guess, you were expecting dark crosses, voodoo dolls, pentagrams... that sort of thing," he says in a forced mocking tone, his attention more focused on my shoulder.

The living room had been simple, nice, even elegant, but I thought that was just for the sake of appearances.

"Maybe a skull and cross sort of theme."

He lets a laugh out as he smears something over my shoulder. His perfectly crisp blue eyes find mine as I take a deep breath. The concern I see is genuine, which makes me genuinely confused.

"Be glad Isolis doesn't come from a strong sire. His venom is weak," he says to break the awkward silence.

His eyes fall back down to my wound, and I flinch as he starts pressing harder against the open bites I still refuse to view.

"He sure as hell felt pretty strong to me."

He laughs at my candor, and then shakes his head as he eases off the bed. His soft, satin bedspread is almost slippery. The vibrant red goes well with the trickle of blood still falling off me. It's a good thing he has magic, otherwise getting the blood stains out would be a bitch.

"He is strong. I guess I should elaborate. Just because his venom is weak, that doesn't mean he's weak. It means he comes from a lesser bloodline. The stronger bloodlines have much more painful venom. Once, I spent days on my back screaming in agony."

I shiver as my mind falls back to the second, almost fatal bite I received. I too spent days on my back, screaming out my torture.

"What did he mean by something big is coming? And what rituals were you talking about?"

He shrugs, as if he's not dwelling on the fanged beast's spewed threat.

"They always say something big is coming. As for the rituals, we don't know what they were for. That's kind of why I asked him."

His playfully poking tone makes me roll my eyes, and then he kneels before me to start bandaging my newest set of bite marks.

"How am I going to explain this to Kane?" I huff out.

"It'll heal within twenty minutes. That medicine is some of my aunt's best work."

It's obvious he's a little closer to his aunt than his mother. Should I pry?

"So, you and your aunt are close?"

He smiles, and then he pulls off his shirt, as if he's trying to make me blush and squirm.

"Very. She should have been my mother. Life sure as hell would have been simpler. Now, let's get back to you. How did you control the energy orbs?"

He turns to me as he pulls out another, clean, blood-free shirt and pulls it over his head. His bottom lip folds between his teeth - the metal ring included - as he waits for me to answer the question I never usually do.

"Do you remember that trust conversation we had?" I ask curiously.

"I think it's time you start trusting me so I can start helping you. That's a lot of power, and Isolis just saw you use it. He got away tonight. Though he'll surely flee town now that he's lost his mignons, he'll be back. You need to be ready. Now trust me."

Hearing a dark user tell a light user to trust them is almost comical, but I really don't have a choice. He can't allow his friends to tell his council what I'm already capable of.

"It's my father's magic. I can control energy just as he does, but it's already strong enough to do some serious damage. If your guys tell-"

"They won't. They don't even know your name or your face so it wouldn't do them any good to tell. You seemed so in-control over it, but I could tell you were holding back. Why?"

Because it makes me a psychopathic freak to use it at full strength.

"It's... well, it's my father's power. Do I really need to say more than that? Just as the use of it gets him high, drunk, and leaves him completely encompassed by the seduction of its force, the same happens to me. It's not something that can or should be used if there are options. My mother's power is from the earth, which is why I can only assume my blood was swallowed up. That's actually new to me. The earth was trying to keep me safe. As for the rest... well, I don't trust you that much."

I don't trust anyone to tell them how strong I really am... how damn crazy I can get. The dark would look light if I ever lost control. I dread being immortal. My power will grow stronger, even stronger than Drackus's power, and who knows what a peril I might become.

"Fair enough," he murmurs while sitting down on the edge of the bed to join me. "For the record, red suits you. I prefer the blond, but you can pull off the extreme change."

I laugh a little as I stare at the ends of my hair bearing the foreign color.

"So, you never speak to Drackus? Care if I ask why?" he asks, seeming hesitant in his approach to the touchy subject.

So, so, so many reasons come to mind, but I only share a tidbit about my estranged father.

"You've heard the stories. Though I know my father would be here if I ever needed him, it wouldn't be because he loves me. Drackus thrives on chaos and power. He'd love nothing more than if I called him and asked him for help just so he'd have an excuse to show the world and me how powerful he really is. To be honest, I'm considering asking for his help. Mom's been missing for far too long."

He shifts uneasily. Most people don't say my father's name above a whisper. I suppose I use it a little too casually.

"I think you should give us a little more time. If Drackus comes out of his-"

"I know. The light and dark would unite to fight against him, and it would be war all over again. My father has just as many friends as he does enemies, so when I say it would be a war, I mean that very literally. I'm just reaching the point of desperation."

Before I realize I'm doing it, the tears are flowing down my face. Gage pulls me into his arms, and I shiver against the unexpected contact.

He's been rude, obnoxious, aggravating, and recently flirty, but this is the first time he's ever been... sweet? Considerate maybe?

Oddly enough, his embrace is comforting, but it only makes me ready to get back to Kane. Those are the arms I want to be in right now.

"We'll find her. I'll keep calling all my contacts and we'll find her."

I pull back to see the truth in his eyes, and I tilt my head.

"Why do you care so much? I thought you were only here to clear all accusations of it being your people."

His lips tighten as he looks away.

"That's how it started, but then you kind of grew on me." His words make me bite back a grin, but his lips etch up slightly upon seeing my reaction. "I know. Crazy how things work out. Besides, you need my help, and I happen to enjoy helping people out. Who knows, maybe once you're immortal, the two of us can even try to be friends."

I lean forward, my eyes teasing him lightly. "Even if I'm light and you're dark?"

His eyes flash a devious glow before he murmurs, "They're just definitions of power, nothing else. If lovers can be on opposing sides, so can friends."

I just laugh at that while shaking my head.

"I'll be glad when my face and hair get back to normal," I say in an effort to shift the topic.

I'm ready to get back to Kane - more than ready. I'm also a little curious about where he went and what he was doing.

"Your face has been back to normal for a while now. That's why I said you could pull off red. It wouldn't be *you* pulling off red if you were still wearing another face."

Reflexively, my hands pop up to feel the familiar skin pulled in all the right places. I glance to the mirror on the wall to see how very bizarre it seems for me to be wearing this brazen color.

"I'm definitely not rocking red. Thanks for the lie though."

He laughs lightly, and then he plops down on the bed to rest his hands behind his head. With him lying that way, it makes me feel uncomfortable to be sitting here. This is too intimate a setting for us, but before I can disengage, he draws my attention to him.

"That'll still leave a mark. The meds just stop the bleeding and kill the worst of the venom. It'll close the wound, but I'm afraid it'll still scar. Sorry."

His eyes hold mounds of guilt to prove the authenticity of his apology. I pat his leg, and then I start to stand.

"That's no problem," I sigh out, and then I wave my hand over the mark while chanting the secret medley of words my mother formed in spell.

Before his eyes, my skin shifts, and an invisible veil drops to cloak the hideous mark I'm not yet prepared to see. His eyes widen, and a smirk forms as he stands and lowers his head to be level with my little miracle.

"That's pretty nifty for a newbie. How long will it last?"

I shrug, trying to ignore the heat of his breath finding the skin on my chest.

"I'm really not sure of its limitations. It's worked on my other one for several years now. Mom seems to believe it'll always work."

He stands up, seeming too impressed for such a seemingly simple feat.

"You don't even realize the significance of this, do you?" he asks while touching the skin.

Chill bumps form when he caresses the hidden bite, and then I shakily murmur, "It's just for small sections. Nothing too big would work."

"It even feels smooth. No different from the rest of your skin," he says while letting his hand trail down my shoulder to my arm.

I shiver this time, and he smirks, obviously reading my aura again. Damn warlocks.

"Um, how much longer until my hair changes back?"

His smirk grows as he pulls my hair between his fingers and draws it in front of my face.

"It just did."

I stare at the blond and sigh in relief. I *really* need to get out of here. I know Kane and I can't be together forever, but I still want him. Being around Gage, someone who has my immortal destiny... it's just confusing me. Confusion is *not* something I need right now.

"I should get back to Kane."

Gage smiles bigger, and then he winks at me while holding his hand over my head. My ripped sleeve mends in front of my eyes as the blood stains covering my clothes disappear. Within seconds, my entire ensemble looks like I just walked out of the drycleaners.

I take it a step further and make it different, changing back into what Kane saw me leave in.

"Call me if you need me," he murmurs with his grin still intact.

Then something dawns on me. "Why did you soundproof your house? You mentioned you were... er... next door... and insinuated you overheard... um... stuff, but your house is completely shut off from the outside and so is Kane's."

He laughs loudly at my stammering attempt. I couldn't just say he mentioned overhearing my bedroom tousles with Kane.

"The house was soundproof when I got it. It wasn't something I added to it. It's rather obvious this is a hotspot for immortals. I'm sure one owned it at some point in time. There are quite a few houses like this one. As for overhearing your passionate screams, I'm not always inside and you don't always shut your balcony door."

My face floods crimson, and he laughs ridiculously hard when I drop my eyes instantly.

"I'm definitely leaving now."

Turning on my heel, I head toward the door, leaving behind the rambunctious cackles flowing freely from the dark user's mouth. He's enjoying this way too much.

Chapter Sixteen

The loud, thumping music is vibrating the house. The lights are dim, like this is some sort of a club instead of a home. I can see a group of boys clicking away on the remotes while playing one of the violent games.

Amy is the only one I recognize and know. There are so many people that it's impossible to find Kane right now.

"Blonds are my thing," a drunken goon slurs from behind me.

I whip around, quickly tossing his stray arm off my shoulders and take a step back.

"Sorry. Drunk strangers *aren't* my thing."

He smiles, his eyes dancing with the thrill of a chase.

"Well, let's make them your thing. I'm Craig."

"She's taken," Deke says while popping up out of nowhere, standing close to me in a protective sort of manner.

"Yo, man. I though you were with Sierra. That babe single now?"

What a jerk.

Deke's eyes narrow, and then he lets out a derisive scoff. "Even if she was, you wouldn't be able to handle her. Sierra's still mine. This is Kane's girl. You really want to keep playing with fire?"

The guy's eyes widen, as if he's sobering a little, and then he stumbles backwards.

"No. Sorry. Tell him I didn't know."

Without another word, he disappears from sight, leaving his balls behind apparently. I've never seen anyone so quick to bow out.

"Where's Kane?" I ask, having to yell over the music.

"He's out looking for you. I just sent him a text to tell him you're here. He's heading back now."

Looking for me?

"Why did he go looking for me?"

"Because there was another attack in town. We got a call a few minutes after you left. Two girls were found dead in their homes, and it wasn't pretty. He went to track you down and bring you home until daylight. But you're an expert at vanishing into thin air. Where'd you go?"

Crap.

"I just walked around mostly. There's a spot at the edge of town I like to go. When will he be back?"

Before he can answer, strong arms are wrapped around me and pulling me into a glorious embrace. I breathe him in, enjoying his smell like he was made for me. Those incredible lips find my neck and trail across my hidden wound as he kisses me through the fabric.

I stifle a wince when he presses too firmly against the still tender bite left behind. Though it can't be seen, it can sure as hell be felt.

I turn around, and he draws me in closer just before his perfect lips find mine. I smile behind the kiss that is far too passionate to be displayed in front of so many.

"No more late night romps through the town, please. My heart still isn't steady," he murmurs against my lips.

I smile bigger as I lean into him.

"I take it you were worried?"

"Very. I've called your phone at least a dozen times. Did you lose it?"

Oh shit.

I left my phone at Gage's before we even left to go set the trap that went terribly awry. I completely forgot it.

"I'm sure it'll turn up. I'm sorry you were worried, but I'm a big girl. I managed."

By the skin of my teeth, that is.

"I heard about those girls they found in town, and it scared the hell out of me. I left shortly after you did, but we couldn't track you down. Since then, I've been worried sick. I sound like a total control freak right now, don't I?"

I smile involuntarily to the point it almost aches. Giggling like a fool, I shake my head. The noisy room makes it hard for us to hear each other, but I can tell he likes the fact I'm more turned on than freaked out.

It feels good to have him care so much, since I feel the same way.

"I love the fact you went all over town looking for me, but I hate you missed your party full of drunk, smitten-with-you women."

He laughs at my insincere remark, and then he cups my face in his hands before leaning down and kissing me lightly once again.

"I need to go check on Zee and tell him your back. I've got him missing out on all the drunk women, too. I'll be right back. Don't move."

I just nod, my foolish grin remaining intact, as he shuffles back through the mass to head outside.

I look over to see Deke has claimed Sierra's attention. I almost smile, but then my mouth fills with the taste of bitter when I see Amy making her way toward me.

Inhaling a sharp breath, I ready myself for whatever cruel, unnecessary thing she spews through her jealous lips. This past month, I've heard it all.

"I really don't feel like hearing it, Amy. Just enjoy the party and leave me alone," I grumble as soon as she reaches me.

"I don't want to fight. I just came to tell you... look, there's a lot about us you don't know. If you love your family, your friends, your life in general, you need to give up Kane."

My blood almost boils. How dare she threaten me.

"You start making threats against my family, and I'll-"

"I'm not making threats, Alyssa. I'm telling you that choosing Kane has consequences. You'll belong to him. If you don't like the way that sounds, you need to give him up, because he's never going to give you up."

She walks away before I can form some well mastered retort. I glare at her back as she mingles into the middle and starts dancing between some drunken men. I wish she'd just stay away from me.

"What'd she say this time?" Kane asks as he comes up behind me. "I saw her talking to you through the glass. I couldn't get in here before she said anything."

I just shrug it off the same way I always do the things she says.

"Nothing that changes anything. I really don't want to talk about Amy."

His eyes burn against her back, and I'm sure she can feel his glare. She's either enjoying his attention or avoiding his scowl. Either way, I'm sick of his eyes being on her.

"How about showing your girlfriend some attention and forgetting about your ex."

His eyes fall on me as he sighs. "She's not my damn ex."

If you say so.

"Then stop worrying about her. Let's enjoy the night."

As someone cuts the lights up a little, I notice something that had averted my attention earlier. Blood stains his shirt in various places.

"What happened? Are you bleeding?" I panic.

He drops his gaze and his eyes widen as he lets a few curse words flow out under his breath. It's obvious he didn't expect me to overhear his swearing, since he said them so low, and then he starts walking toward his room.

I follow him quickly, still waiting for a response.

"Kane," I prompt.

"It's not mine," he says, finally easing the knot tensed in my stomach.

"Whose is it?"

I shut the door behind me as he strips off his shirt. The light stains don't reach his skin, and I sigh in relief when I see it really isn't his.

"There was a hurt girl with a bloody... nose. I helped her out. I didn't realize it had gotten on this shirt, too."

"Too? Did you have on another shirt?"

He ignores me, but I quickly drop my inquisition when I see the divine lines of his body calling to me. Without noticing my gaze on him, he starts rifling through his closet for another shirt.

He finally catches my scandalous eyes and my lip clutched between my teeth, and a dark grin appears on his beautiful face.

"Feeling the weight of a few weeks?" he teases, though it's obvious he's just as turned on as I am right now.

"A little."

Just as he's about to make his way toward me, a loud crashing sound breaks free on the other side of the door. He rushes out with me on his heels to go investigate.

Amy is standing over the blond I saw draped around Kane earlier. The pretty girl has a bloody mouth, a reddened eye and a swollen lip. Her body is a tangled mess of disaster as she lies unconsciously on the ground.

The music halts and the lights come on quickly.

"What the fuck?" Kane scolds, his arms angrily flailing to emphasize his fury.

"I told you she better not taunt me again. I don't deal with that female drama shit."

My ass. That's all she fucking does is start drama.

"Amy, you can't-" Kane stops short of whatever he was going to say as his hands go through his hair.

Sierra walks up, and Deke joins her to scoop the limp girl off the floor.

"Crank the tunes back up. It's not like it's the first time someone has gotten laid out in here." Deke laughs, but his eyes narrow at Amy as if he's silently scolding her.

The sound kicks back in, and Amy goes so far as to wink at Kane. My fists clench at my sides as I hold my breath.

I'm so sick of her!

"We'll talk about this later," he growls, but she just shrugs and smiles before walking off.

He turns back to me to meet my scrutinizing glare burning into him.

"Please don't," he says before I even start to speak.

"What? Tell you how old this has gotten? It's always the same. She acts out to gain your attention, which you always give her immediately after. And people say I have daddy issues."

My sardonic release isn't lost on him even under the deafening music that has resumed. I walk away, pushing through the partiers on my way to grab my own drink. One second things are really hot, but Amy is good at icing the flames.

I grab the first empty glass I see and pour some of the chilled rum into it. Kane catches up to me just as I draw in the first sip.

"Alyssa, I really don't want to fight about this. I don't know what to say besides I'm sorry for upsetting you."

I just shake my head as I stare at all the oblivious people enjoying their short lives. This isn't my world. This isn't my place. I shouldn't be here with him, messing up his short life while he has time to enjoy someone he can be with.

"Kane, I'm sorry, too. I'm going back to my place tonight. This was all... It was crazy. We barely know each other, so me moving in was a stupid move to begin with. I've got a lot going on with my mom right now, and it's obvious you have stuff to deal with as well. I'll come get my clothes tomorrow."

I put the glass back down and start toward the door. Before I can reach it, he's pulling me back, halting my retreat.

"I understand you're mad, but why does it feel like you're breaking up with me?"

My chest becomes heavy and each breath is painful. Staring into his perfect emerald eyes, I want to tell him how I really feel. I could lose myself in him forever if I had the choice.

I would happily give up immortality and keep a short life span just to be with him. Unfortunately, even if I could do such a thing, there aren't any guarantees. I'd rather leave without anything souring our memories... even though Amy is sour enough.

"Because... because..." Damn this is so hard. My tears start breaching my eyes as I walk out onto the deck.

"Because you think you are," he says as he shuts the door behind him, blocking out the music.

The quieter air outside leaves us alone with what's about to happen. The weight on my chest grows to be unbearable as I nod and let a few tears trickle free.

"Because Amy's a bitch? Baby, we can get out of here for a while. I'll let the others deal with housebreaking Amy. Just come back in with me, and we'll pack a bag right now."

He's making this so much harder. Why does he have to be so perfect for me if I can't be with him? It's not fair.

More tears fall as I stare at the dark lake in front of me. His hand slides up my back, and I fall apart.

"Alyssa, I know you've got a lot on you right now," he coos. He pulls me into his arms as I continue to weep into my hands, shielding my pain from his eyes. "Don't push me away."

I have to.

"Kane, let's end this before it gets too hard to end. Before we get hurt," I whimper.

He just pulls me tighter, bringing me so close he's all I can smell, feel, or taste. My tears just fall that much harder.

"It's impossible to end, Alyssa. As for getting hurt, you're already crying, and

I'm already in love."

My heartbeat stops momentarily before springing back to life and rushing around in a frenzy. My ears buzz, making me worry I've lost my mind. There's no way something this incredible yet catastrophic is happening right now.

"Kane, don't say something you don't mean just because you're afraid of losing-"

His lips find mine before I can finish. The heated trails of tears on my cheeks only grow in abundance. He lifts me up and puts me on the rail of the deck as he slides between my legs.

"I'm not," he murmurs against my lips. "I mean it, Alyssa. I'm in love with you."

My head spins like I'm on some ride where gravity is manipulated and toyed with. My stomach is in my head, and my heart is in my toes right now. I'm a disarrayed arrangement of complicated emotions to go along with all the rest of the crazy.

My brain, heart and mouth don't converse before impulsively releasing, "I love you, too."

That's all it takes for his soft kiss to become devouring, desperate, and completely overpowering. His hands slip to my hair to pull me in harder, and I taste blood when the bruising kiss becomes too much.

My heartbeat quickens as the inflaming desire for him suddenly intensifies all the more - the flames becoming almost surreal in comparison to anything I've ever felt. Everything in my body burns for his touch with a depth I've only ever felt once before.

My legs tighten around his waist as all my weight becomes his to bear. He effortlessly pulls me away from the railing as he carries me back into the noisy house. Some wild song about rough sex blares as our entangled passion continues, only adding to the ambience.

"Kane, I'm sorry," Amy's voice interjects as we make our way to the bedroom.

If I could pull back, I would. The moment should be soured after hearing her speak, but it's as if my mind has left me alone with my hormones that have kicked into overdrive.

He does pull back, almost breathless as he does so, and mutters, "I don't care."

Her eyes narrow at me, but I don't acknowledge her. His lips find mine again as we finally find his room. The door slams behind us, and the bed slaps my back as he tosses me to it.

Greedily, I grab at him, ready for him to be melded to my body. His devilish smirk pushes me into a desperate gasp, until his mouth finds my body. I reach for his zipper, but he pushes my hands to the side.

"Not yet," he murmurs against my neck as he slides my shirt over my head.

His lips trail down my chest, paying my breasts some attention just barely before going farther down. His hot breath dampens my skin as he hovers over my pants.

I finally feel the relief of my pants being slid down, and then I feel his warm mouth covering me at the apex of my thighs. His tongue... oh his tongue is incredible.

I moan before I realize what I'm doing as he comes to fully rest between my legs. Grabbing me at the hips, he presses his face against me all the more, making me try to buck in response, but he holds me down.

Forced to endure the ecstasy, my hands tangle in his hair to draw him into me even more. That only stirs his wicked tongue that much more as he pushes me to the brink of heaven. My legs stiffen, warning me I'm almost there, and I'll use my magic on anyone who tries to break up this moment.

My cries are drowned out by the hellacious party music, and my shaking body turns overly sensitive to touch as I fall off the peak of surrealism. I shiver as his lips brush against the insides of my thighs, kissing me with a much lighter touch than I crave right now.

I start to get up, ready to end this teasing game, but he pushes me down and pins my hands above my head with just one of his strong hands. With his free hand, he starts undoing his pants. The sound of his zipper sliding down almost hurts my ears with the building anticipation.

My whole body is throbbing for him, ready to be claimed as he slowly takes his time.

"Please," I release in a pathetic whisper as my hips arch to try and meet his.

He smiles, clearly enjoying my desperation, and then he bends down to bring those soft, perfect lips to my neck. He nips at me, bringing my skin between his teeth, and I moan without even knowing why.

"You sound like you really want me."

He's toying with me, reveling in my desire for him. My hunger only grows with each drawn out moment, and I start shivering as though I'm a junkie dealing with a need for the high.

The second I'm about to release a painful cry from the absurd reaction, he plunges deep inside of me, releasing my hands simultaneously. It's so forceful, so sudden, and so painfully perfect that it takes my breath and forces a grunt through my lips.

"Damn, you feel so good," he murmurs as he pulls back and surges in deeper.

Again, my breath is forced out in a grunt as our bodies collide with the forceful impact. I claw at him, desperate to feel him even closer, as if that's possible.

"Tell me again," he murmurs into the crook of my neck as he claims my body with his.

"What?" I moan out, gripping him even tighter.

"What you feel for me."

I try to catch my breath so I can release a well articulated line, but it's pointless. Half moaning, half gasping, I murmur, "I love you."

His rhythm quickens, letting me know that was the magical phrase he sought, and then he tangles a hand in my hair to jerk my head back, exposing my neck. The pain is sublime and welcome. I'm not sure what's wrong with me, but I'd let him do anything he wanted to in this moment.

He nips at my neck over and over, making my body all the hotter as he punishes me with the most exquisite, rough thrusts. He releases his hold on my hair as his hand slides down to my throat in a choking motion, making all the blood rush to my head in an arousing high.

I start to cry out, almost reaching my peak once more, but he slows his rhythm and releases his hold on my throat as I lose the edge.

"Kane," I plead, desperate to fall into that incredible release once more.

His smile is dark, exciting me to my core. I've never seen him like this, but damn it's sexy.

"Not yet. Tell me you're mine," he murmurs as he arches my hips to start owning me from a different, more salaciously divine angle.

I cry out, the force being just painful enough to be incredibly intoxicating.

"Tell me," he prompts, threatening to slow his rhythm once more.

"I'm yours," I gush out without hesitation, and suddenly that rhythm he's set becomes all the more surreal.

I hold on as though I'm on some hellacious ride that holds my life in its hands. He grips me tighter, pushing me farther with each incredible stroke, until I finally scream out my release and shudder in his hold.

His warmth fills me, making his strangled moan come out in a delicious huff as he stills himself at the deepest point within me. Collapsing to my side, he pulls me into his arms and kisses me so sweetly.

"I have got to stop doing that," he murmurs as if to himself.

"Stop doing what? Making me feel as though I've been lifted ten feet off the ground while having an epic out of body experience?"

He lets out a laugh, and then he shakes his head while kissing me once more.

"I need to go tell the guys to wrap this party up. I'm exhausted, and I just want to hold my girl in silence."

I smile as I snuggle into him. I don't know how I'll ever let him go, but right now isn't the time.

"Hurry back. Your girl is ready to fall asleep in your arms."

His smile is breathtakingly perfect, leaving me enamored as he slips free from the bed. I almost forgot he walked around the party shirtless. No doubt, every girl in here is green with envy right now.

I stand up with the sheet clutched to me, and his brow raises quizzically as he pulls his jeans back on.

"Where do you think you're going?" he jokes.

"I'm thirsty, and I need something to eat. I'll just bring it back to the room."

He lets a small laugh free and nods.

"Definitely bring it back. I don't want to share you tonight."

He kisses my forehead, and escapes into the rowdy room, quickly shutting the door behind him.

With a snap of my fingers, my clothes are back on, and I follow his exit. I really wish he had at least put on a shirt. I hate seeing all the girls drooling over him the way only I should be able to do.

He laughs with Deke, who I'm sure saw our passionate disappearance from the party. I blush lightly as I make my way into the kitchen. Amy's secret art room door is cracked ever so slightly, and curiosity invites me in. With a quick glance over my shoulder, I quietly push through and head in.

Artwork decorates the walls in abundance, but one really grabs my attention in an infuriating manner. There's one of Kane displayed proudly. The attention to detail would be amazing if not for the fact she's a psycho stalker.

One thing strikes me as odd. She colored in his eyes as blue, and there's a dark aura surrounding his beauty. I'm sure to the scorned woman, he does seem dark. To me, he's absolutely stunningly light.

My witch senses kick in, and I feel the faintest trickle of air coming from a hollow wall. It piques my interest enough to draw me in, and I kneel before it to find the slightest bit of a gap from the baseboard.

"False wall, perhaps?" I mumble aloud.

This home obviously belonged to immortals before, and every good immortal has a hidden room designed to be a safe-room. What troubles me, is that it's usually not meant to be *safe* in the same sense a human defines the word.

Secret rooms are designed for discreet killings and disposal thereafter. Torture rooms, holding cells... so many different things could lie below. I'm sure Kane and his friends have been oblivious to all of the dark things that could be hidden beneath, but I can taste the darkness embedded in the wall beyond this point.

With a steadying breath, I step back and bypass searching for the hidden switch that would open this. Using my abilities, I slide the wall open.

A dark stairwell lies in front of me, warning me to drop this search. There's no reason I should need to see what's below. I know darkness once etched this place. I can feel it.

And Kane thinks my house has darkness lurking within.

Against my better judgment and the voice in my head screaming for me to stop, I start my descent, closing the false door behind me as the darkness cloaks me. I push a piece of magic out of my body to light the room.

The glowing ball resembles the sun as it floats to the center and rests high overhead to cast a light on all the hidden, ghastly sights.

My footfalls echo through the silent room. The music can't reach this heavily padded portion of the house, further proving my theory that nothing good ever came from this room.

As I head down, I start seeing many different chains, steel collars, shackles of all kinds, and heavy bars lined up like cages. There are enchanted crests on all of them, making this seem like a prison for the immortal world as opposed to a torture room for human victims.

"Shit," I gripe aloud.

Kane lives in a home where creatures such as myself were probably held and bled... or worse. This is not good. The darkness that owned this place could always return to claim its rights. Immortals are deadly serious about their possessions. Though this house has been sold, the prior tenant might decide to be sentimental and come to reclaim their memories. And they'll take the lives of anyone in their way.

Swallowing hard, I cast a hand forth to draw in the remnants left behind. It's hard to tell what was trapped in that cage because I suck at this, but I finally see the aura staining the ground. There are a few, dried drops of blood to help me cipher what once stayed in here.

"Lycan," I almost whisper to myself.

Someone had a lycan trapped in here. I can almost feel the hatred burning through the bars from the lycan that tried to escape numerous times. Oddly enough, I don't sense a death. This place is full of darkness, but no death? How is that possible?

A shudder passes through me, and I decide I've seen enough to know my house is much, much safer than this one. I don't care if it is against the light law to intentionally use magic against a human. I'll do it to push Kane out of this place if I have to.

I rush back up the stairs, and I close my eyes to check for any presence on the other side of the hidden door. When I feel it's safe, I push through and quickly seal the door behind me, extinguishing my magical light that had lit the room.

Just as I reach the door to escape the art room, Kane steps in, gasping when he sees me.

"What are you doing in here?"

Finding out you live in a dark house I have to save you from.

"I was curious. Then I saw the um... picture of you with the wrong eye color. For such a stalker bitch, you'd think Amy could get that one detail right."

His eyes flash to the oversized sketch of himself, and he shakes his head while cursing under his breath.

"Come on. Let's get out of here. I don't like you being so close to such... craziness."

I laugh a little. If he only knew the *craziness* we're close to. He'd probably flip the fuck out. Maybe I should show him. It might make him think some twisted serial killer lived here and he would probably leave on his own.

I wouldn't scar him with that though.

"Yeah. Right behind you. I still need something to eat and drink."

He frowns, realizing I've been in here for a while now, and then he nods as I walk out in front of his ushered hand.

"Go on to the room. I'll bring you something."

"I can get it."

"Please. I don't want you in this madhouse any longer. This party has gotten out of control, and I don't know all of these people. Deke has started clearing them out, but it'll take a while. Just head on."

With a shrug, I do as he says after he kisses me on top of my head. His breath warms me through my hair, and I smile before making my way back through the sweaty bodies. I'm really glad I can't see their auras right now. I can smell the sex in the air without seeing how desperate this crowd really is.

Shutting the door behind me, I head to the bed. Sudden panic consumes me when I feel a hand clamp over my mouth and strong arms pulling me to a body. I've tasted this scent before, and I know it well.

Heath.

The same pervert who trapped me not long ago has me in his clutches once more. I struggle, but he's so frigging strong. Unless I use my magic, I can only pray Kane steps in soon.

"Easy, girl. It's just me."

The alcohol on his breath floods my senses and makes me sick. When he's drunk, he's a fucking psycho.

"Let me go," I try to say, but it's so muffled by his hand that it's completely lost on him.

"I only came here tonight because I knew you'd be here. We never finished what we started, and damn you look good enough right now to make this trip worthwhile."

I feel his erection in my back, and it almost makes me gag. His teeth scrape my neck as he trails his tongue over my skin.

I squeal out in a cry, but his grip tightens on my mouth. I don't care if I do get sentenced, I'm not letting him touch me anywhere I won't recover from.

Right as I've found my resolve, the door bursts open, and darkening the doorway is my human hero.

"Let her the fuck go before I tear your head off your shoulders."

The venom in Kane's eyes is unmistakably scary. It even scares me, and I know he'd never hurt me. He stalks toward us, and I feel Heath starting to tremble, almost convulsing as Kane nears with a steady approach.

There's something... I don't know what. The air seems to be thicker, as if there's some magical... it's so odd.

The hand over my mouth falls free, and before I realize what's going on, Kane is on top of Heath. His fists are already bloody, and Heath is unconscious as Kane continues to brutally pound the life out of him.

"Kane!" I scream when I worry how far he might go.

A rush of wind stirs, and suddenly Deke and Zee are ripping Kane off Heath who is a bloody mess of lifelessness.

"Is he-"

"No, but he's not far from," Zee interrupts. "Get Dray in here."

I don't know who Dray is, so how do I get him in here?

"Okay," Sierra answers from behind me, and then I realize his eyes weren't on me, but on her.

Kane fights the two of them, and for a second, I'm worried he really is going to break free and finish the job.

"Damn it, Kane! Let it be! You proved your point," Zee pleads.

"Obviously, I didn't, or he wouldn't have tried touching her again. Stupid mother fucker. He has *no* idea who he's fucking with."

I swear there was a low growl in his throat. I've never seen anyone so pissed in all my life.

I walk over to step in front of him, and my arms go around his waist without hesitation. I bury my head in his chest as I fight off the tears that have been teetering.

He stops fighting his friends, and then his arms wrap around me almost too tightly as he pulls me close, breathing me in.

"I'm sorry, baby. I had no idea he was here."

I shake my head, wanting his comfort instead of his guilt.

"I'm fine. He didn't-"

"This fool just doesn't know when to stop, does he?" a stranger asks as he comes into view.

"Thanks, Dray. I sort of lost it," Kane says through gritted teeth, not sounding apologetic at all.

"No worries," he says while swatting away the guilt exuding from Kane. "I'll get him patched up and then I'll ship him off to the hospital. This creep deserved much worse. See you after while."

Dray's eyes catch mine briefly, and he tilts his head, smirking slightly. Then he throws the bloody heap of a man over his shoulder, and leaves just as quickly as he came.

It's as if it's no big deal Kane almost killed a guy. Granted, Heath had it coming, but none of them seem very affected by the whole ordeal.

"We'll leave you to it," Sierra says as she ushers the guys out. "Sorry about this, Alyssa."

I start to speak, but the door closes before I can. Kane lifts me from the ground, his lips closing over mine as he carries me to the bed.

I give up on food and drink. I'm too tired to even try to process all the events from this horrid night.

Since the sun set, I played bait and nearly ended up being devoured by a fanged demon. I was saved by both of my enemies - dark user and night stalker. I tried breaking up with my boyfriend, told him I love him instead, had insanely hot sex, found a dungeon full of dark play toys, and I was nearly.... well, I don't even want to think about that last bit. Not to mention, I almost watched Kane kill a guy over me.

A shiver spreads over me as the soft bed swallows me up. Kane's arms tighten around my waist, and my eyes instantly feel too heavy to hold open.

Again, I feel... something, but I don't know what. I've got to get him out of this house. I think the dark energy is starting to affect his human mind.

Chapter Seventeen

"Kane," a voice whispers into what's left of the night, rousing me from my sleep.

I stay still as Kane stirs.

"What the fuck, Zee?" he whispers back.

"It's Amy... again. I don't know what we're going to do with her if she keeps this up. She's gone though, and we need your help."

"Fuck," he mumbles, and then I feel him leaning over as if to check on my sleeping status.

I remain perfectly still, keeping my breaths even to ensure him I haven't woken up.

"Fine. I'll be out front in a second. Make sure nothing can get in here. Keep her safe."

"I'll stay. It's you they need. You're the only one she responds to when she loses it."

"I think that's just the game she's playing. She's doing everything she fucking can to break me and Alyssa up. I'm sick of this shit. I plan on making that *very* clear."

Their conversation halts as Kane's warmth disappears from the bed. I silently scramble to my feet the second the door shuts behind him.

I'm tired of this shit, too. I'm desperate to see what the hell is going on with Little Miss Crazy Bitch. I want to know why they need his help so fucking bad.

"If she wakes up, tell her I won't be long," Kane says from the living room.

"What should I tell her? You got a good lie lined up?"

Lie? What the fuck?

"No. Don't lie to her. I don't want to do that. Just tell her I'll be back. It's time to explain this shit anyway. I told her I love her."

My heart beats fiercely. The way he says it... it's almost like he's worried about something. Is he worried he said it too soon?

"Shit, Kane. You know she'll be coming for you now. What are you going to do?"

What? Who? Huh?

These guys are more confusing than immortals with their constantly cryptic conversations.

"What I have to. No matter how bad it gets, I won't lose Alyssa because of her. Lock up. I'll be back soon."

Who the fuck is *her?*

As soon as the door shuts, I pull on my shoes and sneak onto the balcony. I'm still wearing my wrinkled clothes I never changed out of, but spy missions don't really have to have a prepared ensemble.

Kane quickly disappears into the woods, and I have to jump from the balcony to keep up.

At the last minute, I use my magic to call to a tree limb to me. It wraps around my waist and halts my fall, turning it into a graceful landing.

Kane's already gone, obviously on his way to town. I can't even sense his trail at all. It's as though he's just disappeared. I'm not giving up though.

I head out deeper, straining to hear one crunch of leaves or one snap of a twig. I'm met with only the stir of the wind against the trees. How in the hell did I lose him that quickly?

Scowling, I trek on, but I quickly learn the woods are trickier in the dark than in the light. After an hour, I'm completely lost. This should have been a quick trip - twenty minutes at most - but now I've somehow wandered into a never-ending circle.

Then I sense it - eyes on me. I look around, casually gauging my surroundings as I inconspicuously search for the creature lurking in the shadows, waiting for their chance to pounce.

Glowing orange eyes appear behind a pile of brush, and my stomach flops against my sides.

Lycan.

I turn around, and after a heavy breath, I start running with every ounce of energy I have, regretting my thin-soled shoes immediately. I hear the furious growl and the fierce roar, and then the chase is underway behind me as the beast launches itself out of hiding to pursue its prey - me.

I risk a glance over my shoulder to see it's too fast for me. The monstrous size of the she-devil behind me makes me gasp, and I lose my balance, pummeling to the ground with a loud thud and an accidental scream.

I leap to my feet just as the vicious beast catches up. It swipes at me before lunging, and I hurl my body out of its path just before impact. Back on my feet again, I don't hesitate. Using mother nature's energy, the ground jumps up and pins her into place.

The vines and plants spring to life to act as natural restraints. I'm both surprised and impressed at the power that fell out at my fingertips. I've never used my mother's power with such success before, and I'm not conflicted with the dark high that follows my father's power.

Shock seems to cloak the glowing orange eyes. Obviously, it hadn't known it was fucking with a witch.

I hear the cracking of the vines restraining the creature, and I start running again before it has the chance to escape. Breathless and terrified, I reach the edge of the woods, coming out behind Gage's house.

I start to rush to the door, but Kane's voice jars me out of my attempt.

"Alyssa! What the hell are you doing out here?"

Shit! I have to get him out of here before that lycan catches up.

"Kane! Go! We have to go! There's a-"

Before I can speak again, the lycan crashes through the threshold of the forest in a mad dash for me. The desperate desire for my death radiates in its eyes. I start to summon the power, knowing I'll forever scar my love, but I don't have a choice.

But before I can release anything, Kane appears in front of me, catching the airborne beast by the throat. I gasp in disbelief as the lycan cries out in pain from his crushing force.

No. No. There's no way. Please, God, no. No!

Kane's eyes glow blue as he growls at the lycan.

"What the fuck are you doing, Amy? I'll kill you for this!"

Amy? Oh no.

My heart breaks and the pieces plummet to the ground. This can't be happening. This has to be a nightmare. *Wake the fuck up, Alyssa.*

With a grunt from his exerted effort, Kane launches Amy backwards, throwing her lycan body back into the forest. Trees crack and break against her as she disappears into the darkness.

I scramble backwards as Kane turns to me, his glowing blues dulling back to green as his vampiric side slinks back into hiding. Sickness attacks me without mercy, and I double over to expel the contents of my stomach in the most ungraceful manner.

"Alyssa, baby, it's just me. I know this is a lot, but-"

"Night stalker." The hushed words flow through my lips like a blasphemous whisper.

He tilts his head, confusion seeming to gather in his traitorous green eyes as I back away again.

"What did you just call me?" he asks, a touch of disbelief and anger mingling in his tone.

"Kane!" Amy screams, her human body back intact as she runs toward us with a robe covering her nakedness. "She's a fucking witch!"

Pain, anger, and so much more flashes through his eyes. All of this was an elaborate hoax. I was tricked into loving the enemy. My hands burn with fury as the silver grabs me and tries to pull me to the darkness, begging me to release my devious power.

"Gage!" I cry out, but he doesn't come... doesn't hear me. I turn to Kane, my eyes watering. "It can't... You can't... I've seen you... How? Why?" I sob out, my tears pouring down.

"You damn witch! You fucking trickster bitch!" Amy growls, and suddenly the sound of shredding fabric rings out as her body distorts and changes in front of my eyes.

Her flesh turns from a tanned glow to a gray ash as the lycan rises to the surface. She launches herself at me again, but Kane grabs her, and rips her back. I don't give him the chance to take me down himself.

Using the energy around me, I slash through Gage's bedroom window, shattering it as I scream once more. "Gage!"

Within a blink, he materializes in front of me, and his eyes gauge the craziness as Kane's glowing blue eyes jump forth to show his defensive stance before he slings Amy behind him.

"You," Kane whispers.

"What the fuck?" Gage gushes, but I jump into his arms and throw my legs around his waist.

"Get us out of here!"

He doesn't waste time. We vaporize into the air and split the planes of life and death as we rush away, retreating in complete disbelief.

The head-rush consumes me, forcing me to be even sicker than I already am as we reach the porch of the safe home I abandoned to live with the devil. No doubt, he didn't like the magic surrounding my home. I gave my innocence to the enemy, and he took much more than that.

"What the hell is going on?" Gage demands as we start walking in.

Before he can cross the threshold, he's launched backwards as the protective spell from my house kicks him in the chest.

I squeal as he crashes into the cliché white picket fence and crushes it to pieces beneath his forceful slam.

"Ow," he grumbles, no real sense of pain in his tone.

"Sorry," I mumble numbly. "Gage can come in."

He stands and warily makes his way back onto my porch. Skeptically, he touches the air of the threshold with the same caution a human would exert to check for an electrical current on a wire.

Finally, he steps through without being battered again.

"Now, I repeat... what the fuck just happened? Kane's a damn night stalker?"

The tears almost choke me, making it impossible for me to speak, so I nod vigorously instead. He runs a hand through his hair to ruffle it as he shakes his head.

"I thought you checked him out. How the hell did he not reveal himself under the influence of your mark?"

I steady myself enough to answer, though my voice is hoarse and pitchy as I speak. "I couldn't use my mark. If he had been human, it would have killed him. I saw him at midnight over and over... he should have-"

"Damn it, Alyssa! When will you learn? Magic isn't old anymore. Midnight doesn't mean shit nowadays. Midnight reveals them if they've taken the lives of *innocent* victims. Heavy emphasis on the word *innocent*. In this day and age, such a fucking thing doesn't exist anymore, unless they kill a child. Fuck! And your damn mark won't kill a human! Stop being so-"

"Mine will! I've seen it, you asshole! My power comes from Calypso Coldwell and Drackus Devall. The two combined gave me more power than what should exist. Most people just don't know how fucking strong my mother is. Her mark kills too, just as my father's does. Do you understand? I couldn't risk it."

He frowns as he lets out another exasperated breath. He grips his head as if it aches, and then he plops down on my couch.

"Fine. Sorry. I didn't know. I knew Drackus's would kill, but I didn't know it was because of the power within. Why didn't Frankie use his?"

The onslaught of tears I'm facing is merciless, ravaging my cheeks with their acidic flow.

"Because he thought I used mine. Frankie doesn't know how strong I am either. Mom keeps it quiet. She's worried the world will shun me like they do my father. I'm not supposed to exist, Gage."

His eyes soften, and he stands to walk over to me. His bare chest glows under the lone light in the room. He pulls me to him, and my tears dampen his chest.

"I don't know what he wanted from me. I don't know why he had to make me-"

My sobs become too uncontrollable, making speech no longer an option. Gage coos in my ear as he pulls me tighter into his embrace. His soft touch is all the comfort he can offer, but it's not enough to hold me together.

"I'll stay with you tonight. At least we know why your spell failed at his house. You were trying to keep out the dark, when that's all that surrounded you."

Fuck. I'm so, so stupid. How could I live with a night stalker for a month and not know it?

I just nod as he scoops me up and carries me to the bedroom. He gently places me on the cold, forgotten bed, and I curl up like a child afraid of the dark. Drawing my knees to my chest, I cry into the pillow.

"Alyssa, I can stay in here if you need me to."

He stands uncertainly by my bed, but I shake my head. I don't need his pity for my stupidity.

"No. Just go."

He sighs out, reluctance shining in his aura. With heavy footsteps, he makes his way toward the door.

"I'll be on the couch if you need me."

A strangled sob comes out as I nod, and then I pull the cover over all of me, trying to vanish from the misery the world holds ready. I've never felt so broken.

Waking up to a new day doesn't ease the burden from the night of tears. It's at least noon, but I feel as though I could spend weeks in bed. Frankie isn't answering my calls on top of everything else. Still no word on my mother.

I can feel her though. Her life is still there. The earth answers my daunting question everyday, letting me feel the air she breathes in, keeping my hope alive.

"So I've gone over everything, and according to my notes, Kane is one hell of a master of disguise. They all are," Gage grumbles as he tosses his pen and paper to the table.

"You were checking him out?" I ask, a crackled lilt to my voice.

"No, but I have a habit of documenting things. Nothing ever once stood out. Why keep a mortal witch alive when you have every opportunity to drain her clean without anyone stopping you?"

I cringe at his heartless release. Kane held my life in his hands for a month. I was his to do with as he wished. Fortunately for me, he apparently enjoys dragging out the game.

"We need to worry about my mother, not my devil-in-disguise lover. I don't ever want to hear his name again."

A knock at the door interrupts our conversation, and Gage motions for me to stay back as he goes to answer it. He's greeted with a vacant, empty porch. He cautiously pokes his head out, but pulls back, seeming confused.

Then he picks up a note that lies at the threshold. With tight lips, he brings it to me.

"It's for you."

I recognize Kane's handwriting immediately, and my heart pounds heavily in my chest as I stare at my name on the front of the envelope.

"I can't read it."

He pulls back the proffered note addressed to me, and then he opens it himself. His eyes scan the contents quickly, and then he releases a sigh.

"Alyssa, we need to speak. You've opened a door you should be prepared for. Thirty minutes. Meet me at the diner. It'll be neutral grounds where you can't touch me."

"Where *I* can't touch *him*? He can't be serious," I squeal out. "He's the enemy. He's the fucking dark night stalker that preys on my kind, damn it. He tasted my fucking... oh damn."

My mind flashes back to the first time he tasted my blood, and then last night jumps up, too. He knew I was a witch. He was sampling the goods before devouring me whole. I'm so fucking ignorant.

"I'll call Cade and the others. We'll need backup. Grab your clothes and get changed."

"You can't be serious," I gasp. "I can't see him. I'm barely keeping myself together as it is, Gage. I don't want to hear whatever evil falls through his lips."

He tenses as he steps toward the door.

"We need to know what he was after. Alyssa, whatever it is, I need you to stay calm. If you lose it at the diner, you'll be putting both of us at risk. I need to grab a shirt. Stay here until I get back."

Before I can argue, he vaporizes into the air and vanishes from sight. I can't see Kane. This can't be happening.

Chapter Eighteen

I walk into the diner with a begrudged and trembling motion. I've drunk all the chamomile tea I can stomach, along with some of my mother's relaxing medleys of potions, but trepidation still claims me.

Kane and his entourage are assembled in the oversized back booth. They all turn to stare at me and Gage as we approach with his own entourage following our lead.

Kane leans back, his eyes burning through me as his jaw clenches. I can see his hatred and disgust teeming in his deceptive greens that are masking the killer blues lurking in their depths.

"Well, We're here," Gage says while standing beside me, clutching my hand.

Kane's eyes flash down to our grip on each other, and a huff of disgust flows through his lips.

"You were the redhead that night, weren't you?" he growls.

My heart flutters in my chest at the very sound of his voice. Just hours ago I was telling this monster I loved him.

"It was you? You are the pack that showed up to help that night?" Gage asks as if he's as baffled as I am.

"You mean the ones who saved your asses? Yes, we were," Amy scoffs while scooting in closer to Kane.

The twisted, psychopathic part of me cringes in jealously as Kane allows her closeness. I can't stop loving him this quickly, but I hate myself for the inability to do so.

"What's this about?" Gage grumbles.

"Have a seat. We've got a lot to discuss," Kane says through tight lips.

I glance at the very unwelcoming seats across from Kane and next to Sierra who doesn't seem as warm and friendly as she pretended to be all month. Her eyes flash an orange glow as her defenses kick in.

Lycan. Unbelievable.

"If it's all the same to you, we'll stand," Gage murmurs.

"You'll draw attention if you stand," Kane gripes, and then he nods to Sierra and Deke who slide out of the booth to allow more room for us.

Zee sits on the opposite side of us, next to Amy who is between the two night stalkers. Zee's and Deke's eyes both flash blue temporarily, warning us to behave.

With a shudder, I allow Gage to guide me into the booth. I sit as close as I possibly can to him without being in his lap. I pray he can vaporize us both for escape if this gets out of hand.

Deke and Sierra climb into the booth adjacent to us, and Gage's friends take the booth behind us.

"Now, talk. Let's not drag this out," Gage prompts, seeming in control.

Kane leans back, a bitter grin cocking up as he shakes his head in disgust.

"What did you want? To get at Castine? You'll sure as hell have your shot now. You have no idea what you've done."

Who?

"Castine?" Gage asks in disbelief. "What the hell does that demon bitch have to do with this?"

Kane laughs bitterly, sounding delirious and livid.

"Don't play me. The two of you have done that quite enough. I've been made a fool, but I won't be allowing you to do such a thing anymore."

"You were played for a fool?" I'm jumping in before I even realize what I'm doing as my anger takes control. "I fell into your bed, gave you everything I had to offer, and you took it without remorse, you monster."

Kane's eyes narrow, venom seeping through his glare.

"Don't play the innocent victim, Alyssa. You were the one who pushed for that, not me. Now, there are consequences to the trap you lured me into."

I want to take him and shake the fuck out of him right now. How dare he try to play this game.

"Answer me about Castine," Gage prompts, ignoring our sparked feud.

"Hey, Alyssa, Kane," Mel says as she walks up to take our order. Her eyes glance between us, and then they fall to Amy and Gage. "Did you two break up? I just saw you together last night at the party."

I never even saw her. Of course, I was wrapped up in the devil's arms for the entirety of the time.

"Yeah. We're definitely not together," Kane says while snarling. "Coffees all around for now. Nothing else, unless you carry liquor these days."

She lets an uncomfortable laugh free to add to the awkward tension before shaking her head.

"I'll be right back with those."

I glare at Kane with complete and utter contempt. How dare he act so disgusted with me. It's I who has a right to feel disgusted, repulsed even.

"Get on with your explanation about Castine," Gage prompts again, impatience shining in his tone.

Kane sighs, leaning back as he starts his explanation. I look away when Amy rests her hand on his leg.

"I broke almost every bond with Castine years and years ago, but until last night, she didn't have a reason to track me down. Now, Alyssa tricked me into telling her I loved her, and that last bond tethering me to that bitch has been severed. She'll be out for blood. Just thought I'd give you a heads up that your dreams of taking a shot at her are about to come true, but you'll regret going for this."

Bond? Tricked? *That bastard.*

"I didn't trick you, you son of a-"

"Castine is your sire?" Gage asks, interrupting me as the color rushes from his face, stealing his calm composure.

"Like you didn't already know, *hunter*. The Somage have wanted her dead for quite some time," he snarks, carrying on with his charade. "I couldn't exactly kill her without first falling in love. If I had of, it would have killed me, too. She knows that I've said it now, and she'll fear I'm coming for her. Since I'm one of the few strong enough to do so, she'll go on the offense. The two of you should leave, because despite what you think, you won't be able to take her on. When she gets her hands on a mortal witch, she'll be merciless. Though I don't give a damn if she bleeds her fucking dry, I don't feel like trying to kill damn Vampiress that is already much stronger than me while she has a witch's blood coursing through her, giving her added power."

His words cut like daggers in my heart. He's so cold and callous. I want to hate him so badly right now. Why can't I?

"Fuck," Gage says under his breath. "When will she be coming?"

Kane leans forward, his eyes finding mine once again.

"I don't know, but Alyssa is living in her house. That gives her all the power in the world over her. That little protection spell she cast won't do a damn bit of good. You should know how possessive my kind is. That house belongs to the dark, and so will the blond witch if she stays there."

"You knew the whole time, you slimy bastard. You knew what I was and you-"

His eyes narrow as he interrupts me. "The spell threw Deke off your porch. That's how I found out. It let me through, ironically enough, considering I'm the one who wants to see you suffer for what you've done."

"What *I've* done? You're as psychotic as your pet," I scoff, my eyes cutting toward Amy.

A beastly growl slips through her snarling lips, and Gage stands to pull my hand in his.

"Let's go. We've heard enough."

Mel returns with the coffees and her eyes clock Gage's hand on mine.

"Wow. The night really changed things," she gasps while putting down the tray.

"One night didn't do anything but reveal the true depths of deception Alyssa has," Kane angrily releases while standing and tossing a few bills to the table. "Keep the change."

He walks off with his dog on his heels. It makes so much sense now. Lycans don't mingle with night stalkers unless they find solace in one. That *one* usually ends up being its owner... sort of. Lycans were meant to be guardians to the night stalkers, and only after the rebellion did they cut ties.

The door jingles an annoying tune as the bells above it clank together. Just like that, they're all gone, leaving us behind to deal with the heavy air.

"We need to go. If you're living in Castine's home, he's right - no spell will keep you safe enough. You'll stay with me."

"Right next door to him?" I scoff. "Hell no. If she comes, I'll rip her heart out."

"Alyssa, damn it. You don't understand how this shit works."

"No, *you* don't understand what he did to me. I won't let him take me from my home just because he has a crazy ex. I'm sick of this ridiculous bullshit."

He pulls me down the road and to my walkway as we near my tainted house. He glances around, suddenly wary of his surroundings as he urges me in. His companions break off and head into the woods to vaporize and disperse.

"You didn't even ask him what he wanted from me. You let him dictate the conversation and blame me for it all. You even interrupted when I tried to pry the truth out of him," I scold, crossing my arms in front of my chest like a sullen child.

I'd stomp my foot, but that might be a little too immature. I'm not sure why I ever thought a dark user would actually help me get the truth from my mortal enemy. Of course, Gage is technically my other mortal enemy. How the fuck did all this happen?

"He gave us the answer without meaning to, Alyssa. He used you. Let's face it - you're the kind of girl a guy can fall in love with without having to try too hard. Night stalkers are possessive, but they hate to be possessed. Almost all night stalkers dream of being able to kill their sires, but breaking the bonds it takes to do such a thing is painful and damn near impossible.

"He would have had to break the bonds one-by-one. Some are excruciatingly painful, so much so that most night stalkers refuse to attempt breaking more than enough to distance themselves from their controlling sires.

"Castine is the most notorious among the night stalkers. She has bonded spawn all over the place. She's possessive, just as they all are. It's their nature to be so. Her creations are her pets. Most all of them manage to distance themselves by breaking enough bonds. Few ever break all the bonds they have to in order to kill their sires themselves.

"There's no telling the pain he went through to break the first of those. Though this last one would have been painless, it was still a wall that crumbled between them. She would have felt it, and she'll be coming for you. Her venom is the most toxic there is."

I shake my head in disbelief. Kane comes from the most vicious sire in the frigging immortal community. Fuck my luck.

"So Kane's venom is just as toxic. I guess it's good he didn't get the itch to bite when he tasted my blood."

Gage's face pales, and then he stands to be closer to me.

"He tasted your blood? Fuck, Alyssa. You're more than lucky he didn't use his toxic venom."

"He didn't bite. Did you miss that part?"

"Damn you're so naive," he grumbles while walking away from me as if in exasperation. "Venom isn't in the fangs, it's in the saliva. You won't be affected by it anywhere other than the bloodstream. Even if they taste your blood from a cut, you still get their venom. What did you feel after he tasted your blood?"

Hot as hell. I'm so ashamed and disgusted with myself right now.

"Oh," he says, as if he's reading my aura's tell-all colors. "Poison's kiss. Figures. That's one way to coerce a confession of love."

"Poison's kiss?" I ask, still choking back my cruel, taunting tears.

"Seductive venom. It's highly intoxicating and you almost drown in lust."

It all makes so much sense now. I was just the dummy pawn.

"He never really loved me, so it's possible his bond is still intact," I whimper, giving into the tears when I can't hold them back.

"He didn't have to really love you. He just had to believe it enough to sever their connection. It's a fucked up world we live in. You can't be here. I can't protect you from her. She wears an amulet around her neck that was given to her before the rebellions. It's blessed by several of our kind, and it enables her to shield herself from our magic. She can harness any energy you use against her, and she can use it on you."

Realizing just how fucked up this all is, I finally drop my shoulders in defeat.

"Fine. I'll move, but not to your place. I'll just have to find a new home in a less vampy town."

He releases a breath of relief, as if he's genuinely concerned.

"Sounds like a reasonable compromise. The sooner the better. I'll stay with you until you do find something. I can at least try to get us out of here if she does come. Your spell might slow her down enough to give us that time... if it works on her at all. With her amulet, I doubt it will give us more than a few seconds."

Sighing in disbelief, I fight off the wave of tears beating at the backs of my eyes. My phone rings just as Gage plops down on my couch and pulls up my laptop to start searching for homes.

"Hello?" I almost mumble.

"Alyssa, it's me."

Frankie's voice is soothing, though right now I just want to fall apart.

"Frankie, I've got so much to tell you. You're never going to believe –"

"Alyssa, this is about your mom," he says in interruption. My stomach plummets to the ground as my breaths stop. I reach out to the earth, still feeling her presence, which relieves me somewhat. He finally kills the suspense. "Lyss, she's back."

End of Book I

ACKNOWLEDGEMENTS

Thank you to everyone on Facebook. I love you all so much for your support.

Thank you to my two wonderful sisters, Tonya and Danielle. I love you both so much.

And thank you, Daddy. Your faith and encouragement has helped me be stronger than I thought I could be. I love you so much.

ABOUT THE AUTHOR

What does C.M. Owens write? A little bit of everything as long as the central focus is romance.

C.M. Owens is an escapist, and loves to stretch the imagination. Writing is more than a passion – it's a necessity. It's a means of staying sane and happy.

Where do her ideas come from? Usually it's a line in a song that triggers an idea that spawns into a story. Though she came from a family of musicians, she has zero abilities with instruments, she sounds like a strangled cat when she sings, and her dancing is downright embarrassing. Just ask her two children. Her creativity rests solely in the written word. Her family is grateful that she gave up her quest to become a famous singer.

C.M. Owens

Printed in Great Britain
by Amazon

65211099R00154